Season's Readings

Season's READINGS

More
Sweet, Funny, & Strange® Holiday Tales

Editors
Marianne H. Donley and *Carol L. Wright*

BETHLEHEM WRITERS GROUP, LLC
BETHLEHEM, PENNSYLVANIA, USA

Season's Readings
More Sweet, Funny, and Strange® Holiday Tales

Published by Bethlehem Writers Group, LLC
https://bethlehemwritersgroup.com

Copyright © 2024 by the Bethlehem Writers Group, LLC. All rights reserved. No part of this book may be used or reproduced in any form, or by any electronic or mechanical means, without written permission of the copyright holder.

The copyright of each individual story is retained by the author.

The contents of this publication are works of fiction. Names, places, products, businesses or organizations, events, and incidents are either products of the authors' imaginations or are used fictitiously. Any resemblance to actual persons, living or dead, businesses, organizations, events, or locales is entirely coincidental.

Sweet, Funny, and Strange is a registered trademark of the Bethlehem Writers Group, LLC.

Cover design by Marianne H. Donley and Carol L. Wright
Cover and interior images licensed from Depositphotos.com

Trade Paperback ISBN: 978-1-954675-03-2
Ebook ISBN: 978-1-954675-04-9

Library of Congress Control Number: 2024946290

Printed in the United States of America

*In celebration of
all the glorious holidays
that bring
spice and seasons to life.*

Also from the
BETHLEHEM WRITERS GROUP, LLC
SWEET, FUNNY, AND STRANGE® ANTHOLOGIES

A CHRISTMAS SAMPLER:
SWEET, FUNNY, AND STRANGE HOLIDAY TALES (2009)
Winner of two 2010 Next Generation Indie Book Awards

*

ONCE AROUND THE SUN: SWEET, FUNNY, AND STRANGE
TALES FOR ALL SEASONS (2013)
Finalist, 2014 Next Generation Indie Book Award

*

A READABLE FEAST: SWEET, FUNNY, AND STRANGE
TALES FOR EVERY TASTE (2015)
Finalist, 2016 Next Generation Indie Book Award

*

ONCE UPON A TIME: SWEET, FUNNY, AND STRANGE
TALES FOR ALL AGES (2016)

*

UNTETHERED: SWEET, FUNNY, AND STRANGE
TALES OF THE PARANORMAL (2018)
Finalist, 2019 Killer Nashville Silver Falchion Award

*

FUR, FEATHERS, AND SCALES: SWEET, FUNNY, AND
STRANGE ANIMAL TALES (2020)
Winner of two 2021 Next Generation Indie Book Awards

*

AN ELEMENT OF MYSTERY: SWEET, FUNNY, AND
STRANGE TALES OF INTRIGUE (2022)
Finalist, 2023 Next Generation Indie Book Award
Finalist, 2023 Killer Nashville Silver Falchion Award

OTHER PUBLICATIONS

OFF THE RAILS: A COLLECTION OF WEIRD, WICKED,
AND WACKY STORIES (2019) by Jerome W. McFadden
Finalist, 2020 Next Generation Indie Book Award

*

LET IT SNOW: THE BEST OF BETHLEHEM WRITERS ROUNDTABLE
WINTER 2015 COLLECTION (2015)

*

BETHLEHEM WRITERS ROUNDTABLE
https://bwgwritersroundtable.com (since 2011)

Table of Contents

Thanksgiving, 4th Thursday in November
Narragansett Nellie and the Transferware Platter—Mary Adler 11
Next of Kin—Dianna Sinovic 17
As Simple as That—Emwryn Murphy 30
First Thanksgiving—Sally Milliken 55
The Heart Needs a Home—D.T. Krippene 61
Best Laid Plans—Carol L. Wright 72

Krampusnacht, December 5th
He Sees You When You're Sleeping—Diane Sismour 85

Pearl Harbor Day, December 7th
Creating a Memory with Gran—Debra H. Goldstein 95

Hanukkah, 25th day of Kislev
Latkes and Sour Cream—Peter J Barbour 103

Christmas, December 25th
High Tech—Dianna Sinovic 109
A Winter Wonderland ... Well Sort Of—Jeff Baird 114
Flue Shot—Jerome W. McFadden 125
Oh! Christmas Tree—Rhonda Zangwill 129
The Catcher—Kidd Wadsworth 134
Just Ask Santa—Bettie Nebergall 147
The Tour—Ralph Hieb 153
Millie's Christmas Wine—D. T. Krippene 159
Hagemeier's Christmas Ale—Christopher D. Ochs 168
The Goblin King's Music Box—A. E. Decker 171

New Year's Eve, December 31st
The Star of the Party—Paula Gail Benson 193
Ringing In the New Year—Peter J Barbour 198

About the Authors 203

Acknowledgements 209

Thanksgiving
4th Thursday in November

Narragansett Nellie and the Transferware Platter

Mary Adler
Third Place Winner, 2024 BWR Short Story Award

Dawg, a border collie, aptly if unimaginatively named, greeted me at the entrance to the McClain turkey ranch. He waited while I opened the gate, drove through, and closed it. Then he raced me to the house.

"Mornin', Steve," McClain called. He nodded toward the trucks loaded with Narragansett turkeys on their way to the butcher. "It's hard to see them go. I try not to get to know them, and I certainly don't name them—" His tone said only a fool would do that. "—but I'll miss them."

While writing an article on the turkey ranch, I'd watched the affectionate and social turkeys care for their brood and knew I could never eat one. Unfortunately, my article had convinced Angie, my wife, that we should cook a Narragansett for Thanksgiving.

McClain stuffed my three fifty-dollar bills into a pouch he could barely close. No checks, no credit cards. Definitely no electronic transfers.

"Wow, Mac. That's a lot of money to have hanging around," I said. The ranch was isolated, and people knew McClain was a cash-on-the-barrelhead old timer.

"Don't worry. It's safe." He tucked the pouch inside a feed sack. "Pick your oven-ready bird up tomorrow after ten a.m."

I abandoned worrying about his fiscal practices and pondered my own problem: telling my wife I couldn't eat the Narragansett turkey I'd just bought.

*

As I drove away from the ranch, hoping Angie would understand, a cannonball hit the side of my van.

I slammed on the brakes and jumped out. A turkey shook her bluish colored head as if momentarily stunned. I approached her, wary of her powerful wings and claws. She darted around me, jumped onto the driver's seat, then hopped into the back making the chirp-like sound that signaled danger. I listened for thundering hoofbeats or revving all-terrain bikes. Nothing. Maybe the turkey wranglers hadn't noticed she was gone.

How could I take her back? She'd escaped, fair and square, and I *had* paid McClain for a turkey. Why not this one?

I called her Nellie, with a wry nod to McClain's statement about naming animals.

*

When I got home, I left Nellie in the van ruffling her black and gray feathers. Probably not the only feathers to be ruffled today. Angie didn't like surprises, especially one that could turn her carefully planned Thanksgiving feast upside down.

The rat-a-tat-tat of chopping drew me to the kitchen.

"Hello, Darling." Angie looked up and frowned. "Where's the turkey?"

"About that."

"Oh, no. Don't tell me McClain ran out."

"Funny you should say *ran out*." I considered embracing her, then light glinted on the knife she held. "A turkey escaped. I rescued her. Like we did Finn, remember?"

"You rescued a turkey? A live turkey? And you think reminding me that we voluntarily took a demented Golden Retriever into our home is helping? Madonna, Steve." She dropped the knife and shook her bunched fingers at me. "What were you thinking?"

Did I mention she's Italian?

Finn, our dearly loved Golden, mistook her open arms as an invitation and launched his exuberant sixty pounds at her. Luckily, Angie landed on his orthopedic dog bed where he often drooled while she cooked. He pinned her, the better to lick her face.

He'd bumped the table on take-off, and a bottle of locally sourced, free-range milk teetered at its edge. Finn would find a glass-dotted puddle of milk even more enticing than Angie's ear. When I dove for the bottle, I nudged a colander. Cranberries rained down like garnet hailstones.

The rattle of berries attracted Clarence, our African grey parrot, who soared onto Finn's back and bobbed excitedly as his favorite treats rolled across the floor.

"Help me up!" Laughter leavened Angie's fur-muffled demand.

I gave her a hand, and after order was restored, resumed pleading.

"Come out to the van and meet her, Angie. I can't bear the thought of her being killed."

She clasped her hands together as if in prayer and moved them back and forth in front of her face. "All you had to do was pay McClain the exorbitant sum of $150 for a turkey. A nicely dressed, featherless turkey. One that should be prepared to fulfill her destiny"—she pointed a finger at the transferware platter handed down from her great grandmother—"on that!"

I opened my mouth. She showed me both palms, silencing my protestations, and went on.

"Before your article, I would have been happy with a turkey in a box. A regular old turkey, even one with a pop-up thermometer, dressed, plucked, trussed, and most important, *dead!* Not a live run-away turkey from farmer McClain's."

"Rancher McClain."

"Farmer, rancher. What's the difference?"

"If you plant it, you're a farmer; if you chase it, you're a rancher."

"Who cares? Not the twelve people coming to Thanksgiving dinner, where a roasted turkey is usually the main attraction. One they can pour gravy on, not one looking at them with beady eyes."

"Eleven people," I said. "Lois doesn't expect a turkey."

Mentioning Lois, a vegetarian, was the last straw, and I'm not hinting at any turkey-in-the-straw puns. Angie scowled and shooed me to the van where Nellie snoozed on Finn's blanket. She woke when Angie slammed her door, and I reluctantly shifted into drive. Destination, McClain's ranch.

*

I tried to tune out Nellie's distressed clucking.

At the ranch, I slowed. Dawg wasn't waiting at the gate. The gate that yawned open. I stopped the van and cut the headlights.

Angie thumped the dashboard. "Quit stalling, Steve! That turkey's going back no matter what—"

"Something's wrong."

I got out of the van and listened. At first, I heard only the familiar nighttime noises: a screech owl, the whistle of a train. And then a whimper, like a dog having a bad dream.

The sound of Nellie beating her wings thundered in the van, and Angie burst through the door.

"What's she doing? Make her stop."

"Sounds like Dawg whimpering. Nellie probably hears him, too. Get back in the van. She's upset, but she won't hurt you."

"If it's all the same to you, I'll take my chances out here with coyotes and mountain lions."

I eased my door closed, then crept through the dark. I found Dawg lying on the road breathing shallowly.

I carried him to the van. "I think he's been drugged."

Angie overcame her distrust of the turkey long enough to help me put Dawg on Finn's blanket. Nellie gently rubbed his muzzle with the side of her beak.

"She's trying to comfort him," Angie said in wonder. Then she shook her head as if remonstrating with herself.

I showed her my phone. No bars. "Take Dawg to the vet and call the sheriff as soon as you have service. Tell him something's not right here."

"You made it out of Afghanistan." She made the sign of the cross. "I don't want to lose you on a turkey farm, ranch, whatever." Her flippancy failed to mask her real fear for me.

"I'll be careful."

Before we closed the sliding door, Nellie jumped out and crash-landed beside me. Angie climbed into the van. She was almost out of sight before she turned on the lights.

"It's just you and me, Nellie." The turkey wagged her head and shook out her feathers. We set off toward the house, keeping to the shadows. She stayed close, not able to see in the dark any better than I could although in daylight turkeys saw much better than humans. Ask any hunter.

Lowered blinds prevented me from seeing inside the lighted kitchen. Judging from the old Mustang parked by the back door, McClain had company. The kind of company that might not bother to close a gate.

I hunkered down, and Nellie fluffed her feathers as insulation against the chill. I was hungry, tired, cold, and worried. Other than that, I was just fine. At least I wasn't under fire.

And then a shot exploded inside McClain's house.

"Guess we can't wait for the cavalry, Nellie." I ran toward the house, keeping low. Twenty-five pounds of angry fowl raced along beside me.

"Stay here," I whispered. "Stay."

I might as well have been talking to Finn. She knocked my hand away and clucked. I didn't know the lyrics, but I knew the tune. She was with me for the duration.

"That was a warning shot, you old coot." A man's arrogant voice came through the kitchen window.

"I'd give the money to you if I had it. My son deposits the cash. Why would I keep it here?"

"People say you have the first nickel you ever made and don't hold with banks."

"I don't."

"Then where'd he take the money?"

"The credit union."

"That's a bank."

"No, it's not."

When McClain started to explain the differences between banks and credit unions to the man holding him at gunpoint, I peeked around the blind.

"Shut it, old man." The intruder waved the gun at McClain, who was tied to a chair. "Where's the money?"

I looked at Nellie. "If we survive this, you'll never end up on a platter."

She shook her wings, like a boxer flexing his muscles. I stumbled, and a metal watering can clanged against the house.

A gunshot shattered the window.

I ran and threw myself at the kitchen door. It wasn't latched. I stumbled into the kitchen and Nellie hurtled past me into the gunman. He threw his arms up, and the gun went off.

McClain toppled the chair. The rattled gunman spun back toward him.

I seized a yam from the counter, pulled the pin, so to speak, and let it rip across the room. It hit the robber but didn't bring him down.

I hefted a can of cranberry sauce and put everything into the throw. It glanced off his shoulder as he turned and pointed the gun at me.

Nellie flew at him as I hurled the can of mushroom soup. It caught him right between the holes in his ski mask. He crumpled. The gun went off.

Nellie plummeted to the floor.

Sirens approached the house as I cradled her limp body.

*

We were lucky that night. The sheriff dragged the would-be robber off to jail. Nellie is recuperating at a farm animal sanctuary where Angie and I visit her often. Dawg suffered no lasting effects from being sedated, and McClain has retired from the turkey business. Says it has nothing to do with Nellie helping to rescue him.

We sat down to Thanksgiving dinner without the traditional pièce de résistance. I looked around the table at our good friends, at the roasted root vegetables, the mashed potatoes, the citrus salad, the grilled portobello mushrooms, and the transferware platter piled high with Parker House rolls.

As each guest arrived, I'd told them about Nellie's heroics. They agreed that under the circumstances we could hardly eat a turkey. Everyone was happy save Finn, who wasn't eager to embrace a vegetarian lifestyle.

I raised my wineglass.

"I'm thankful to be here about to share this bounty. Most of all, I'm grateful Nellie survived. Thank goodness the shot—"

"—only winged her!"

Our guests finished the line I'd said to each of them.

Maybe more than once.

Next of Kin

Dianna Sinovic

"Can you come home for Thanksgiving, Riley?"
"Maybe," I told my mother.
Like a monoculture field that's been depleted of nutrients, my family is barren of interest. They didn't get me, never have. I wanted to stay on campus and spend the holiday with the dean of the Agricultural School—he'd invited me and the other Aggie "orphans" who couldn't afford to go home . . . or didn't want to.

"Your brother will be here, and I've invited your aunt and cousin. He has his kids with him this holiday." Mom thought she was tempting me. "It will be a family reunion of sorts." When I didn't take the bait, she tried another tack. "Your father and I are worried about you. You haven't been home since early spring—with no explanation except that you have research to complete."

That I *couldn't* go home was not on her list of reasons. But she didn't know that. And I wasn't going to tell her.

"Your Great-Aunt Garnet will be here." Mom had pulled out her ace of spades. "She hasn't visited for . . . must be at least fifteen years."

I looked at the stack of postcards on my desk. My great-aunt, a thin woman with a shock of wiry hair who smelled of soap and stardust. I might not have seen her since I was a kid, but she had sent me a postcard every year since then—from Belgrade, Lodz, Medellin, Canberra, Cebu, Lagos, and a handful more. They arrived precisely on my birthday, no matter where she was on the globe, and no matter what my address. Except for this year. November seventh came and went without my hearing from her.

And I knew why.

My mother mistook my silence for hesitation. "She's asked to see you."

And so I packed up my laptop and notebooks—finals were the following week—and drove my Civic from the Finger Lakes to Southeast Pennsylvania, hoping I was brave enough to trade a low-key (read: boring) weekend in the Ag lab for a reckoning I knew was due.

*

In the irony of life, my family, the Bucks, lived in Bucks County, about an hour north of Philadelphia. It made for never-ending jokes from friends and family. That Thanksgiving weekend, Pippin, my younger sister, was still at home. My older brother, Theo, was flying in with his partner, Pax, from Chicago. My mother's widowed sister, Roseann, would be there, and my first cousin and his kids. And then Great-Aunt Garnet, my father's aunt.

"Theo and Pax are staying in your brother's old room," my mother reported as she led the way up the stairs, me trudging behind. "Pippin, of course, will stay in her room. She has a friend over."

My sister lounged in her doorway, the friend hovering just behind her, and held her nose. "Wily Riley, home from the farm."

I shrugged at her attempt to needle me. "Manure can work wonders, if you let it."

She giggled and closed the door to shrieks of laughter. *Ah, the joys of being fourteen.*

"Girls," my mother warned, then opened the door to my old room, now converted into the guest room, that overlooked the front yard. "I've put Aunt Garnet in here with you."

Two twin beds, quilted coverlets, lace window treatments, on the wall the framed photo of me astride Two Hatchets when I was twelve and thought horses were my gods. But no Garnet—yet. My shoulders relaxed and my heart stopped doing cartwheels.

"I can sleep on the couch downstairs." I'd hoped for a private oasis from the chaos that was traditional Thanksgiving at the Bucks'. If that wasn't possible, I would rather tough it out alone in the living room than share the bedroom.

"Your great-aunt is seventy-seven. She said she was fine sharing the room with you. And I quote, 'I've had worse roommates.'" My mother straightened a coverlet that didn't need straightening. "You'll get along fine."

I said nothing. There would be no hiding this weekend. I still had time to jump back in my car and drive back to campus. To my own tiny apartment, my own dedicated plot.

When my mother left the room, I plopped my overnight bag on the bed nearest the front window. My choice; I was there first. Great-Aunt Garnet could take the other bed, nearer the door and the noise of the house.

On my pillow sat a square, white envelope. It was addressed to me in the flowing old-school cursive of past generations. With a glance toward the doorway to make sure Pippin wasn't spying on me, I slid a finger under the flap and tore the envelope open. Inside was a greeting card and on the cover a patch of rudbeckias in full bloom, my favorites in a summer garden—with their deep black center and joyous circle of yellow petals. Lucky guess for her to choose that card.

My dearest Riley, the message inside began. *I look forward to seeing you at Thanksgiving. We have much to discuss, especially about Tanner.*

It was signed, *Aunt G.*

With a gasp, I stuffed the card back in the envelope and buried it deep in a pocket of my bag. Of course, she knew. Why had I thought she wouldn't?

"She's been a mercenary soldier." My sister, now in the doorway, whispered this news. "I heard she was also a spy."

"Great-Aunt Garnet?"

"And she cut off a guy's dick once who tried to rape her."

I tried to gauge Pippin's level of truthfulness on this point. She seemed sincere, but she was prone to exaggeration. "Good for her," I said. Those occupations seemed as reasonable an explanation as any for the peripatetic trek Garnet had chronicled on her annual postcards.

*

I sequestered myself in the kitchen, helping with the dinner prep and anticipating Aunt G's arrival. The air smelled of fresh rosemary and yeasted dough. My mother assembled the candied sweet potatoes and checked on the rising dinner rolls. I could see my father through the kitchen window, tending the turkey on the gas cooker set on the patio. Despite a temperature in the thirties, he wore a green Eagles tee and kept rubbing his arms. The rest of the family maintained a rousing conversation in the living room, talking loudly to hear over the TV, tuned to the Cowboys pregame show. My second cousins romped through the kitchen and back out into the living room, playing a game of tag.

"Isn't Pippin going to help?" I groused to my mother. My assignments were the salad and the roasted portabellas —"you're the farmer in the family," my mother had said in explanation.

"She's got that friend over. Her parents are off on a trip to Barbados. Ellie had nowhere to go, so Pippin invited her to spend the weekend with us." My mom said this proudly, as though my sister was a saint. "Sweet, don't you think?"

"Yeah," I said dryly. The youngest in the family was always the spoiled one. The oldest got the acclaim, and the middle one? They got to make salad while their stomach churned with dread.

From the living room, even over the TV, I heard a voice that cut through the air like a foghorn.

My mother stopped stirring the sweet potato mess. "Aunt Garnet is here." She glanced toward the kitchen window. "Go tell your father."

Before I could move, a woman half a head taller than me strode through the swinging doors into the kitchen holding a wrapped bouquet of flowers. If I had expected a matronly woman with gray hair pulled into a neat bun, I would have been quite in error. Great-Aunt Garnet had my father's same slim, muscular build. She wore not a shapeless shift but a jumpsuit of dark green and over it, a vest of a lighter olive; her hair was as dark as mine but with a stripe of white that ran from her forehead back. Her gray eyes assessed me and found me . . . wanting, I guessed. She frowned briefly before bursting into a wide smile at my mother.

"Melissa!" Her voice came out graveled, as though she smoked a daily pack of cigarettes, but she smelled of musk, not tobacco. "You don't look a day older than when I saw you last—must have been back when I just made port from Canberra." She laid the bouquet on the island and air-kissed my mother, then turned to me. "And there you are, Riley Buck."

She enveloped me in a hug that left me gasping, then stepped back to hold me at arm's length. "All grown up and then some," she said, her eyebrows raised as if to ask me a question. Then seeming to remember something, she surveyed the kitchen. "Melissa, where's Frank, my baby? It's been forever."

"Patio," my mother said. "Freezing while he arm-wrestles the turkey."

Aunt Garnet whooped with laughter and left the room.

And then some? The churning in my stomach ramped up as I sliced tomatoes and cucumbers for the salad. The last time we met I must have been all of five, but her gaze just now had reflected back all the years that had elapsed since. Somehow, she *knew* me, more than either of my parents did, more than anyone else knew me. It was frightening but at the same time, a relief.

"She's had a hard life," my mother murmured. She slid the tray of sweet potatoes into the upper oven; the rolls were earmarked for the lower one. "As a spy? A soldier? All those postcards. She never said why she was in those places. I could only guess." And each one had offered a kernel of advice exactly appropriate to the challenge I faced at the time. *How did she know?*

The salad was done, and I moved on to the mushrooms, painstakingly scraping out the gills.

"Postcards?" My mother looked surprised. "You know, she's not really your great-aunt."

I stopped scraping. Waited.

"Your father grew up in the house next door to Garnet, over in Perkasie. She babysat him, and he adored her. Then Frank went off to Penn State, and Garnet disappeared—or he lost track of her. She turned up at our wedding, out of the blue, and of course, we welcomed her." My mother gave the counter a few swipes. "Or, Frank did. I had no idea who she was.

"She got into trouble later, but I never heard the details." My mother took out the canned cranberries from the pantry and opened the lid. "She's kept in contact with us off and on over the years. Frank considers her his aunt."

Digesting this revelation, I finished the mushrooms and tackled the bouquet brought by my maybe-not-great-aunt.

More rudbeckia, plus bee balm, wild lupine—the delicate scents made me smile. Where had she found these in November? Those on the outer perimeter of the bouquet had started to shrivel, most likely touched by the crisp air outside. *A pity.* I retrieved a vase and arranged the blooms, surprised that each petal I brushed perked up slightly. Or had they? Intent on touching the other blooms, I didn't hear the buzzing until the honeybee stung me. "Aaa-ee!" I rubbed my hand, and watched the bee die on the counter.

My mother came to the rescue and quickly removed the stinger, then applied a cold pack. "A bee? How odd," she said. "It should have been hibernating by now." She gently touched the bouquet. "These will look lovely on the table."

Then she was back to her rolls and cranberries. Several minutes later, when I lifted off the cold pack to check on the sting, black specks dotted my reddened skin, forming a name: *Tanner.*

I rubbed my hand, trying to erase the word. How had Garnet magicked the bouquet? Or, my mind argued, it was my guilt serving up a reminder, like leaf rust nodules on wheat.

*

The bedlam in the house kept Aunt Garnet occupied until dinner. She never stepped back into the kitchen, for which I was thankful. It was when we moved to the dining room that I reappeared on her radar.

"Riley, come sit with me," she said. The command in her voice stopped the movement toward seats around the table. Theo shifted over one chair, so I could reluctantly take the one to Garnet's right. The rest of the group sat down as though mesmerized. My father headed up one end of the table, my maybe-great-aunt at the other. The spaces in between filled with Theo and Pax; my mother; my Aunt Roseann; my first cousin; my second cousins, and Pippin and her friend, Ellie.

My father cleared his throat. "Before we begin this meal, I'd like each person at the table to offer something they're thankful for." My cousins giggled and whispered. "I'll start. I am thankful that Garnet could join us today."

And around the circle we went, thanks given for: the Eagles season so far; pizza; Taylor Swift; earthworms (to laughter); Barbies; the roast turkey; good neighbors; Pax (from Theo); Theo (from Pax).

Then it was Aunt Garnet's turn. She looked around the table. "I am thankful for secrets."

All eyes turned to me. *Do they know?*

"Riley?" my father said. "You're last. What are you thankful for?"

I took a breath. Garnet's response had emptied my head. "I'm thankful for . . . my family."

My great-aunt chuckled and unfolded her napkin on her lap. "You are, are you?"

And so we began the feast.

Garnet's presence put a damper on conversation. I felt unnerved by the force that emanated from her. When I glanced at her, she was staring at my plate.

"You don't like the turkey?" She put a forkful of the bird into her mouth for emphasis.

I didn't answer and nibbled at the portobellos.

"She's vegan," Pippin said, smirking. "Ellie is, too."

Garnet held my gaze. "You're majoring in agriculture, but you don't eat meat?"

The rest of the table snickered.

"I'm in the plant science program, not livestock management." My cheeks burned, but it wasn't the first time my family had ribbed me about my dietary choices. "My emphasis will be on developing new crop strains. Sustainable agriculture is the wave of the future."

Theo coughed politely. "My sister would rather eat a brussels sprout than have a strip of bacon pass her lips."

This time there was laughter, and I shot daggers at my brother.

"When I was fighting in Serbia, we ate whatever we could find, to survive," Garnet said. "We didn't ask where the food came from—or even what it was." She buttered her roll and took a bite. "It might have been the scrawniest chicken in the pot or perhaps a rat. They were tasty, with enough pepper and thyme."

Forks paused in midair around the table.

"So, you *were* a mercenary." I wanted to redirect the conversation away from me.

Garnet's smile was crafty. "I was known as Gemstone—my *nom de guerre*—and I'm sure you all can figure out why."

Uneasy chuckles this time, as though the group wasn't sure she was serious—or done talking about rats.

Despite my wariness of her—she would be the invasive species in a field, trying to choke out the soybeans—I felt admiration as well. She wasn't afraid to speak up. I had trouble defending myself, preferring to stay silent rather than argue.

"Were you wounded, in the fighting?"

She patted my hand, my un-stung one. "Not all injuries are physical, my dear. But I'm sure you know that."

Tanner.

I drained my wine glass and motioned to Theo to pass the bottle for a refill. Anything to drown the reminder.

"And you were a spy, too, weren't you?" Pippin said this tentatively.

"Hardly," my father said from the other end of the table. "Your great-aunt has led a busy life, but it has not included espionage."

Garnet arched an eyebrow. "Frank, I love you to pieces, but you don't know shit."

Theo laughed loudly and slapped Pax on the back. "Score one, Aunt Garnet."

With her passive-aggression on full display, my mother rose and began to clear the table. "Coffee anyone?" It was as though nothing untoward had been said in the previous few minutes.

"I'll take a shot of Jameson," Garnet said, passing her plate around to my mother. "The same as Riley."

And yes, Jameson was my choice when I wanted to get seriously smashed. Which I did that night.

*

The final football game was in its last quarter, the kitchen was passably clean, the second cousins had exited, screaming in tiredness. I placed each foot on the stairs carefully, pushing off to the next riser, while my head swam.

Garnet, whoever she was, had traded shots with me for the last two hours, or was it three? Hands down, she was a pro on the drinking circuit. Where I could barely keep my eyes open after the third round, she kicked them back while telling stories to those who weren't focused on the TV. She'd been an inveterate traveler, a dressmaker, a mercenary, a spy—the list went on. I had difficulty concentrating as the evening wore on and might have the sequence out of order. She did not mention babysitting my father, the trouble my mother alluded to, or the incident with the would-be rapist Pippin had shared with me.

At the top of the stairs, I paused to listen for Garnet. Her gravelly alto continued from the living room below, speaking with my brother and Pax, the only ones still standing.

I washed my face and brushed my teeth, putting off as long as possible the conversation that awaited me once Garnet came upstairs to bed. I could feign sleep, but I knew that would be futile.

In my old room, Garnet's suitcase lay on the bed I'd assigned to her. Its scuffed appearance spoke of many miles of travel. Had she been telling the truth about her past? Or was she just an excellent storyteller? My brain was too soaked in alcohol to decide on that.

When I turned to my bag to pull out my sleepwear, I froze. This time my pillow supported not a white envelope but a shriveled red apple marked by several broad lesions. I poked at them. Bitter rot, a fungal disease.

"Yes, you recognize that," Garnet said, taking it from me.

I pushed my bag aside and sank onto the bed, suddenly exhausted. "Why that?"

Garnet pulled out a plastic bag and rolled the apple into it; the bag disappeared into her suitcase and another appeared in her hand. "Perhaps you'd like this sample of black knot on a plum tree instead?" She held out the bag.

I batted her arm away, and the bag fell onto the carpet. "What do you want from me? After all this time, why now?"

She sat on the other twin bed, and we stared at each other for a few moments. The house beyond the room was silent, and my head was spinning. The room carried a whiff of stardust. Outdoors, through the closed window, a great horned owl hooted in the distance.

"Because it's now that you need me," she finally said.

"Need you?" I tensed. I didn't *need* anyone.

"The corn stalk looks healthy to the untrained eye, but the expert knows that the true measure of health lies below the surface. That the longer the malignancy of red root rot remains untreated, the greater the chances it will spread and overtake the entire plant."

She paused and then changed her timbre. *"The world is blind to my pain."*

That she'd said those words—*his* words—made my head swim even worse. "Stop it. Stop it." I held my hands to my face. I would *not* cry.

*

Tanner had cornered me in the library, his hang-dog face drooping even more than usual. I was annoyed; mid-terms started in three days and I had to study.

"Why do they hate me?"

I shushed him. "Nobody hates you."

"Bullshit. T-tell them to leave me alone. P-please." He was stuttering, as he did when he was upset.

"Tell them yourself." Had I enjoyed watching Brett bully Tanner? Part of me did because Brett and I were a thing. But only Tanner and I were plant folks; the rest were engineering or pre-law. He and I had bonded during our first week on campus, sharing our fascination for all things green and growing. We had crammed for tests together and spent hours in conversation about what we saw as our botanic destinies.

"They'll listen to you." Tanner's gaze was pleading. "You're part of the pack. Don't you care?"

Pack? Maybe, but I hadn't *done* anything. I wasn't like them.

"Can't help you." I stuffed my books in my courier bag. Tanner would latch on for the afternoon if I wasn't careful. "I've got to study. Don't you?"

I walked out into the March afternoon, leaving him there. And yet. As I reviewed my notes later for my plant pathology test, my thoughts dredged up the cruel tricks the group had played on Tanner—always, I realized, at Brett's instigation, just because Tanner was easy to pick on. But wasn't Tanner a friend? What did that make me?

He didn't answer the texts I sent that afternoon. His phone went straight to voice mail. On my way to the lab early the next morning, his text showed up: the words that Garnet had intoned. Opening the door to the lab, I stopped: He was there, hanging by a belt strap looped over a steel supply pipe.

*

A sob escaped my throat before I could stop it. "Yes," I whispered. "I cared."

"And now the malignancy is eating at you, that you cared, but not enough to intervene," Garnet said.

I wanted to climb into bed and pull the covers over me. "What can I do?"

She sighed. "It's what you *can't* do that's more critical."

I waited, sure that she had arrived on this national holiday of thanks to tell me I was cursed to an awful fate.

"What you can't do is turn back time," she said. "You can't bring Tanner back no matter how much you want to. And you can't change your former inexcusable behavior." She smoothed the already smooth coverlet. "What you *can* do is forgive yourself."

I shook my head. "I don't deserve forgiveness." There. I'd said it. The curse I couldn't erase.

Garnet tsked. "Our actions always have consequences, but we are also human. Forgiving yourself doesn't absolve you of what you've done; you'll carry that onward. What matters is your honest acknowledgement of that."

"Thank you," I said, not sure I agreed with her.

She seemed to sense my thoughts. "Each day you rise, as the sun rises. Each day you take one step forward, and the past grows a little more distant. And each day you remind yourself that you have a choice: to remember or to forget."

Choice? My thoughts refused to focus, instead grasping at a question I'd been aching for years to ask her. "Why the postcards?"

Garnet smiled and picked up the bag of black knot that had fallen to the floor. "Ah, yes. The postcards. I hope you've like them. I may need to step up the pace a bit."

"But why me? We're not even related."

"Oh, but we are." She looked around my old room. "I'm sorry that our reunion this weekend was so long overdue. But I have followed you since we first met all those years ago. Do you remember what you told me at that time?"

I had no real memory of any interaction with Garnet aside from that hug filled with stardust.

"No," I said.

She stood again and paced the length of the twin bed and back. "You said, in that wonderful wisdom of a small child, 'I am you. You are me. We are one.'"

I returned to my original question: "But why me? You know what I've done. I'm a disappointment."

She stopped pacing. "I owed your father." She held up a hand. "I'll say no more than that. And I sensed in you something that day that blossomed as you grew into the dazzling young woman you are today. The changes you sensed in the bouquet—that was you. You made that happen. Your sister and brother are well and happy and will live satisfying lives, but you, you're almost there, almost at the point where your path diverges. You'll continue to go your way, and they'll go theirs." She paused and looked sharply at me. "And you are not a disappointment. I can't excuse your actions, but what you learn from them will make you stronger."

I didn't feel stronger just then. Sleep was pulling at me, and the ache that guilt had carved in me left me hollow. "The flowers. Am I—are *we*—some kind of magic people?"

She looked at me. "I'm close to the Great Divide, with no cure, they say."

"You're dying?" My great-aunt had walked back into my life only to be called to a quick exit? "You're strong, too. You can beat it."

Garnet smiled and reached out her hands to mine. "Here," she said, and in my right palm she placed a dull blue marble that seemed to have materialized out of thin air. Another trick?

I closed my fist around the marble's coolness and when I relaxed my hand, the object gleamed, with swirls of maple brown, ocean blue, and blinding white—an aggie. Limestone reborn through the forge of the Earth as marble.

"What does this mean?"

"Our magic, if you want to call it that, lies in what we do well. For me, every destination is a place where I can solve a single problem. For you, every successful lab study is a solution to keep famine from our door." She turned to her suitcase and unpacked her nightgown. At the doorway, she paused. "The marble is my legacy to you. You'll figure out soon enough its purpose."

Garnet was absent from the room long enough that the alcohol finally dragged me down into a deep sleep.

*

When I woke, Garnet and her suitcase were gone. The bed was as neat and tidy as though no one had slept in it, but the faint scent of stardust lingered.

Maybe I'd dreamt the bedtime conversation. In any case, my head throbbed with a hangover, and I padded down to the kitchen for a glass of water.

It wasn't yet dawn. Too early for anyone but me. No one else was stirring.

Back upstairs, I sat at the window looking out on the suburban street. The window's broad sill had been my favorite spot to sit and read or think while growing up. The rising sun was behind the house, which kept much of the front yard in frosty dimness. The shadows there reminded me of the morning I'd discovered Tanner: the silence, the lifeless form, my guilt.

"I'm sorry, sorry, sorry," I said to him, to the world. I made my choice: to remember.

I'd been gripping my hands into fists, and when I relaxed them, I discovered in my right hand the marble. The more I rotated it, the more the swirls came to resemble the Earth. A minuscule dot of silver glowed in southern North America, heading south. It was, I knew, Garnet. In the same moment, a gravelly whisper touched my ear: *You will be fine.*

*

After that weekend, back on campus, I plunged into my research. The harder I worked in the lab, the more I paid back Tanner for my crime.

The first postcard arrived just before New Year's. She was in Belize, headed to Peru.

Nitrogen. Give it another look.

My room chilled as I read the words, and the marble, set in a shot glass so I could easily see it, swirled. Sure enough, the tiny dot of silver lay over eastern South America. She was right: I'd dismissed the effects of nitrogen in my latest work. But how had she known this?

The second postcard appeared in my campus mailbox in early March, when the test fields lay under a melting blanket of snow. The card featured a tomb and shrine in Kyoto.

Death is only one step away. For everyone.

I escaped to the campus greenhouses, warm and thickly humid against winter's bite. Walking the aisles, I felt and then saw the seedlings turn toward me as I passed. Just my imagination, I told myself.

*

Despite Garnet's morbid missive, more postcards arrived over the next few months, through the heat of summer and into fall. I allowed myself to hope.

My great-aunt lasted until my birthday, in early November. It had been almost a year since she had reappeared in my life.

At Thanksgiving, gathered once more around the table, we took turns sharing our thanks. The marble rested deep in my pocket. There would be no more prick of silver darting across its tiny expanse.

"I owe Garnet a debt of gratitude," I began, and my father, sitting red-eyed at the other end of the table, nodded. "She saw something in me many years ago, something I would not be aware of myself until much, much later. She cared for that seedling, knowing it would thrive if given enough time and love. It has. I'm thankful for that. I will not let her down."

My brother, Theo, sat next to Pax, bouncing an infant on his knee. A girl. I would need to watch her carefully as she grew up. Tease out what she was good at. Help nurture that. And maybe send her a postcard from time to time.

As Simple as That

Emwryn Murphy

Riley (I/me)

"Wake up!" The hissed words wedged themselves into my dreamless sleep. "Riley, wake up!" I cracked one eye open. The November morning was still pitch dark; the house silent except for distant snoring audible through the walls.

"What? Tina, geez—" I squinted at the glowing red numbers on the alarm clock. "—It's six a.m. I'm sleeping." I rolled away from her and pulled my grandma's quilt up over my head, already drifting back to sleep.

"I can see that." Urgency laced Tina's voice as she grabbed my shoulder, rousing me back to consciousness. "But you have to wake up. There's a *man* on the sofa."

The way she said, *"a man"* reminded me of that scene in Roger Rabbit when the faux Jessica turns and shouts *"A MAAAAN!"*

I stifled a laugh at the image of Tina as Jessica Rabbit and peeked at her over the edge of the quilt. "Did Phil and Cam have a spat?"

"What? No. I mean, probably not." Tina shook her head. "It's not Phil." She paused. "You really think they'd fight like that? Wait... you really think I'd wake you up at the butt-crack of dawn to tell you Phil was on the sofa? And why'd you say Phil and not Eric or Stevie? Phil isn't the only man here, ya know."

My eyes drifted shut while Tina talked to herself.

"Riley!"

"What?" I moaned, pulling the covers back over my head.

"The man!"

I sighed. There was no way I was getting to sleep. Groaning, I pushed myself up to a seated position to try to trick my body into believing I was awake. "Okay, Tina. I give up. Who's on the couch?"

Tina threw her hands into the air and shook her head in a dramatic gesture that sent her long box braids flying around her head. "If I knew that, why would I be waking you up?"

I traced my finger along the quilt's hand-stitched violets as I ran through a mental guest list. Cam and Phil were downstairs in the green room, with easy access to the downstairs exit for Cam's dog, Wolfgang's, calls of nature. Next to them, Norma had her own space in what she called the Indigo Room—which I always thought was blue—because she loved the built-in bookshelves filled with my bibliophilic grandparents' extensive library.

Upstairs, Eric, Stevie, and June had the yellow room, which June picked because of the *Yellow Submarine* song. That left Tina, Taz, and me in here, the purple room. I glanced at the still-empty twin-size bed against the opposing wall of the room. "Did Taz arrive overnight and bring a friend maybe?"

"That's what I thought, too," Tina said, pushing my knees through the covers. I moved over so she had room to sit on the edge of the bed. "But no, Taz isn't here, and 'Subaru' isn't in the driveway. There aren't any new cars in the driveway. Riley . . . who's on your sofa?"

Fully awake now, I sat cross-legged and pulled the covers up for warmth. The November morning was frosty, and the heat from the lake house's woodstove didn't quite reach the upstairs bedrooms. "Who else is awake?"

"No one. I just got up to pee and heard snoring in the living room thingy and went to see. Damn, I still need to pee."

"You pee; I'll check the couch."

I got out of bed and followed Tina down the hall. Somehow it was even colder out there than it had been in the bedroom. I walked with Tina until she peeled off to use the bathroom, then continued alone toward the space that Nana called the Life Room, a multipurpose kitchen/dining/living room space where, as she put it, life happened.

But right now, it was incredibly dark. The little plug-in nightlight in the hall was no match for the early morning darkness partnered with the faux wood paneling on the walls.

As I drew closer to the Life Room, the faint snoring grew louder. I paused. Had I locked the door last night? I meant to. But maybe Phil left it unlocked and someone snuck in? But, why would someone break in just to take a nap? I reminded myself that I was far from alone in this house. One yell, and my friends would have my back. I took a deep breath and moved through the tiny puddle of orange light toward the dark maw ahead.

I paused again as I reached the end of the hall. The snoring was just around the corner. It was loud, even, and undisturbed. Whoever it was, they were fast asleep.

Leaving my feet planted, I placed a hand on the wall to steady myself. The familiar smooth and grooved texture of the paneling was somehow comforting. I leaned forward to peek around the corner and squinted through the darkness. As reported, there was a man wrapped in one of Nana's crocheted afghans. Hesitant to move closer, I pressed my shoulder against the wall and leaned as close as possible. He looked like—

*

CAM (xe/hir)

"—poop?" Cam asked before Phil was even through the door. Phil stepped aside to allow Wolfgang, Cam's dog, inside first. A gust of frozen air blew in as he slid the door shut against the cold.

"Good morning to you too." Phil said, a wry smile spreading across his face. "You didn't have to get up just because I did."

Cam rolled hir eyes. Clearly Phil was not taking this issue seriously. "Well?"

Phil shook his head. "Not yet. I'll take him back out when the sun is up."

Exasperated, Cam lifted hir cast-encased leg from the ottoman and reached for hir crutches. "Pass me the leash. I'll try."

Phil put out a hand. "Let me try again later. I don't want you to get even more hurt trying to walk him on crutches.

Cam opened hir mouth to say something more but was interrupted when rapid footsteps hurried down the stairs behind hir. Cam turned to see Riley, still in pajamas, scampering down the stairs.

"I'm so glad you're awake." Riley hissed. "Houston, we have a problem!"

*

GREG (he/him)

"Why are you sleeping here?"

Greg's eyes snapped open to find a child hovering over him as the first rays of golden sunlight peeked in the windows.

"Woah!" He threw back the afghan and jumped to a seated position, placing his hand on his chest to calm his racing heart. The child seemed unbothered.

"This room is for being awake, and you're not wearing jammies. Did you forget to go to bed, or did you wake up too early? Usually, the grownups aren't up before me. You probably need more coffee, hmm? When you make coffee, can you make me hot cocoa? It's probably okay because it's a special occasion." The child looked hopeful, but then slumped slightly. "I should probably ask my dads though. Even though it is a special occasion. I mean, how often do you find someone sleeping on a couch, right? And we're on vacation." The child's expression brightened again. "Maybe if you make it with water instead of milk, because then it's not as special, right? Just a little special? No more special than apple cider, and I was allowed to have that for breakfast yesterday, but it's so cold here that I want something warm to drink, and hot chocolate is medicinal, right?"

After a pause, Greg realized it was his turn to speak. He ran his hand through his short hair in an effort to stimulate his sleepy brain cells.

"I—uh—I didn't forget to go to bed," he said, scratching his overgrown scruff and making a mental note to shave later. "I arrived while everyone was asleep, and I didn't want to bother anyone by going into the bedrooms."

The child nodded. "Are you Taz?"

"Am I what?"

"Taz? You look different. Wait," the child's eyes narrowed. "Who *are* you?"

"I'm Greg. Who are you?"

The child—girl?—frowned. "That's private information. They said at school that we shouldn't share private information with strangers. So, you don't get to know my name, or that I'm eight years old, or that I have a cat, or that her name is Lily. That's all private. Do you think my dads will let me have cocoa for breakfast, Greg?"

"I have no idea." He closed his eyes, wondering if he was still dreaming. When he looked again, the child was still there. What was going on? "You have multiple dads here?" He asked, feeling like he was missing something.

The child nodded vigorously.

"Who are your dads?"

"Eric and Stevie. They're married, but not gay married. They could be now, but they got married before two dads could get married, but it was okay because nobody knew Dada was a dad then. They thought he was a mom. Even he thought he was a mom! Can you believe it? I mean. He wasn't actually a mom then because I was born later, but you know what I mean, right? Wait, are you a dad or a mom?"

"Neither," Greg said. "I don't have any children."

"Oh. I mean would you be a dad or a mom? Like, what are your pronouns? I'm June and my pronouns are he/they today, but I'm still a girl because that's how I feel on the inside. How do you feel on the inside?"

Confused, Greg took a moment to parse out June's actual question. "I'm Greg," he said at last, "and my pronoun is . . . he . . . I guess? It's nice to meet you, June."

June stepped backward, eyes narrowed. "How do you know my name? That's private information."

"You just told me your name. You said you're June and you're a girl."

"But my pronouns are he/they today."

"Junie?" an androgynous voice came from the hallway. Greg turned on the couch to see a teenage boy enter the room. "I hope you're not bothering—oh—" He stopped midsentence as soon as he saw Greg. "Sorry, I don't think we've met."

"This is Greg." June said, jumping over to the boy. "I thought he was Taz, but he's not Taz. He's Greg. He . . . wait. . . . Did you used t'be Taz?"

Greg shook his head. "Always Greg."

"Do you even *know* Taz?" June asked, shifting from one foot to the other, then spinning in a quick circle.

Greg shook his head again. "Taz is a person?" He guessed.

The boy grabbed June's hand and crouched down to look the child in the eye. "Junie," he said, his voice soft but firm, "that's a lot of private information that you just shared, including my private information. What do we say about that?"

June's face fell. "Sorry, Dada."

Greg studied the boy. "You're her . . . dad?" He tried to do the mental math and it wasn't adding up. "But you *were* her mom?"

The boy sighed. "Is that going to be a problem?" He asked at the same time that June said, "He! Or they! I'm he/they today! The correct way to say it was 'and you were his mom before' or 'you were their mom before.' They is okay, too. Today."

The boy rested his hand on June's shoulder, his eyes not leaving Greg.

Greg realized how his question must have sounded to the boy. "Oh! No, not like that. You just look really young to have a kid."

The boy nodded and seemed to relax a bit. "Ah, that would be the famous second-youth of the trans-masc experience. I'm older than I seem. How do you know Riley?"

*

TINA (she/her)

"Your cousin?" Tina hissed as she scampered down the stairs. "Did I hear that right?"
Riley nodded.
She paused at the bottom of the stairs to take in the scene. Cam, her twin, was seated, broken leg elevated, focused on Wolfgang. Phil, her hopefully someday brother-in-law, was standing nearby holding the dog's rolled-up leash, his attention shifting between Riley and Cam. Meanwhile, Riley was pacing the brown-tiled floor, looking even paler than usual.
"What is your cousin doing here?" Tina asked.
Riley collapsed into a gold-colored vinyl wingback chair that would have been the most dated thing in the room if not for the fact that Cam's chair was the same material in olive green.
"God if I know," Riley moaned. "I have no idea what he's doing here. This was *not* a part of the plan."
"Did he know your grandparents said you could use the lake house this week?" Tina asked, perching on the arm of Cam's chair and letting Wolfgang sniff her hand.
"I don't know," Riley whimpered.
Tina leaned toward her friend. "Is he like, an 'oh yay, my childhood bestie is here' kind of cousin or more of a 'oh crap family drama around the holidays' kind of cousin?"
Riley crumpled forward like an airplane passenger bracing for impact. "I. Don't. Know."
"I know how to find out," Cam said, not looking up from scratching Wolfgang's ears."
Tina slid to the floor to pet Wolfgang and looked up at her twin sibling. "How?"
Cam shrugged. "Ask him."
Phil chuckled softly to himself. "*You'd* ask him?" He asked, his expression a sweet mix of amusement and adoration.

Cam wrinkled hir nose. "I wouldn't," xe said, "because I don't care." Xe reached over and tugged Phil's sleeve. "The sun's coming up and Wolfgang still owes us a big poop."

"What's all this commotion?" Tina turned toward the sound of Norma's voice as she entered the room. Her 6-foot frame was delicately wrapped in a fuzzy pink robe which perfectly matched her pink plush bunny slippers. She held her walking stick like a queen's scepter and somehow seemed to glow as she entered the room. "You youngsters are all far too concerned for this early hour."

"Wolfgang needs to poop and he hasn't," Cam explained. "Not since we left home yesterday. He always poops in the same place, and that place is in Maryland, not New Hampshire. He didn't poop when we stopped in New Jersey, or Massachusetts, and he didn't poop here last night, either. He needs to poop! Bowel regularity is essential to gut health."

"Poor guy," Norma said, leaning over to scratch Wolfgang behind the ears. "Why aren't you pooping, my little boy?"

Cam sighed "Wolfgang's gender is—"

"TBD," Cam, Phil, and Norma said in unison. Tina giggled at the friendly chorus. Seeing her twin among people who appreciated hir made her incredibly happy.

"Oh, I know dear," Norma said, patting the dog on the head. "Old brains forget, you know. My apologies, my canine friend." She lowered herself into the remaining vinyl wingback—this one a dark brown—and rested a hand on the back of Riley's head. "Am I correct in my suspicion that your distress extends beyond your concern for our dear friend's canine's bowel operations?"

Riley nodded without words.

"Riley's cousin is upstairs, and Riley didn't invite him," Tina summarized. "We don't know why he's here."

"Well," Norma said with her characteristic certainty, "it seems there is only one solution to this quandary—" she paused for dramatic effect.

"I already told them to ask him," Cam said with an eye roll. "I mean, if they want to know, that's how to know."

"And?" Norma prompted.

"*I'm* not doing it," Cam said with a shrug.

"Well, you don't have to ask me twice," Norma said. "There's a handsome young man asleep upstairs. What kind of a lady would I be if I didn't greet him?"

"Uh, guys—" Tina started, while Phil said, "How do you know he's handsome?" and Cam growled, "Norma, he's half your age."

From her chair, Norma held out a finger in the way grandmothers do when the young people must pay attention. "I will have you know," she said with all the dignity of a matriarch, "that in transition years, I'm still a young maiden, and any cousin of Riley's is bound to be extremely handsome."

"Guys—" Tina tried again.

"Gross," Cam grumbled. "Come on, Wolfgang. I'll take you outside."

"No," Phil said. "I'll try again. You sit." Wolfgang sat. Cam scowled and crossed hir arms.

"Make sure you walk with him," xe said. "Maybe he wants to poop in some grass. Or near a tree. Give him options—" But Phil was already gone with the dog.

"Excuse me," Tina said, lightly punching Cam's shoulder.

Riley looked up. "I'm listening."

"As I was saying," Tina said with an exaggerated sigh. "He's not asleep upstairs. I heard him talking to June when I came out of the bathroom."

*

Phil (he/him)

"Come on, buddy," Phil said leading Wolfgang back outside into the cold.

The sun was rising over the lake, transforming the darkness into a peaceful, if frigid, pre-winter morning. The drive north yesterday had taken them through all the stages of fall. Maryland still had bright autumnal hues but up here the trees were all bare; the ground covered in crunchy brown leaves.

He led the dog down the hill to the edge of the lake. There was a layer of ice covering the water. He wondered how soon it would be solid enough to skate on. Probably not this visit.

Wolfgang sat quietly beside him, looking out over the frozen water. Phil dropped a hand to caress the dog's head. "What do you think, buddy? Is this a good place to poop?"

The dog's head tipped back, studying Phil with deep brown eyes. "What is it, pal?" Phil asked. But the dog's secrets remained unspoken.

*

Riley (I/me)

If I hadn't been seated already, Tina's words would have sent me to the floor. Greg was up there. With June. Adorable, precocious, *talkative* June. I had to... what? I had to fix this. I had to... my brain wouldn't give clear instructions. I realized Tina and Norma were staring at me. Cam was looking out the window at Phil and Wolfgang.

"He doesn't know." I managed to choke past the lump in my throat. "I'm not really out to my family."

"Is he like your parents?" Tina whispered.

"I don't know." I felt the lump in my throat spread up to my eyes and fought the tears that wanted to spill. "We didn't grow up talking about religion and politics. When we saw each other, we were here where we were safe because the nearest church was so far away that we couldn't attend."

"Isn't there a church about three minutes from here?" Norma mused.

"Yeah," I sighed. "But you know my parents. It wasn't *their* church, so it didn't *count*."

Norma nodded. "Well, I suppose there's only one thing to do then." She planted her cane firmly on the floor and pushed herself to a standing position. I stood and took a step toward the stairs.

"We need to help Cam upstairs," Tina reminded us.

I hesitated and looked at Cam, who was struggling with hir crutches to stand up.

"Let Transma handle this," Norma said, resting a hand on my shoulder. "You go ahead. I'll make sure we all get ourselves dressed and up there."

I nodded and moved toward the stairs, taking a deep breath as I started to climb. I held the railing for support, my hand shaking. I paused to listen when I reached the second floor. I could hear three voices in the Life Room: Greg, June, and Stevie. I felt some of the tension drain from my shoulders. Stevie could handle Greg for a moment.

Rather than turning left toward the voices, I went straight across the hall into the bathroom. I splashed cold water on my face and studied my reflection in the mirror. My face was different, but would Greg notice? The changes were still subtle... probably only visible to someone who knew what to look for.

I looked down at my body. At my chest. Well... that was unmistakably different. He couldn't miss that. Unless—

I cracked open the bathroom door. The voices in the great room sounded amiable. Stevie was still there.

I turned left out of the bathroom and passed my bedroom to tap quietly on the door to the yellow room. Eric opened the door. "Hey," he greeted me. "What's up?"

"Sorry, can I grab something from the closet?" I asked.

"Sure," Eric held the door open and moved aside to let me in. "Where is everyone?"

"Umm, Norma, Tina, and Cam are downstairs . . ." My mind focused on the clothing options in front of me. There. That would do.

I reached for the hanger and remembered Eric's question. "Ummm and June and Stevie—" I turned toward the doorway, but Eric was gone. Huh.

I pulled my grandfather's biggest sweatshirt over my head, inhaling the smell of him and feeling safer for it. My grandparents were the exception to the rule when it came to my family. They were the only ones whom I felt safe coming out to.

"Okay," I said to the empty room. "I guess there's just one thing to do now."

*

Phil (he/him)

"Let's try walking," Phil said, as a shiver shook his body. "At least it will *feel* warmer." He closed his eyes and pictured the route that Wolfgang and Cam took each morning. He led the dog up the hill to the road, then tried to emulate that route, estimating distances between turns.

"Okay, we go this far," he narrated to the dog. "And then we turn left." He looked at the side of the road. Turning left here would take them into a neighbor's yard. "We'll just turn extra left," he said, turning them a full 180 degrees to the left and walking back toward Riley's grandparents' house.

"Funny. Riley has never mentioned a cousin," Phil mused to the dog. "I wonder why he's here."

Wolfgang walked on, sniffing the ground as they went.

"I know Riley's parents are super religious," Phil continued. "But does that mean that the whole family is? And even if they are, would that matter when it came to someone they loved?" Phil thought of his own coming out process. Totally different, of course. His parents were former hippies who took pretty much everything in stride. Sometimes, a little too casually for Phil's taste.

Wolfgang whimpered and pulled against the leash, returning Phil to the present. He let out a long breath and watched the steam from his lungs mingle with the outside air.

"You're right, buddy. It's cold. Would you like to poop before we go inside?"

The dog just stared at him, unimpressed with the suggestion. Phil noticed a snowflake dancing to the ground between them. It was followed soon by another.

"Please poop?" he implored the dog.

Wolfgang's eyes moved from Phil to Riley's grandparents' house.

"You wanna go inside?"

Wolfgang's tail wagged at the word "inside."

"Okay, buddy, let's go back and warm up. We'll try again after breakfast."

*

Stevie (he/they)

"Would you like some coffee, Greg?" Stevie asked, moving to the kitchen portion of the great room.

"Yes, please." Greg stood and stretched; his spine releasing an audible pop.

Stevie pulled an extra mug from the cabinet and opened the airtight coffee tin he'd brought from the queer-owned coffee shop back home.

"Ry!" Greg exclaimed.

Stevie looked up to see Riley swimming in an oversized hoodie, hesitating at the entrance to the room. Greg spread his arms wide as he crossed the space between them, but he hesitated when Riley didn't return the gesture, instead shrinking away from the contact. Well, that answered the question of whether Greg knew about his cousin's transition. Stevie had been in those shoes before.

"Sorry to arrive unannounced . . ." Greg sounded confused. "How are you? It's been too long."

Stevie made a pretense of making the coffee while keeping an ear on the conversation.

"What was it, Great Aunt Edna's funeral?" Greg asked. "We really need to make a point to see each other more often. We're family, after all."

"Dada, may I please have some coffee?" June asked, climbing up onto a bar stool and resting their elbows on the sliver of counter that separated the kitchen from the dining area. They were blissfully oblivious to the drama unfolding nearby.

"Is that why you're here?" Riley asked, echoing the question in Stevie's head.

"What? No." Greg shook his head. "I wouldn't just—"

"Dada?" June's voice drew Stevie's attention away from his eavesdropping. He held a finger up to his lips and tried to piece together Greg's explanation about snow somewhere, canceling his flight.

"May I *please* have coffee?"

Stevie's attention focused on his child's request. "You want coffee?"

June made a show of thoughtfully pursing their lips and tapping their chin. "Hmmm, you're right, I probably am too young. In that case, hot cocoa is probably a better idea."

"—and when I told my parents I wasn't going to be able to reach them for the holiday, they said Nana said that you were here with some friends, and I thought, 'hey, that sounds better than spending Thanksgiving snowed in at Logan.'"

"Do Nana and Pop know you're here?" Riley asked.

"Nah, they were asleep by the time I decided to come. Fortunately, they haven't moved the hide-a-key since last time."

Stevie reached for a packet of hot cocoa as Riley mumbled, "If you'd called ahead, I'd have waited up for you."

"Oh, I tried," Greg said. "Your phone is off."

"It is? Crap!" Riley turned and ran out of the room.

Stevie looked down at his hands, the open hot cocoa packet clutched in his fingers. "Wait a minute. Junie!" He looked at his child's grinning face and laughed.

"It almost worked," June said through a giggle.

"Yeah, kiddo, not for breakfast."

"I missed six calls from Taz," Riley said, returning to the room. Stevie reached for his phone and checked for messages. "Nothing here," he said. Riley motioned for silence and listened to a voicemail message.

"They say they're running late—"

"Is that Taz?" Norma asked, gently moving Riley out of the hallway and into the room. "I didn't see Ms. Rivera in the driveway. Shouldn't they have been here by now?"

"Voicemail," Riley said. "Something about car trouble, but they're on their way and should be here soon."

"And you must be the cousin," Norma said, fixing her eyes on Greg. "Just as handsome as promised." She turned to Stevie. "Your gentleman husband is helping Cam up the stairs and asked that I relay to you his most ardent desire for a cup of coffee."

Riley muttered something about helping and disappeared down the hall as Greg retreated to the picture window overlooking the lake.

"Tina, dear," Norma said to the young woman behind her. "If you would be so kind as to bring in some firewood, we can make use of that charming fireplace. I do so love a Keeping Room with a fireplace."

"That's a deal," Tina said. She grabbed her coat from the hook by the kitchen door and went outside.

*

Eric (he/him)

"You must be the handsome cousin," Eric said as he helped Cam settle at one end of the Chesterfield. Greg jumped and turned toward him as he spoke. "Sorry, didn't mean to startle you. I'm Eric." He crossed the room and extended a hand in greeting.

"Why am I now the handsome cousin?" Greg asked.

"Word travels fast around here." Eric chuckled. He pulled a wooden chair away from the dining table and positioned it so Cam could elevate hir broken ankle.

"Tell me about it," Greg said. "You're not Taz, so you must be the Not Gay-Married Married Gay Husband?"

Eric grinned. "Let me guess. You've met June?"

Greg nodded. "I didn't follow it all."

"This will help," Stevie said, handing a mug of steaming coffee to Greg, and another to Eric. Greg's eyes followed Stevie as he returned to the kitchenette. "Coffee?" Stevie offered Norma.

"If by coffee you mean 'The Best Part of Waking Up,' then I would be delighted. With just a splash of milk, please."

Stevie made a face. Eric knew well his husband's views on instant coffee, but for Norma, even Stevie would prepare a cup of Folgers.

The kitchen door opened and Tina entered with an armful of split wood. She saw what Stevie was doing and said, "Oh, I'll take a cup of the good stuff, please. Black and sweet. Like me. Where do you want this, Norma?" She nodded toward the wood in her arms.

"Next to the Davenport please, dear."

"This is why we're friends," Stevie said, pushing the sugar bowl across the bar.

"I'll take it to go," Tina said, placing the wood between the fireplace and the Chesterfield. "I'm gonna run and get dressed." She brought Norma her Folgers and then took her own mug from the bar and disappeared down the hall.

Eric hesitated. Unsure whether he should offer to build a fire or focus on supporting his husband. Stevie picked up his mug, his face reflecting a variety of emotions and thoughts. Eric glanced at Greg who was staring into his untouched coffee. "Try it," he urged. "You'll be glad."

Greg took a careful sip. "Oh, this is amazing," he said, closing his eyes to savor the flavor as he lowered himself into one of the wooden chairs that surrounded the dining table.

"It's Kona," Stevie said, pulling out a chair on the opposite side of the table. Eric moved to the chair next to his husband. He could feel the tension behind Stevie's casual demeanor and knew his beloved was likely remembering his own cousin's reaction to news of his transition.

Stevie and his cousin, Brie, had been the closest of childhood friends. She had been Stevie's maid of honor, they had talked on the phone at least weekly, they had kids around the same time and even had a joint baby shower. But when Stevie shared the truth about his gender, his cousin had told him, "we can stay friends, but I don't want my child exposed to a transgender situation." *Transgender Situation*—Eric knew those words continued to haunt Stevie years later. He, however, felt ambivalent about the whole thing. He'd never particularly warmed up to Brie and felt that if she was so transphobic that she couldn't see past her own prejudice, Stevie—and especially June—didn't need that kind of toxicity in their life. But, on the other hand, he felt for his husband's pain at the loss, and worried for Cate, his niece, who not only lost a beloved cousin, but was also being raised in a family that could prove unsafe if she turned out to be trans herself.

Eric reached for Stevie's hand and gave it a squeeze. He could tell from the crease in Stevie's forehead that he was doing what they called Safety Math. That mental calculation of who was around, what their views were, what power they might have, and whether it was safe to be his fully authentic self in this space. He lifted Stevie's hand to his mouth and kissed his fingers to remind him that he was safe here, even if Greg turned out to be a massive transphobe.

"Hey, Dad," June called from the head of the table. "Can I have hot cocoa with my oatmeal?"

"No," Stevie and Eric responded in unison.

Greg's eyes opened. "She's quite a talker," he said, a note of admiration in his tone.

"My pronouns are he/they today," June called.

"Thanks for letting us know, kitten," Eric said with a wink.

"I don't understand what that means, I guess," Greg said, cupping his coffee mug in both hands and taking another sip.

"What's confusing?" Stevie asked. Eric felt his grip tighten as he spoke.

Greg swallowed and set his mug on the table. "She said she's a girl," he said, his eyes glued to his coffee, "but she said her pronouns are he/they? Shouldn't she be she? I don't get it."

"*He* said *he's* a girl," Stevie corrected. "And today *his* pronouns are he/they."

Eric glanced at Riley, who was leaning against the kitchen counter, scrutinizing the conversation from across the room.

"He said he's a girl," Greg said, he paused still studying his coffee mug. "So, he's actually a . . . boy? Like, he's a tran—ya know?" He looked up, his eyes moving from Stevie to Eric and back.

"Transgender?" Stevie suggested.

"Yeah, I wasn't sure the exact word and didn't want to say the wrong one," Greg said, scratching his beard. "Thanks. I'm not trying to be a jerk. I'm just . . . wicked confused." An embarrassed smile crossed his face. Suddenly Eric could see the resemblance between Greg and Riley. His heart opened up a bit. Greg might look like a typical cis/het white boy, but Eric could sense there was some hope for this one.

Eric felt Stevie take a slow deep breath and knew he was trying to stay present in this moment and not get pulled back in time to earlier, similar conversations. Emboldened by the hope of constructive connection and careful not to speak to his husband's experience, Eric said, "It's okay for us to be confused, as long as we're respectful of others, ya know? Life can sometimes be the most confusing right before it makes the most sense." He put an arm around Stevie's shoulders as he spoke. "For example, it wasn't all that long ago that I considered myself to be a straight man. Where I grew up, people weren't gay. I mean, of course we were, but no one talked about such things. As a result, I repressed that side of myself so successfully that even I didn't know. I did that until I just couldn't anymore. Not being my authentic self was killing me, even though I didn't know it. Then I realized, or admitted to myself, that I'm gay, and suddenly so many things came into focus. But at the same time, I was even more confused because I was married and was still completely in love with my spouse."

"That was me," Stevie said. Eric was relieved his husband was back with them. "Eric said, 'I'm gay, but I'm still attracted to you.' He was so confused, but for me it was amazing because I knew I was a man by that point, but I hadn't told anyone." He rested his head on Eric's shoulder.

"That's . . . convenient," Greg said.

Stevie nodded. "It meant everything to me that we had a relationship that gave me the space to grow into myself without the fear of losing the one I loved. It still does." He squeezed Eric's hand and snuggled a bit closer.

Eric kissed Stevie's head, inhaling the familiar scent of him. "So that's what we're doing for June," Eric continued. "Only June can know what June's gender is. Only June knows which pronouns feel good for June. We're consciously fostering an environment where June can try on the different options without judgment, and ultimately know that whatever they decide, whoever they are, we're here for June and love June one hundred percent."

"Even if I'm not June," June said through a mouthful of oatmeal. "Even if I'm Elsa, or Rapunzel, or Eliza, or . . . Smurfmobile!" June giggled and shoveled more oatmeal into their mouth.

Greg nodded slowly several times and took another sip of coffee. "Okay," he said at last. "I . . . I still don't totally understand, but also, yeah, I respect that you're June's parents. And I guess I don't . . . need to understand?" His eyes returned to Eric's, then Stevie's, and back.

"Right," Stevie said. "It's as simple as that. Just respect June as he explores his identity and trust that June will figure out who they are."

"You can use she/they," June said, bouncing in his chair. "*If* you give me hot chocolate for breakfast."

"No," Greg, Eric, and Stevie all said in unison.

*

Tina (she/her)

Tina chose an outfit that best highlighted her femme assets. Norma was right, Greg was pretty hot. She wondered if he was a good kisser. She also wondered if there was any more coffee left. The stuff Stevie made was amazing.

She made her way back to the common room. Norma was teaching Riley how to build a fire, Cam was reading a book, and the guys were at the table, deep in conversation. She moved around the peninsula to refill her mug.

The kitchen door opened as she passed it and Phil entered with Wolfgang. The dog shook off a dusting of snowflakes.

"Hey, Wolfie," Tina said, leaning forward to scratch the pup's ears. "Who's the goodest pooper?" The dog leaned into her fingers for a moment, eyes closed, before crossing the room to curl up by Cam's feet. Phil followed Wolfgang across the room and bent to kiss Cam on the forehead. "Nothing yet," he said softly. "I'll try again soon." Phil reached into his pocket and handed Cam hir ear plugs. Phil really loved Cam for hir full self, neurotic tendencies and all. Even if he were completely hideous, which he most certainly was not, Tina would have to love him for the way he loved Cam.

As she refilled her mug, Tina caught Greg staring at the couple from the table. "Adorable, right?" she said, moving toward the chair next to him. Greg looked up at her and blushed when he met her eyes.

She sat in a way she hoped he would appreciate. If he was as straight as he appeared, that is.

Greg's eyes flicked back to his coffee, but the redness in his cheeks remained.

"I'm Tina," she said with a seductive smile, hoping to get another look at his baby blues.

"Hey," he said, looking back toward her and somehow blushing even more. Yup. She had him.

"I'm Cam's twin," she said, gesturing toward the sofa. "Cute together, aren't they?"

Greg looked toward the couple and nodded. Then he looked back at Tina, still blushing. "Um . . . is it okay if I ask a question?"

Tina nodded and rested her chin on the heel of her hand, leaning toward Greg. "Ask me anything, handsome."

Greg hesitated, taking a slow breath. "Are they gay, too? Like . . . is Cam a boy or a girl?"

Oh, that was disappointing, but Tina didn't let her smile falter.

"Cam's pronouns are xe/hir/hirs." She explained. "Xe isn't a boy or a girl. And as for Phil, he's queer, of course, but I don't actually know if he uses the label 'gay.' The only way to know for sure would be to ask him."

"You lost me," Greg said, scratching his scruffy chin. "What do you mean Cam's not a boy or a girl?"

"Well." Tina thought for a moment. "I'm guessing when you were born, they said 'it's a boy,' is that right?" Greg nodded. "Okay, and when you say to yourself 'I'm a boy' how does that feel?"

Greg frowned. "I don't know. True? I guess?"

"Okay," Tina said. "So, imagine you woke up tomorrow and your body..." She gestured toward Greg's belt. "... was completely different, and everyone said, 'Greg's a girl.' How do you imagine that would feel?"

"Um... not good?" Greg shrugged. "Confusing?"

Tina nodded. "Okay, so that feeling of who you are. That internal knowing. That's your gender. For many people, their sex and gender match. But for others, they don't. Your sex is what your body is; your gender is what *you* are."

"So Cam—" Greg's forehead creased as he thought. "Cam doesn't feel like a boy or a girl and whatever... xe?" Tina nodded. "Whatever xe feels like, it's not he or she? It's... something else?"

"Exactly," Tina said, nodding. "Now you get it."

"Well, I wouldn't go *that* far. But at least I feel like I know what I'm not understanding. If that makes any sense?"

Tina looked at Cam and Phil and smiled. "It makes perfect sense."

"And for Phil, he's not gay because Cam isn't a dude?"

"Not exactly," June chimed in from the end of the table. "He's not gay, like the small gay—the one where men want to marry men and only men—because even though Phil is a boy, Cam isn't a girl but also isn't a boy. So not the small gay. But we're all gay in the big way, like queer or LGBTQIAA plus. *Everyone* here is gay in the big way... but mostly not in the little way." June grinned, oblivious to the sudden awkward silence that had fallen on all the adults.

"Hey, we should get the turkey in the oven," Greg said, glancing at his watch.

"Junie, why don't you put your bowl in the sink and go get dressed," Stevie suggested.

"Okie dokie, picka-packa-pokie!" June said. She dropped her bowl off in the sink, and then skipped out of the room singing, "I'll get dressed in the yellow submarine, yellow submarine..."

When she closed the bedroom door, it felt unnaturally quiet. "Um, did you say you brought a turkey?" Tina asked, turning to Greg.

"What? No. I mean . . ." Greg looked confused again. "I guess I just assumed there was a turkey what with it being Thanksgiving?"

*

Norma (she/her)

Norma leaned on Riley's hand as she stood up from the hearth next to a now-roaring fire. She met Greg's eyes across the room just as a door opened and June's voice called from the hall. "Not Thanksgiving. *Friends*giving. Thanksgiving is a celebration of colonization and murder." She slammed the door shut and they could just hear her singing, "It's a-bout col-na-zation and mur-der," to the tune of "Yellow Submarine."

Norma chuckled. Greg smiled and gave a small shake of his head. "No, June's right," Norma said. "Look up John Winthrop. The first declaration of a Day of Thanksgiving was to celebrate the safe return of armed colonial volunteers who had just massacred seven hundred Pequot people of all genders and ages."

"That's why we do Friendsgiving," June said, skipping back into the room clad in a sunny yellow sweater and rainbow leggings. "Friendsgiving is a celebration of chosen family. And that's us."

"How *do* you all know each other?" Greg asked.

"We—" June started.

"Junie," Norma said, pointing to the window. "Look at the snow."

"Snow!" June ran to the window, where Tina joined her in admiring the torrent of flakes falling from the sky. "Can we go out and play please-please-please-please-*please?*" June asked, jumping up and down.

"Your cousin is a special person," Norma said to Greg, sidestepping his question as she eased herself onto the Davenport. "Riley has a way of making everyone feel at home."

"Announcement, everyone!" June called from the window. "It is now time to go play in the snow."

"Excellent idea, my dear," Norma said. "Riley," she said, turning to their host, who was still holding her elbow. "Shall we do some kitchen work while the children play?"

Riley nodded and sent Norma a look of gratitude while Tina, June, and the dads bundled up against the cold and went outside. Greg excused himself to get cleaned up, and with Phil and Cam huddled on the Davenport on the opposite side of the great room, Norma and Riley enjoyed relative privacy in the galley.

At first, they worked together in silence, removing the frozen contributions everyone had brought, and arranging them in the oven and various air fryers so everything could be ready at once. When all the timers were set, and they were satisfied they weren't going to overwhelm any fuses, they sat at the table to make the salad. As she cut up the lettuce, Norma heard Riley sigh.

"Have I ever told you about my brother?" she asked. Riley didn't respond, which she took as license to continue. "We were close as children. Thick as thieves. Birds of a feather. I was like his shadow. Anything he did, I wanted to be right there by his side. This was back in the day when kids ran around outside until the streetlights came on. My parents never worried because I was always with him."

Slicing tomatoes, Riley nodded but didn't speak.

"Well, we grew apart as we aged. He married and had a bunch of kids. We didn't live in the same state. We were busy. You know, the usual things. I missed him very much, but I was also afraid. I knew who I was, and I was afraid if I came out to him, he wouldn't want to be my brother anymore. I thought it was easier to not tell him and just stay away. I thought I could just live with the memories of our childhood together and that would be enough." She pushed the lettuce into a large bowl and set it to the side, then picked up the can opener and a can of olives. "Well, as life has a way of doing, we were thrown together unexpectedly, and that choice was taken out of my hands."

The can opener was the new-fangled kind, so she handed it to Riley to operate. She held on for just a second too long and Riley met her eyes. "And do you know what he said when I came out to him?" she asked. She could tell she had Riley's attention now. "He said 'I am so sorry if anything I ever said or did led you to think that I'd ever hate you for being who you are.'" She paused for effect, before scooping the tomato chunks from Riley's cutting board and sprinkling them over the lettuce.

"Sometimes," she said softly, "people surprise you." She struggled to her feet, untied her iris-printed apron and draped it over the back of her chair. "I will say this, though. We can't live life denying ourselves. Take it from your elder, you're more likely to wish you'd come out sooner than wish you'd remained in hiding."

She heard a commotion outside and looked out the window. "Oh good, it looks like Taz is here."

*

Taz (they/them)

No sooner had Taz eased to a stop and put the car in park than a snowball hit the windshield, completely obscuring their view. "You know what that means?" Taz shouted opening the driver's side door and jumping out.

"War!" June shouted, lobbing another snowball that narrowly missed Taz's head. "But time out. Not actual real war, like the bad kind. Just snow war, right?"

"You got that right, kiddo," Taz said, stooping to gather snowy ammunition.

"Junie," Eric said, jogging around the house. "Let Enty Taz acclimate before declaring war on them."

"But what if the snow melts before they're acclimated?" June asked.

Taz looked at the ground. At least five inches had fallen, and the air was still thick with flakes. "This isn't going anywhere fast," they assured the child. "And if my drive here was any indication, neither are we."

"How were the roads?" Eric asked, moving behind the car to help with Taz's bags.

"Terrible," Taz said. "Fortunately, nothing 'Subaru Rivera' couldn't handle. She's one feisty broad." They patted the roof of their car. "Ended up giving some folks a ride to Concord when their Honda went off the road. That's why I'm late."

"Taz!" Stevie chided them, shaking his head. "Leave it to you to pick up hitchhikers in a snowstorm. I wish you'd be more careful."

Taz chuckled. "Well, I'm here now, and none the worse for wear. The world needs every bit of kindness it can get. Plus, they were so grateful they gave me this." They hefted a pre-cooked turkey breast into the air.

"That's good Karma," June said. Then, with a glance toward her dad's disapproving expression, added, "But it wasn't very safe. I would have called an adult." She wagged her finger at Taz like a cartoon schoolmarm.

"As well you should, my dear. Do as I say, not as I do. Sneak attack!" Taz lobbed a snowball, gently hitting June square in the chest.

"Hey! Cheater!" June giggled, tossing snow back.

Fifteen minutes and countless snowballs later, Taz finally made it inside. Norma welcomed them with a steaming mug of hot cocoa. "Don't tell the boys," she said with a wink. "I have some for June, too, when they come inside. By the time you reach my age you learn a few things. Perhaps the most important is that everyone needs hot cocoa after a snowball fight." She hooked a thumb toward Riley. "That, and 'let people show you who they are.' Tied for most important."

Taz shook their head. "Well, I clearly missed something, but I will say, at my age, I've learned that listening to Norma is generally a very good idea." They gave her a big hug, careful not to spill cocoa on her blue dress.

"Speak of the devil," Norma said, gesturing over Taz's shoulder. "Greg, meet Taz."

Taz turned to see a clean-shaven young man with damp hair enter the room wearing sweatpants and a Red Sox jersey. "Hey," Greg said, extending a hand.

"Hello, new friend. Do you hug?" Taz said, spreading their arms wide.

Greg froze for a moment but then said, "Sure, why not?"

Taz wrapped him in their arms. "Welcome to Friendsgiving. Glad to know you. You a member of the Alphabet Mafia?"

"Am I a . . . what?" Greg said mid hug.

"Excuse me, folks, coming through," Phil said. "I can feel my toes so it's time to take the dog back out, but then I'll be back for my hug, okay?"

"Sure thing, brother," Taz said, releasing Greg and moving to the side to let Wolfgang pass.

"Greg's my cousin," Riley explained.

Phil opened the door and stepped back as June, Eric, and Stevie tumbled inside. "It's getting nasty out there," Eric said. "Be careful."

"We'll stay nearby," Phil promised.

"June," Norma stage whispered. "Transma made you cocoa."

"I don't keep secrets from my dads," June stage-whispered back with a grin.

"Of course not, dear," Norma said. "What do you think, dads?"

Stevie shook his head in resignation. "Who are we to disagree with Transma?"

"There you go, my dear," Norma said. "Let's sit at the table and you can tell me all about third grade."

"After we change into warm clothes," Eric added with a wink, ushering his family through the room.

"Can I help you settle in?" Greg asked Taz, picking up the suitcase at their feet. "Which room, Ry?"

"Uh, purple," Riley said. "Twin bed."

"Righto, cuz," Greg said, leading the way.

Taz followed but stopped short when the kitchen door flew open.

*

Riley (I/me)

The door crashed open. "I'm so sorry," Phil shouted. "He got away from me. He was right there with me, but then there was this cracking sound and a branch fell nearby, and I jumped and he jumped and the leash broke and I need help finding him!"

"I'm going," Cam said, jumping up from the couch. "Ow!"

"No, you are not," Tina said, catching her twin as xe teetered on one foot.

"I'm coming," I said. "Tina, you stay with Cam. Taz, Greg, come on."

I ran out into the snow, trusting they'd be right behind me. The flakes outside were so thick and furious that it was impossible to see more than a few feet away. Fearing the worst, I walked toward the road. "Wolfgang," I called out. "Here boy, er, girl, um, dog! Here doggo! Wolfgang, where are you?"

Excited barking drew my attention. Glancing back at the house, I saw that someone thoughtful had turned on the outside lights. While they didn't make anything clearer on the ground, they at least offered a helpful landmark. And the barking was coming from the other side. *Wolfgang must be down by the lake.*

I ran past the house and followed the sound of barking. Eventually I could see the faint outline of a squatting dog. I slowed my pace and inched closer, not wanting to spook him into running again. I heard distant voices calling his name. "He's here," I shouted. "And he's pooping."

"Where are you?" Greg called back. He sounded far away.

"Um . . . here," I said. "I don't know. Somewhere between the house and the lake. But it's fine. I'll grab him and head back to the house."

I was close enough to reach for Wolfgang's collar, but when the dog finished squatting, it pushed past me and ran back toward the house.

"Ingrate!" I yelled, turning to follow him. Then the ground below me gave way and I crashed through the ice.

*

Greg (he/him)

Greg heard the splash and instantly knew what had happened. He raced in the direction of the sound, passing Wolfgang on the path toward the lake.

"Ry," he yelled. "Riley!"

He heard another splash and then, "Oh god, it's so cold!"

"Are you okay?" Greg could just make out Riley's outline through the snow. It took all of his willpower to keep himself from rushing to his cousin's side. With the layer of snow, he wasn't sure where the ground ended, and the lake began. "Can you get out of there?"

"I'm fine. I—I'm just stuck on something."

"I'll come get you."

"No" Riley shouted. "I just—what if I—oh fine." There was another splash as Riley disappeared back under the water.

Greg took two steps forward, hitting the ice as Riley reemerged.

"I'm fine," Riley said through chattering teeth. "My hoodie is just stuck on something."

"Leave it," Greg shouted. He took another step toward his cousin and fell through the ice, but only up to his knees. He glanced back toward the house and could just make out the outdoor lights.

"Leave it, Riley. It's freezing here. Come on."

"My fingers are numb. I can't take it off." Riley's voice was so close that Greg realized his cousin was in far more danger from the cold than the depth of the water. He pushed his way through the icy water until he was close enough to help ease the hoodie over Riley's head. He wrapped his cousin in a hug. Riley was shivering so hard they both shook with the force of it.

"Let's get back inside." Greg pulled Riley toward shore.

*

Riley (I/me)

By the time I was warm and dry, the house was full of the smells of everyone's favorite foods. Norma gave each of us a mug of cocoa and lamented that she hadn't brought matzo meal to make her mother's soup.

June and her dads were all in matching yellow long johns and slippers. Tina was assisting Taz in the kitchen where they were heating up the turkey they'd inherited from the hitchhikers. Cam and Wolfgang were huddled together close to the fireplace while Phil made sure they each had everything they needed.

Greg returned in red flannel pajamas, once again wrapped in Nana's red afghan. "Mind if I sit?" he asked, gesturing to the cushion beside me.

"If you want to," I said.

Greg sat and put an arm around my shoulders. We stayed that way in silence for a long time. I didn't know what to say or where to start. Greg knew. He had to know. There was no way he could have missed it. But he was also still there. And he didn't seem mad.

"You . . . okay?" I finally asked. "With . . . ya know?"

Greg rested his head against mine. "Of course, Ry—er—Riley. It makes sense in a way. And, well, even if I don't fully understand it all, I respect you. Hell, I love you. Nothing changes that."

"Of course you do!" June interjected from across the room. "Friendsgiving is for family, and family are the people we love no matter what."

Greg squeezed me close and nodded. "That's right, June," he said, adjusting Nana's afghan to cover me as well. "It really is just as simple as that."

First Thanksgiving

Sally Milliken
First Place Winner, 2023 BWR Short Story Award

The frozen turkey didn't fit into the microwave. I knew that but had to try anyway and gave it a forceful shove. It slipped out of my hands like the greased watermelon we used for one of our childhood pool games. How many other people were trying in vain to thaw a turkey on Thanksgiving morning? I couldn't be the only one.

My new mother-in-law was arriving in less than two hours and would expect the smell of a cooking turkey as soon as she stepped inside the door. She was an amazing cook. Me, not so much. Luckily, my husband didn't seem to mind. Or at least he never said so. He also never complained about splitting the cooking duties with me. We never would have gotten married if he had.

My lack of talent in the kitchen was inherited. My mother was not the most adventurous of cooks either, but she successfully fed our family on a basic meat and potatoes diet. However, if anyone asked her friends about their favorite moments with her, it would involve sharing a huge chicken casserole. For at least twenty. That was her superpower: creating magic out of a can of Campbell's mushroom soup and a twenty-pack of chicken thighs. I learned early that one doesn't need to be a gourmet cook to create a community. Just a large casserole dish, overcooked steamed broccoli, and rice. And good friends and family.

Reluctantly accepting that the microwave would not work, I considered my other options. Was there such a person as a MacGyver for Thanksgiving dinners? If only I could salvage a meal with duct tape and a Swiss Army knife. If I wanted to impress my new relatives, then I needed to figure it out.

When we invited his mother and sister to celebrate the holiday with us, my husband and I divided the tasks. He successfully made a pumpkin pie—with a perfectly imperfect-looking crust—and mashed potatoes—with just the right number of lumps—so that there was no question they looked, and would certainly taste, homemade. I volunteered to do the turkey, gravy, stuffing, and cranberry sauce. My mother-in-law and sister-in-law were arriving with everything else: green veggies, squash, and an apple pie.

I cursed at myself again for not removing the turkey from the freezer earlier.

"How's it going, Suze?" My husband asked as he entered our tiny kitchen. I'm not sure how he kept a straight face. The wreckage on the countertop left no question as to what I'd been trying to do. The dressed bird should have been tucked into the oven over an hour ago.

"This is not going to work," I said, as I dropped the frozen bird in the sink with a loud *thunk* and closed the microwave door.

"Hmmm." Closing his mouth, he did not offer the words of advice ready to burst. Smart man.

Most days my independent streak was a strength, but this was not one of them. We were now a married couple, a team, a crew on a ship out at sea, and I knew, if I asked, he'd go down to the bottom with me without a second thought.

I was about to admit defeat when I said, "I'll figure it out." I'm not sure who was more surprised, him or me. I chewed on my bottom lip and stared at the bird.

"You don't want help?"

"Nope, I got this. You'll see, it'll be the best Thanksgiving meal you've ever had."

"You sure?" Checking his watch he added, "They'll be here soon."

"Yep, no problem."

"Okay. I'm heading out to rake leaves. Let me know if you change your mind."

Before he'd even closed the door, I began Googling for locations that sold cooked turkey. Was anything open on Thanksgiving Day? I was about to call the phone number of a local restaurant when I received a text.

Mom: Happy Thanksgiving! Good luck today. I'm sure it'll all go well.

She included a photo of her and my dad in the kitchen. In it, she held a plate with her famous cranberry bunny: the sauce was shaped with her grandmother's ceramic rabbit mold. Every Thanksgiving, my gaggle of twenty or so cousins used to fight over who would get the ears or tail first. She'd given me my own rabbit mold for our wedding, and I hoped my attempt chilling in the refrigerator would look even half as good.

Me: Happy Thanksgiving! It's going great! Thanks for the recipes. Miss you!

I took a photo of James's pie and sent it. Then added a photo of the outside of our oven, imagining the bird inside. If only. There was a lot to be thankful for on Thanksgiving, and I was thankful she couldn't see the partially defrosted turkey that I'd stuffed back into the fridge. She would have been highly amused watching me try to wrangle the frozen lump as it skittered across the granite countertop like a hockey puck sliding on ice.

I was getting desperate. I continued to dial. I tried the fifth restaurant. Or was it the tenth? I'd lost track. I'd already tried our local grocery stores. They were all closed. Anything open was thirty minutes away. Could I get there and back in time? It was looking like I didn't have a choice.

My phone chimed. My mother-in-law, Anne, texted: On our way!

Decision made, I grabbed my keys and slipped out the back door. Our first major holiday together, and I was well on my way to messing it up.

I was about to back out of the driveway when the phone rang. "Hi, Mom."

"I could tell from the tone of your text that you might need a little help."

"Um—the tone of my *text?*"

"Well, yes, that, and the oven light was on in the photo. I could see there was no turkey inside."

"Oh—well." I inhaled and the words tumbled out. "The turkey took longer than I thought to thaw. And James's mother and sister will be here in less than an hour and now it's too late. No restaurant is open and the only store where I can find a cooked turkey is too far away to get it back here in time." I exhaled. "I'm not sure what to do."

"Take a breath. It's okay to ask for help, you know."

Slouching in my car seat, I gripped the steering wheel. "I wanted everything to be perfect."

"For whom?" Before I could answer, she asked, "Do you want to hear about my first holiday with your father's family?"

"Sure." I shut off the engine. "Why not. I'm on a futile errand anyway."

"We went to your grandparents' house for Christmas. Before dinner on Christmas Eve, I spilled an entire bottle of wine, red wine, on their oriental rug."

"Oh no. What did Nana and Grandpa do?"

"Nana didn't bat an eyelash. Just laughed, soaked up what she could with an old towel, and dumped an entire container of salt on it. Your Grandpa was more restrained in general, but he opened another bottle of wine and moved the other guests into a different room."

"Accidents happen."

"They do." She paused and I imagined her smile. "It may have happened decades ago, but the memory is still fresh. Luckily, the stain was hard to see because of the pattern. From then on, the rug was called 'The Fumble Rug.' I look at that stain now as a lovely memory of your grandparents."

I realized what she was referring to. "That's the rug in our living room."

"*Mmmhmm*. And every time I see it, I'm transported back in time to when I was a young wife, and soon-to-be mother, and how your father's family welcomed me."

"That's very sweet." I grinned at my own fond memories of my grandparents, now long gone.

"That was just the first day. You remember how your grandmother loved her raspberry Melba sauce? Well, during dessert, I dropped a gigantic dollop of the sauce on myself. It left a trail of red down the front of my shirt and the more I wiped at it, the worse it got. I looked like I'd been stabbed."

Covering my mouth, I could not squelch the bark of laughter. "What happened?"

"I was about to excuse myself to change when your grandmother spilled her coffee. In nearly the same spot on herself." The sound of my mother's chuckle tickled my ear. "I never saw her spill anything after that day. It wasn't until years later that I guessed she did it on purpose. And her silk blouse was certainly far more expensive and difficult to clean than mine."

"Wow, that's above and beyond. After that weekend, they must have thought you were a klutz."

"They saw how much I loved your dad. That must have been enough."

"And I'm sure how much he loved you—So, did Nana ever admit she spilled her coffee on purpose?"

"I never asked her. Likely she would have denied it anyway. I just appreciated how hard she tried to make me feel comfortable. Not every family is like that—I think I was especially fortunate—but your mother-in-law seems a similar sort. She certainly has been kind when I've been around her."

FIRST THANKSGIVING

"That's true. But she's so good at cooking. Every meal she makes is like we're at a five-star restaurant."

"Everyone has different strengths, honey. And you know my favorite saying." We said the words together. "All you can do is all you can do." My mother laughed again, asking, "So, now, what are you going to do? About your Thanksgiving meal, I mean?"

Taking a deep breath, I exhaled long and slow. "You've given me an idea. Thanks, Mom. Love you."

"Love you, too. Good luck."

After ending the call, I glanced at my phone to check the time, then Googled, 'What to cook for Thanksgiving if you don't have a turkey.'

A long list appeared, including a story from The New York *Times* called, "Thanksgiving Main Dishes That Are Better Than Turkey." Perfect. I smiled when I scrolled past "Mushroom potpie" thinking of my mother and her Campbell's-enhanced casseroles. I made a note to try that dish another time. Picking the recipe with ingredients we had on hand as well as the one that would take the least amount of time, I returned to the house and dug around in my freezer. Finding a ten-pack of chicken thighs—I truly was my mother's daughter—I thawed them easily. Following the directions, I tossed them into the oven with the rosemary I'd purchased to season the turkey.

My husband returned ten minutes later. He sniffed. "Yum."

"Thanks." I leaned into his kiss and relaxed against his body for a long hug. "You called my mother, didn't you?" I mumbled into his shirt.

"Um, yes. I hope you don't mind. You were getting more and more upset, putting pressure on yourself and taking the whole idea of a 'perfect Thanksgiving' far too seriously. I wasn't sure how to help." Stepping back, his eyes searched mine. "How'd you know?"

"You gave up and went outside too easily. Thank you for not saying, 'I told you so.'"

"It doesn't matter what we eat. I'm just thankful to be married to you. To be here together with you."

"And that we'll spend the day together with your family—"

"Now *our* family."

"Yes, of course. Our family." My breath hitched and I cleared my throat. "And I'm thankful for you," I whispered, tucking my head back against his shoulder.

Holding me tight, he shrugged. "Plus, I knew you'd find out a solution. And likely come up with an idea far better than I ever could." Sniffing again, he added, "And I believe you have. It smells delicious."

"*We* came up with it. You and my mom helped."

A knock on the door interrupted us. My new family was here. He kissed my cheek and went to welcome them.

The Heart Needs a Home

D.T. Krippene

Nate peered out the window at the mid-November haze of airborne Nevada dust. Almost two years had passed since he left the staid world of historical archiving to seek a fresh start and help open a tiny museum in Southern Nevada. An hour ago, a former Bostonian colleague called with an offer of a prestigious position back East. It was his dream job, but did he really want to go back? The Board of Directors wanted his decision by the week after Thanksgiving.

He sighed when a wind gust knocked over a potted plant outside. Some Nevadans called these storms "haboobs," a romanticized Arabic word for the strong winds of a weather front that carried particulate sand instead of rain. While exploring saguaro cacti in a remote area last spring, he got caught in one and ended up hunkering behind a sandstone boulder until the storm ended.

"Not exactly the falling leaves of Connecticut," he mumbled with a smile. *But it was quite an adventure.*

"You say something, boss?" asked Hector Morales.

"Nothing." Nate turned to his museum technician, who fiddled with another supposed family heirloom dropped off the day before as a potential exhibit from Nevada's mining days. "What's your conclusion on that pickaxe?"

"Modern-day tool someone left out in the elements too long." Hector set it aside, put his foot up on the desk, and sighed. "Man, this place is dead."

"Maybe we'll get some traffic during the holiday week. Why don't you go home? I'll lock up later. Just be careful driving out there."

"We Nevadans have sand in our blood." Hector stretched. "You coming to the Indigenous People's Festival on Saturday?"

The festival was Parhrump's most prominent cultural event. Native American tribes statewide convened at the local park the weekend before Thanksgiving to display artistic craftsmanship, share stories, and offer indigenous foods.

"I'm meeting Sandy there. She's bringing some of her students."

Hector fitted a faded Arizona Cardinals baseball cap on his noggin. "You two got plans for the holiday?"

While still adjusting to being a widower in his forties, Nate had skipped last year's dinner invites. But since Sandra Duran, strikingly handsome in her thirties, had brought her fourth-grade class to the museum to leave fingerprints on every glass surface, he'd found her ebullient individuality enchanting. Their first unofficial date, when she introduced him to hummingbirds in a high desert environment, became the prelude to many more.

"Sandy wants me to come to her place for Thanksgiving dinner to meet the family." Nate coughed. "I understand she has a sizable number of kin coming as well."

"Uh, oh. Hispanic family trial by fire. If you pass muster, they'll expect a wedding date."

"Not helping."

When Hector reached his car, clutching his cap to keep it from blowing off, Nate could still hear him cackling.

Nate swallowed, wondering which was worse: meeting Sandy's family for the first time or telling her about the job offer. "I'm not ready for this," he whispered to the wind that howled through the building's eaves.

The tinkling of the bell on the entrance door shook Nate into the present. In walked the man who'd dropped the "heirloom" pickaxe off yesterday. "Hey, Dr. Beekman. Got a verdict on the axe?" He brushed the dust off his coat that powdered the room like the Pigpen from *Peanuts*. "I was kind of hoping to show the kids when they visit next week."

Nate eyed the dust settling on the exhibits. *Should have closed early.* "Why don't we go to my office and chat."

*

Nate spotted Sandy at the Native American Festival with a group of her fourth-grade students. Beth Windflower, an elder from the Pyramid Lake Reservation, was explaining the Shoshone and Paiute tribal histories.

The moment the kids spotted him, they yelled, "Hi, Dr. Beekman." They swarmed him with hugs and high-fives.

"Okay. Let's give Dr. Beekman a little space to breathe," Sandy smilingly scolded. She clapped her hands. "All right, follow Ms. Windflower. Chief Shadowmountain is about to start his talk about harvest celebrations."

Sandy watched her students chatter and skip toward a makeshift stage before turning back to Nate. "They really like you."

Nate smiled. "They're a great bunch of kids."

She slipped her arm into Nate's. "Whenever you arrange a field trip, my last year's class wants to come too. You make learning fun."

"I enjoy working with them. They are so different from the college students I used to teach. Most of them were only there for the required credit."

He cleared his throat to change the subject. "I'm curious about the connection of indigenous people to Thanksgiving. I sometimes wonder if we over-mythologize the Pilgrim story. From a historical perspective, why would any Native American want to be a part of it after the atrocities committed?"

"According to Beth and her tribal family, long before European settlers arrived, their ancestors had longstanding traditions of giving thanks throughout the year in appreciation for the good things in life, like family, community, and the gift of Mother Earth's abundance." Sandy wore an indulgent smile. "They didn't wait for one long weekend of the year."

She squeezed Nate's arm. "You might consider adding a seasonal exhibit at the museum to help people understand that different cultures celebrate the holiday in different ways. You could advertise it in Las Vegas to attract vacationers looking for a diversion. Beth and I can help if you want."

Nate wandered to the exhibit table when Sandy opened a folder to make notes. Her idea had tremendous merit. *But I'd have to be here to make it happen.*

Beth Windflower returned. "Well, I got the students settled. Have you sampled this year's holiday offerings yet?"

"If you have stinging nettles on the menu, that's a hard no," Nate grumbled. Traditional edible plants of Southwest indigenous people consisted of vine-grown vegetables, foraged wild greens, and pine nuts. How did a plant that made his lips swell like over-injected collagen make the list?

"Young nettles are very nutritious," Sandy replied. "There might have been a few stray hairs left on the sample you ate last year."

Nate wrinkled his nose. "Think I'll stick with the grilled fish and rabbit."

Beth barked a laugh. "You men. It's always about burning meat on an open fire."

Sandy giggled. "I'm going to check on the kids."

Beth winked at Nate when Sandy headed toward the stage. "My fellow elders have wagers going on you two."

Where gambling is practically the state religion, people bet on anything. Beth wandered away before Nate could conjure a retort. First Hector, now Beth. What should have been a friendly chide sank into Nate's belly like a stone.

He'd grown fond of the community that disregarded his stiff New England ways and embraced him without hesitation, but they had expectations. His feelings for Sandy had developed into a deep love he hadn't felt in years. But to give up on his dream job pulled on him like an East Coast undertow. *What am I going to do?*

He spotted the curmudgeon who owned the not-so-historical pickaxe approach with a burlap bundle in his arms. *Oh crap. He's back.*

*

On the Wednesday before Thanksgiving, Monty Contreras, Nate's buddy and fellow treasure hunter, threw a rancher Thanksgiving before he and his girlfriend, Marianne, headed to Utah. Nate parked behind one of many pickup trucks lined up near Monty's ranch house. Country Western music mingled with loud cheers filtered through the driver's side window. He switched off the engine and sighed.

Nate almost bailed on coming and just wanted to get some sleep before facing Sandy's family tomorrow and her mother's inevitable queries like, "when are you going to make an honest woman of my daughter?" He skipped the open front door that was blocked with area ranchers clutching beers and walked around to the backyard. With his trademark tan Stetson and white, bushy mustache, Monty held court by pouring whisky near a crackling firepit.

Nate wandered to the rusted barbed wire fence that separated the ranch house from the many acres of dusty range Monty owned behind it. The horizon glowed with fading tangerine orange, hovering above the blackening silhouettes of distant mountains. Nate leaned on a fence post, careful not to catch his shirt on the prickly barbs, and inhaled the cool, dry breeze that drifted from the west across the rock-strewn, grayish sand. Unlike the constant humidity of the East Coast, there was something about the arid desert air that instilled a sense of calm.

THE HEART NEEDS A HOME

Monty sauntered alongside and handed Nate a brimming tumbler of whiskey. "I've lived here most of my life, and gazing at those mountains at sunset never gets old."

"I've seen a lot of sunsets, but nothing like Nevada," Nate replied.

Monte raised his glass in a toast. "True spoken." He took a healthy swig and wiped his mustache with a finger. "Where's Sandy?"

"Helping her mother set up for tomorrow. She sends her apologies."

Monty scratched the stubble on his cheeks. "I wanted to thank her for helping me organize my notes last week."

"I've seen how you make notes," Nate chided. "You owe her a public testimonial."

"Been thinking we'd have better luck with our treasure hunting if she helped us more often. Surprised I hadn't thought of it before." Monty swallowed another big gulp of whiskey.

"You know, it's okay to savor a drink. Your liver isn't exactly a spring chicken." Nate glanced back at the merrymakers. "I didn't see Marianne," he added, thinking her presence might tame Monty's tendency to imbibe himself blind.

"She's still packing. We leave first thing in the morning. That is, if there's room enough for my one bag after we pack her stuff in the truck. I swear that woman has more clothing than an outlet mall."

"Do I detect the possibility of your forever bachelor lifestyle in jeopardy?" Nate teased.

"It's not polite for guests in my house to speak of forbidden subjects. We're just two consenting adults having fun." Monty took another nip. "But since you brought the subject up, rumor has it you're getting the hot lamp treatment tomorrow from Ms. Duran's family."

Nate blanched, took a larger-than-advised slug of whiskey, and coughed. "Appears we're the talk of the town."

"Small town telegraph. Better get used to it." Monty drained his glass. "Come on. Let's get some grub in you before your *inexperienced* liver makes you face-plant in the dirt from that drink."

Sporting a "Grady's Lonestar Shooting Range" ball cap, Walt, a former colleague of Monty's from the bureau, tended a grate over a mesquite fire, flipping steaks that had to be at least two pounds each.

"How do you like your beef, Dr. Beekman," Walt asked.

"Medium rare, please."

Walt grinned. "One *wipe its ass and put it on a plate,* coming up."

The Texan riff for doneness would shock the Ivy League crowd, but Nate only laughed. He eyed a table with mashed potatoes, large boats of gravy, greens with bacon, barbecue beans, roasted yams with prickly pear cactus jelly, and three kinds of fruit pies. "I gather turkey isn't on the menu."

Monty chewed on a piece of mystery meat jerky. "If you're referring to that mutant "Frankenbird" basted in its own fat, you'll find many of us with roots in the region aren't into eating an oversized chicken. But if you have a hankering, Walt bagged a wild turkey last weekend." He pointed to a scrawny bird perched on a bed of smoked sausage that resembled an overcooked roadrunner the wily cartoon coyote might have finally caught.

"Doesn't look like anyone's touched it," Nate observed.

Walt plated a steak that left little space for side dishes. "With that in your belly, who has room for poultry?"

*

Nate considered getting a slice of pie after he dropped his empty plastic plate in a garbage can, but the congealing brick in his stomach rumbled against it. He grabbed a cup of coffee and found a folding chair near the campfire where a young woman sang soft country ballads to the accompaniment of two guitars. Her soulful melodies of love among those who scratched a hardscrabble existence in the Old West conjured thoughts of his relationship with Sandy.

Nate admired Sandy's tranquil persistence and infectious curiosity that instilled admiration and respect. She kindled a flare he thought was not possible at this point in his life. He continued to struggle, however, with the question of whether a hometown woman with Western mores in her veins would be content with a middle-aged East Coast man set in his ways. He should have told her about the job offer by now, and it feathered his insides with guilt.

Sandy could easily find a higher-paying teacher's position, but would she be willing to leave everything behind and find happiness in a city like Boston? Nate rehearsed the many options of how he'd break the news. What kept him from doing so was a question he didn't know the answer to, and it scared him.

*

Thanksgiving Day warmed to unseasonably temperate mid-seventies. Sandy arrived a little after noon at Nate's apartment in her off-road Jeep Challenger. She preferred jeans on their weekend excursions or a modest skirt and matching blouse for dinner dates. The vision that graced the doorway wore a white, sleeveless, floor-length dress of linen embroidered with vibrant multicolored flowers and sashed at the waist with a sky-blue lace belt.

She reached to his chin and gently pushed his open jaw closed. "I clean up pretty good, don't I?"

"Um—let me grab my blazer." He returned to find Sandy scanning the tiny living room.

"Have you ever considered getting a bigger place?" she asked.

Though she was no stranger to his apartment, her question threw Nate off guard. "Might be a little small, but I've found it adequate since it's just me."

Their typical chatty banter was subdued on the way over, and Nate wondered if the town gossip about them could be stressing her. He sometimes wondered about former beaus or why she never married, but mentally filed it in the don't-ask category.

They pulled up in front of a single-story house with colorful paper banners the locals called "papel picado" decorating the front porch—a departure from New England's yard embellishments of scarecrows, bundled hay sheaves, and shrunken pumpkins left over from Halloween.

Before going inside, Sandy adjusted his tie. "Are you ready to rumble?"

Nate coughed a chuckle at her reference to contact sports. "Do I look that nervous?"

With a sparkle in her luminous brown eyes, she pecked Nate on the lips and took his hand.

The living room was crowded with people. Kids darted between sitting and standing adults like in an old-fashioned pinball game. When they spotted Nate, the buzz of Spanish conversation dropped to silence.

An older, frailish woman resembling Sandy threaded through the crowd and took Nate's hands. "Bienvenido, Dr. Beekman. I've been looking forward to meeting you."

"Thank you for inviting me into your home, Mrs. Duran."

"In this house, everyone calls me 'Mama.' It would warm my heart if you did, too."

The living room gatherers burst into smiling cheers and took turns welcoming Nate with hugs and back pats. Sandy guided him to an elderly couple sitting near a window and introduced her *abuela* and *abuelo*. Sandy's grandmother's face split into a toothy grin. She pulled him down to bestow a kiss on each side of his face.

Weaving through a sea of well-wishers to reach the kitchen, Nate observed Sandy gently but firmly giving orders: "Mama, sit down; you've been standing too long. Daniel, get your fingers out of the pie. Manuela, can you grab the large jar of salsa from the garage refrigerator?"

Nate pressed himself into a corner nook when Sandy braced herself with an akimbo posture and berated a tattooed young man twice her size. Nate knew enough Spanish to interpret her use of acerbic scolding phrases that had the big guy cowering like a misbehaving schoolboy.

Nate ambled over to Sandy after the big guy skulked out the back door. "I take it you rule the roost here."

"When my dad passed away years ago, Mom bore the duty of managing family dynamics. With her getting older, it's up to me now to keep order." She exhaled loudly. "I love my cousin, but sometimes he needs a quick kick in the *culo*."

Nate followed Sandy outside to the spacious backyard and festive linen-covered tables that groaned with hearty Mexican fare. She loaded a plate with braised turkey in a green mole, fried cornbread speckled with chorizo, and homemade tortillas.

"Just for you, Mama didn't make it too spicy," she said while spooning charro beans with tomatoey chili peppers. "I know you're not fond of guacamole but try the cranberry-peach salsa. I made it myself." She pointed toward an empty table by the back fence. "Let's grab those chairs."

"I can't remember the last time I felt so welcomed by a family I barely know," Nate said before he took his first bite.

"I come from a heritage where there's no such thing as strangers. Just friends we haven't met yet." She nibbled the edge of a flour tortilla. "The acceptance of Thanksgiving customs was an easy transition for us. It's all about love, family, and togetherness."

They watched the children laughingly stumble through a dance routine while they ate. Nate smiled at the contrast between this and the New England traditions of a Norman Rockwell holiday he'd grown up with.

His parents went all out on the holiday decorations to make up for him being an only child with no close relatives. Thanksgiving and the lead-up to Christmas was his favorite time of the year, with the nippy air scented of conifers and the continuous recycling of Christmas music. When he married his late wife, Pam, she continued their tradition of enthusiastic holiday cheer, even after his parents passed on. Pam's apple sausage stuffing and chiffon pumpkin pie were unmatched. Though they didn't have kids, there was no shortage of friends and colleagues to join them for holiday meals.

When Pam died, the joy of the season passed with her, and he avoided holiday gatherings. The last thing he wanted was to be the guest of honor at pity parties, where everyone would try to cheer him up.

Nate's musing bubble popped when Sandy asked, "Do you think you'd ever be happy here?"

Her unanticipated question stunned him. "What makes you ask that?"

"I've come to know you well, Nate. I can sense a spirit that hasn't found its way yet."

"Oh, come on. I've enjoyed every moment I've been here, especially with you. Except maybe the solar furnace in summer."

She bit her lip and looked away. "I feel a 'but' hiding in you."

Add extrasensory perception to her remarkable traits. His words momentarily stalled under her intuitive bullseye.

"I ... wanted to talk to you about something. A former colleague back East called the other day." Nate swallowed to clear phlegm from his throat. "There's a tenured position open at Harvard for the Museum Sciences graduate program, and they want me to take over."

Sandy blinked. "Wow. Harvard."

The late afternoon air had cooled, but Nate's collar heated and itched. "I haven't accepted the offer yet."

Sandy's lip quivered. "I had this dumb schoolgirl fantasy that you'd never leave."

His throat constricted. "Sandy ..."

"You're the most remarkable man I've ever met," she interrupted. "For a prestigious institution like Harvard to tap you is an opportunity of a lifetime. I should have known a little desert town wouldn't be enough to keep you here." She released a shuddering sigh. "Who else knows?"

"No one. I wanted to talk to you first." Nate's mouth went dry. "I know it's a little sudden, but would you consider ... maybe ... coming with me?"

"It's not that I don't want to consider it. Mama is getting more fragile. As her only child, I have to help. She'd be heartbroken if I left." She looked away. "I love you, Nathaniel Beekman, but my place is here."

Her mother called from the back porch. Sandy wiped her eyes. "I should go see what she needs. I'll be right back."

A powerful sadness pulsed through Nate as she walked toward the house. The lure of returning to the familiarity of New England and a coveted position in academia he'd always dreamed of pulled with immense weight.

And why would Sandy even consider going with him? He brought nothing to the table regarding a family. Unlike the folks he'd befriended here, Bostonians weren't known for embracing newcomers.

He remembered what Monty said when they'd collaborated in a search for lost gold. *The desert can bare a man's soul. Challenge one's reasonings and purpose. The only way to handle it is feet forward and never look back because there's nothing to see.*

Observing the joy of Sandy's kith and kin as they laughed and made merry, the impact of Monty's folksy parable now made sense. Nate's personal and professional life centered on the past, but it dulled his ability to see the present.

"What the hell am I doing?" he mumbled to himself.

Wearing a jacket to ward off the chill of sunset, Sandy returned with a bowl of flan. "It's Mama's famous recipe. She'll be upset if you don't eat it."

Nate caught Mama watching him from the back porch. He polished the dessert off, scraping for any last remnants. "That's better than crème brulée."

Sandy flashed a thumbs-up to her mother. "You just made her day."

Nate set the bowl aside. "You know, I've always wondered what you saw in a middle-aged introverted archivist from the East Coast. You deserve better."

"I *found* better." Sandy placed her palm on his cheek. "But I don't want to be responsible for holding you back. You've earned this opportunity, and you'll finally be going back home."

Nate swallowed hard. "While you were in the house, it dawned inside my thick skull that New England isn't home anymore."

"What are you saying?"

Never look back because there's nothing to see. "There's a cheesy saying that home is wherever your heart is." He took her hands. "My heart belongs with you. If your home is here, then so is mine."

Sandy wrapped her arms around Nate's neck and kissed him, wetting his cheeks with her tears. Breaking the embrace might have required the fireman's jaws of life—until the gathered family erupted into boisterous cheer. Nate sheepishly faced them when Sandy turned her back and wept into a napkin. People slowly dispersed to give them privacy.

Sandy's muted sobs broke down the last remaining bricks of Nate's forty-plus yesteryears. When she finally composed herself, she laughed. "God. Don't remember the last time I lost it. I must look a mess."

"Never." Nate extracted a wrinkled handkerchief from his blazer breast pocket when she sniffled. "I promise. It's clean."

She blew her nose in it. "In front of my family, too."

The adults and a few kids had shuffled out to dance on the lawn. Soft Hispanic ballads wafted from a boom box.

"They don't look too concerned," said Nate. "I see Mama in the kitchen window. On a day that embraces thankfulness, I'm thankful she's still smiling." He stood and offered his hand. "M'lady, I recommend a diversion. If thou art willing to risk thy feet being trod upon, may I have the honor of this dance?"

As they swayed to the music, the delicate floral scent of Sandy's shampoo, the feel of her arm on his shoulder, and the gentle press of her body made his soul soar.

Sandy touched her nose to his. "I was thinking you haven't had much of a traditional Thanksgiving. How about I fix up a proper roast turkey and all the trimmings this weekend? No stinging nettles, barbeque, or tacos."

"After orchestrating this amazing feast?"

"Hmmm. I expected a bit more enthusiasm," Sandy teased. "Are you questioning my culinary aptitude for colonial cuisine?"

"It seems too much to ask."

"You didn't ask." She leaned into his shoulder and kissed his cheek. "I think it's time we created our own Thanksgiving traditions."

Best Laid Plans

Carol L. Wright

Once all three of her oldest friends had settled at their usual table at their favorite Lehigh Valley, Pennsylvania coffee shop, Desiree cleared her throat.

"Dears, I've been thinking," she said. "There's something I have always wanted to do, but never had the chance."

"How is that even possible?" Geraldine muttered, barely audibly.

Desiree gave Geraldine a side-eye but was not deterred. "Ever since I was a kid, I always wanted to go to New York to see the Thanksgiving Day Parade." She paused, apparently expecting agreement from her friends. When no one reacted, she prodded them. "Haven't you all?"

Betty looked doubtful. "I remember you wanting to go as a teenager, but haven't you ever done it in the last sixty years?"

Desiree sighed. "No. Grant never wanted to go while he was alive. We always ended up taking a trip somewhere, usually to a country that didn't even celebrate Thanksgiving. But I still want to go and follow it up with a grand traditional American Thanksgiving dinner with all the trimmings."

Desiree knew she had led a charmed life. Even as a senior citizen, she had it easier than her friends. Strangers thought she was ten years younger than the others, perhaps thanks to having been married for over fifty years to a plastic surgeon. She now enjoyed freedom from financial worries in her widowhood while her friends ranged from comfortable to just scraping by. But they'd known each other all their lives. Despite their different circumstances, they remained the closest of friends.

Ida, a retired science teacher, brushed a hand through her spiky gray hair and straightened in her chair. "Do you know how long people have to stand out in the cold to wait for the parade to pass by their place on the route? And how many other people they're crushed in with blocking their

BEST LAID PLANS

view?" She folded her hands around her coffee mug and shook her head. "COVID is still a thing, you know."

Geraldine picked her head up. "Not to mention RSV and the flu." Her voice rose as she imagined other horrors. "Why in late November it could be freezing . . . or snowing . . .or sleeting."

Betty shook her head. For once she agreed with Geraldine. "It doesn't sound like much fun to me. And Desi, you're only five-foot-two. How could you see anything unless we are in the front row? Which means getting there extra early. Wouldn't we see it better on television?"

"Oh, sweeties," Desiree said, patting Betty's arm. "I've thought of all that." She surveyed the unenthusiastic faces around the table. "I have the most wonderful idea."

No one asked what it was. Ever since their botched trip north to see the total eclipse, the women had become wary of "best laid plans."

Betty was the first to relent. "What is your idea?"

"Well," Desiree said, pulling papers out of her purse. "I checked, and hotels along the parade route have special packages for rooms . . . or suites . . . that face the parade route."

Again, no reaction from her three chums.

"Don't you see?" Desiree continued. "We can stay warm—and safe from pickpockets and the weather—inside a luxury hotel and still see the whole thing going past us below." She giggled with excitement. "The balloons might even be at eye-level for us."

She laid a brochure on the table. "See?" she continued. "I found this in my mailbox a couple of weeks ago. I've already reserved a large suite at this wonderful historic hotel at the end of the parade route. And I got a great deal. It's known for its luxury, so I thought, why not spoil ourselves a bit? And it includes . . ." She pointed to the words below a photo of a sumptuous banquet table, "An 'opulent Thanksgiving feast.' With Thanksgiving less than a month away, I couldn't believe my luck that they still had a parade-view suite available."

"Have you ever stayed there before?" Geraldine sounded skeptical.

"Not in ages," Desiree said. "Grant and I stayed there in the eighties and loved it. I've been eager to go back one day."

Ida grabbed the brochure. "As long as they have turkey. It's not Thanksgiving without turkey and stuffing."

"That and all the side dishes you could ask for." Desiree pointed to a highlighted box on the back page.

Reading the menu listing, Ida nodded. "Looks like all the essentials are here, and a few things I've never tried. Have any of you ever had chestnut stuffing?"

"I tried it once," Geraldine grumbled. "It tasted like dirt."

"So do truffles, my dear," said Desiree, "but they're nearly as dear as gold."

"Which is why I've never tried them," Geraldine retorted.

"Well, then, lucky for you," Ida said. "They also have cornbread, sage, sausage, and oyster stuffing options."

"What, no tur-duck-en?" Betty said with a laugh.

"That will have to wait for another year," said Ida, handing the brochure back to Desiree.

Desiree sat back and watched as her friends became more invested in the idea. But then Gertude asked the question Desiree knew they were all wondering about.

"How much will this set us all back?"

Desiree cleared her throat. "Well, since this is something I've always wanted to do, and that I really want to share with you three, I plan to host it myself and all of you will be my guests."

She sensed palpable relief from Geraldine, practical assent from Ida, and an uncomfortable reluctance from Betty.

"Oh, no, Desi," Betty said. "That's too much. We should each pay our own way."

"Then I'm out," Geraldine said, placing her palms down on the table as if to push herself away.

Desiree arched a brow at Betty, then turned what she knew was her most gracious smile toward Geraldine. "Nonsense. I insist."

"I'm in," said Ida. "It sounds like it could be fun."

Betty still looked uncertain. "Okay, but I'm the only one of us with a car, and I don't want to drive in Manhattan. I'll only go if we take the bus into the city."

The friends looked at each other, nodding in agreement.

"It's a plan!" said Ida. She drained her coffee mug and placed it on the table with a clunk.

*

In the following days, the friends spent every coffee hour together making plans.

"I see where we can go up to Central Park to see them inflate the balloons on Wednesday," Ida suggested one morning. "Can we get into town early enough to do that?" She brightened with a new idea. "And maybe I can drop by and see my son Keith. The museum where he works is near the park, and he lives up in Washington Heights."

The following week, Desiree volunteered, "I'd hate to go into the city without also seeing a Broadway show."

A few days later, Betty offered, "I've never seen the Christmas show at Radio City Music Hall. Maybe we could still get tickets. And watch the ice skating at Rockefeller Center."

Desiree noticed that Geraldine remained silent as the suggestions raised the total cost of the trip. "I'll look into tickets," she said. "I might be able to get a deal through the hotel package. If so, it is, of course, all on me."

She was glad to see Geraldine finally show some enthusiasm.

"Okay. This ought to be fun."

*

On Wednesday of Thanksgiving week, Betty collected her friends from their various homes and drove them to the bus station. Desiree brought two suitcases, saying she couldn't decide what to wear to the theater, so she brought several options. The others managed to pack in one bag each, but with five bags to transport, it made getting on the bus a longer process than they had hoped.

By the time they boarded, nearly every seat was taken. It seemed everyone was going into New York that day. Desiree was scrunched into a window seat by a burly man who seemed annoyed at having to share his row. Then the person in front of her reclined their seat, wedging her in for the hour-and-a-half trip with no way to shift position.

She leaned forward and asked the reclined passenger in front of her if they would mind straightening their seat back, but was given only a raised middle finger in response. *Not exactly the holiday spirit,* she thought. She wriggled into as comfortable a position as she could find and closed her eyes to shut out the unpleasantness around her. Unfortunately, she could not shut out the sounds . . . or the smells. *I should have hired a limo,* she thought.

The bus made several stops before finally pulling into New York's Port Authority bus station. Most of the passengers stood in the aisle waiting for their turn to get off the bus, but the man sitting next to Desiree showed no interest in moving. With the seat in front of her still reclined, Desiree couldn't even stand up straight, but she was able to get onto her feet and lean over her seat, hoping the man next to her would get the hint.

She watched as the three other women exited the bus, calling after Betty, "Please make sure my bags are taken off, will you?"

Betty nodded and waved. At least Desiree had an ally. She knew Betty would not let the driver leave while any of them was still on the bus.

As the flow of passengers ebbed to a trickle, Desiree spoke to the man blocking her path. "Excuse me. I have to get out here."

He scowled at her and, with much grunting and groaning, got out of his seat. A whiff of perspiration assaulted her when he raised his arm to brace himself against the seat in front of him.

I am so glad this trip is over, Desiree thought as she wriggled past him. *Now the fun can begin.*

The four women rolled their suitcases through the massive building and out to the street where a line of taxi cabs picked up passengers and nosed into the flow of traffic. The glass façade of the New York Times building across the street, the mix of rotting smells along the pavement, and the traffic in the congested street made them know they were not in Pennsylvania anymore.

"Look at that statue," Geraldine said, pointing toward a bronze likeness of Jackie Gleason dressed as a bus driver. "I remember that old show. What was it called?"

"*The Honeymooners,*" Ida reminded her. "I remember it, too. Back before color TV, my parents used to watch it."

"Huh," Betty added. "I remember it opened with fireworks, that all looked white on the screen. What was the point?"

"Better than radio," Desiree chimed in. She was determined that they were going to have fun, no matter what.

When their turn came to hop into a cab, they couldn't all fit in the first one in line. When a minivan came along, they each had their own captain's chair. Desiree, from the back row, gave the cabby the address. "Four-oh-one Seventh Avenue please, driver."

The cabby looked back at her. "Four-oh-one? Are you sure?"

"Of course I'm sure," Desiree insisted. She had checked the address before buckling her seat belt.

"Whatever you say, lady," the driver said and inched away from the curb.

Winding through the city streets, Desiree wondered if the cabby was intentionally making the trip longer than it needed to be in order to increase the fare. *Probably trying to put one over on a bunch of old ladies.*
"I never asked," Ida said. "What hotel will we be staying in?"
Desiree felt smug. Her friends were going to love it. "The one and only Hotel Pennsylvania." She watched them for their reactions. "It's our 'Pennsylvania' home away from home." She giggled at her own joke.
Betty stared at Desiree, her mouth agape. "The Hotel Pennsylvania?"
"Yes, my dear friends. It's one of the finest in the city, right across from Penn Station and Madison Square Garden. And, it's just a few steps from Macy's where the parade route ends. We can go outside to watch the parade, but if you'd rather, our suite will be on a floor high enough to watch the parade as it approaches Herald Square."
The cabby harumphed and Betty still looked shocked as the cab pulled over in front of Madison Square Garden. The other women got out while Desiree paid the fare. When she joined her friends on the sidewalk, they were all gawking across the street where . . .
"Wait a minute," Desiree said when she turned to follow their gaze. "Where'd the hotel go?"
They were staring at a construction site.
"It appears that the hotel is gone," Ida said.
Geraldine added, "Unless it's a David Copperfield illusion."
"It was razed," Betty agreed. "I read about it when it happened. The hotel didn't survive the COVID shutdown and even though people tried to save it as a historic landmark, they failed. Developers bought it, sold off the contents, and demolished the building. They're building a new skyscraper."
Desiree grabbed Betty's arm. "But I have reservations."
"Not here," Geraldine said, leaning on her suitcase.
Desiree pulled several sheets of paper from her purse. "No. Look here. It clearly says the Hotel Pennsylvania is where we'll have our suite and our Thanksgiving dinner," she said, pointing to the first page. Then, shifting to another sheet, she said, "And here is the confirmation they sent for our Broadway theater tickets and the Radio City Music Hall. It's all right here."
Ida grabbed her bag and led Desiree toward the corner. "Here, let's find a place to sit down and figure this out."
The others followed them, dragging their bags. The smell of warm bread and Italian spices drew them to a small table in a pizza place. As

they squeezed in together, Desiree gazed at her paperwork, still unable to believe what her eyes told her was true.

"Oh my gosh, Ida. I've been *scammed.*" She felt tears well up in her eyes. "I'm one of those gullible rich widows you read about, giving their money to strangers who just take it and run." She covered her face with her hands as the tears flowed down her cheeks. "I'm so ashamed of myself. What an *idiot* I am."

Betty rubbed Desiree's shoulder and Ida handed her a tissue.

"Oh, honey. It's okay," Betty said in a soothing voice. "You did your best to give us all a great vacation. It's not your fault there are wicked people in the world,"

"You might have some recourse through your credit card company," Ida suggested.

Desiree sighed. "They had me pay by check."

Geraldine, from across the table remained silent which, Desiree knew, was the best she could have hoped for. Surely by now all her friends realized they had nowhere to stay, no way to see the parade, and no place to have Thanksgiving dinner. She knew crying would get her nowhere, but at the moment, there didn't seem to be anything else she could do.

She dabbed her tears and pulled out her compact to check her makeup. By the time she looked up again, all three of her friends appeared busy. Ida was on her phone, listening to someone. Betty had taken Desiree's papers and was scrolling down a page, and Geraldine was scowling at the pizza menu, apparently alarmed by the prices.

"If we're going to sit here, we should probably order something," Geraldine suggested. "I'll go get some drinks and maybe breadsticks." She eased herself up and wove her way past several tables to the counter.

Desiree watched her go, amazed that Geraldine had volunteered to pay for food. *She must think me really pathetic.*

"Any luck?" Desiree asked Betty, hoping all this was going to turn out to be a huge mistake and that their reservations were someplace else. It was not to be.

"Bad news," said Betty. "I called the number on the brochure, and it's disconnected." She sighed. "I would have been surprised if it weren't."

"I suppose you're right," said Desiree, feeling her emotions getting the better of her again.

"Then I searched for information on this scam. It seems to be well known to the police, and it happens in one form or another every Thanksgiving or New Year's when tens of thousands of people flock to New York." She placed her phone on the table and looked at Desiree with sympathy. "There are only so many hotel rooms and they take advantage of people not being familiar with the city to get them to book rooms that don't exist. A lot of other people are probably in the same boat."

"Is there nowhere for us to stay?" Desiree had held onto hope, but it was rapidly slipping away.

"Don't look so forlorn," Betty said, patting Desiree's shoulder. "What's the worst that can happen? We've lost money, sure, but we're all safe and reasonably healthy for a bunch of old goats. If we need to, we can turn around, go home tonight, and tomorrow we'll watch the parade together on television. Then we'll get out and find a turkey dinner together. There has to be somewhere in the valley that will serve four more turkey dinners."

Desiree patted Betty's hand. "You're such a dear. I'm sure we'll deal with this somehow. But I was so looking forward to this trip." Her voiced choked on the last part of the sentence.

Geraldine returned with a tray filled with paper cups of ice water and a basket of breadsticks with marinara sauce. She placed it on the table and grabbed a straw. "This was all I thought we'd need to rent the table for a while." She nabbed a breadstick and took a bite.

"Thank you, dear," Desiree said as she and Betty each took a cup of water and placed them in front of them.

Just then Ida said, "Thanks, sweetie. You're the greatest," as she hung up her phone. She looked across the table at her friends and smiled.

"Okay," Betty said. "What's with the Cheshire grin?"

"I was just talking to my son." Her smile broadened.

"A-a-nd?" Desiree said wondering how that could help.

"Well, he says his museum is right along the parade route and they invite donors to watch it from the roof of the building every year."

"But we're not donors," Geraldine said, resignation in her voice.

"Speak for yourself," Ida said with a smug smile. "I don't donate as much as the others invited, but he's sure he can wedge me in."

"Just you?" Desiree asked.

"No. I'm allowed to bring friends who . . ." Ida cleared her throat. ". . . who might be future donors?" She looked from one to another of them with a hopeful look on her face.

Desiree sighed, thinking of all the money she'd already lost on this boondoggle. Then setting her jaw with resolve, she said, "I'm sure we can put something together for a good cause."

Betty nodded and looked at Geraldine.

"As long as there isn't a minimum donation required," Geraldine said with a shrug.

"Terrific," said Ida as she typed into her phone. "I'll let him know to save us a table."

"I hate to be a wet blanket," Betty said, "but the parade is tomorrow. Where will we all stay tonight?"

"We could try the YWCA," Geraldine said, under her breath.

Betty scowled. "I already checked it. They're booked full."

"Figures." Geraldine grabbed another breadstick and dunked it in the marinara sauce.

"I've also been looking through other options," Betty continued. "The only ones with vacancies are places with one or two stars—or with bathrooms down the hall—or in the Bronx or New Jersey."

"I didn't know there were hotels with only one star," Desiree said.

"Ladies, I have that covered, too," Ida said, then, looking down added, "Sorta."

All focused on her, waiting for her to elaborate.

Ida shrugged. "Keith has a sofa bed in his apartment that can accommodate two of us. And he is cat sitting for a friend who went home for the holiday. He thinks the friend won't mind if two of us sleep there. He's checking with them now." She looked sheepish as she went on. "Manhattan apartments are notoriously tiny, you know. It won't be a five-star experience, but the price is right, and it beats going home and missing everything."

"Let's go for it," Betty said. "It'll feel like being a kid again. A slumber party."

Desiree tried to imagine staying on someone's couch. She couldn't quite picture it, but she didn't want to complain when the predicament was all her fault.

"And," Ida said, "the museum will offer an early brunch, but they'll have a full turkey dinner buffet after the parade has passed."

"Free?" Geraldine asked.

Ida nodded. "Free for their 'donor guests.'"

"How will we split up for sleeping?" Geraldine asked.

"Desiree and I will stay at Keith's," Ida said. "It's on the third floor, but there's an elevator." She looked down. "I'm afraid the friend's place is a walk-up, but you two packed light, right?" She looked at Betty for assent. Geraldine groaned. "My knees!"
Betty sighed. "I'll help you with your bag."

*

The next morning, when Ida and Desiree arrived at the museum, a lavish continental breakfast awaited them under a caterer's tent on the museum roof. Ample tables and chairs dotted the space filled with well-heeled donors who seemed more interested in hobnobbing with each other than watching the parade.

This is more like it, Desiree thought, trying to loosen the knot in her shoulder from the lumpy sofa bed. Then, noticing a famous author and a popular singer in the crowd, she couldn't help but be relieved she had packed appropriate outfits.

"Hey, Mom," Keith said, coming up to them, a little out of breath. "Sorry I had to leave before you got up this morning, but glad you got here okay. Just pick any table, and make sure to check out the food. It's pretty great."

"This looks wonderful, hon," said Ida, giving Keith a quick hug. "We feel so lucky to be here. You're a real life saver."

"Glad to do it, Mom. But I gotta go schmooze with the donors. Gotta pay the bills, you know." Keith grinned and waved as he moved toward a knot of people at a nearby table.

Geraldine and Betty arrived a few minutes later and made a beeline to the coffee urn.

"Yoohoo," Desiree called as she came up to them. "We have settled at a great table with a terrific view of the street." She pointed to where Ida sat, guarding chairs from a burly man who appeared to want to borrow one of them. "Hurry up. The parade starts soon."

By the time the Tom Turkey float with seated Pilgrims drove by, they had filled their plates and were sipping mimosas.

"This is better than a hotel suite," Geraldine said, signaling to a server for a refill.

The many trademark balloons floated past them at eye-level, and the music enveloped them in the spirit of the holiday.

When Santa finally sailed past on his sleigh, Desiree hugged Ida. "I cannot thank you and Keith enough," she said. "You really saved the holiday."

Ida embraced her as Geraldine stood, saying, "So where's the turkey dinner?"

"I saw them setting it up under the tent," Betty said. "I think we just need to follow the crowd." They moved to join the line of donors.

Ida stood and took Desiree's arm. She leaned in to ask, "So, Desi, was it everything you'd hoped for all those years?"

"Well—" Desiree inhaled the enticing scent of turkey, stuffing with gravy, sweet potatoes, squash, green beans, and cranberry. She thought about her "best-laid plans," the money she had foolishly lost, and the things she had hoped they would do in the city. Then she looked at her dearest friends. The ones she had known almost all her life, on whom she knew she could always rely, and who, despite their varying personalities and situations, were the best people she knew on the planet. She knew Thanksgiving wasn't about a parade or a luxury hotel or five kinds of stuffing. It was about appreciating the friends you love and who love you—no matter what.

Desiree turned to Ida, tears in her eyes. "You know it's not what I expected," she said, unable to keep the smile from filling her face. "But, my dear, in its own way, this is so *very* much better."

Krampusnacht
December 5th

He Sees You When You're Sleeping

Diane Sismour

December, 2019

Our neighborhood doesn't go in much for Christmas decorations other than the blow-up yard ornaments that lie flat during the day and come to life at night. I think the bright lights and gardens downtown look more Christmassy, but that doesn't change Momma's mind. Even though the weatherman forecasts a cold front hitting the South all this week, she's complaining again that the climate in Texarkana never gives her the same holiday spirit that New York City did.

Our Christmas has one tradition. On the first Wednesday after Thanksgiving, we sip hot chocolate as we trim our tree. It's the same day the one in Rockefeller Center lights up.

Momma places a bright-red Santa hat with white trim on her head. Her short, black-as-coal, curly hair peeks out from below. She adjusts a too-large hat on my head.

"You look pretty, Momma," I say.

She cups my cheek with her hand. "That's sweet of you, Millie. I have a surprise for you."

She kneels in front of me so we're face-to-face and bops my nose with a finger. "Remember when I said you were too young to help hang the fancy ornaments? Now that you're seven, you can hang them with me."

"I can! Super cool, Momma." I drag one of the totes filled with ornaments closer to the tree while she goes to make the cocoa.

When she adds the chocolate to warm milk, the aroma wafts into the family room and competes with the pine for the perfect Christmas smell.

"Millie, do you want peppermint or marshmallows?" she calls from the kitchen.

"Marshmallows, please."

When she carries two hot mugs of cocoa into the room, she gives a real smile, not the strained one she wore while Daddy carried Britney's boxes to his car earlier today. In one cup is a candy cane and the other has my gooey deliciousness.

The melted marshmallow reminds me of last year, when Britney wanted three marshmallows in her cup. The melted sugar oozed onto her face and left a sticky mustache.

"It's weird not having..." *I can't say my big sister's name.* I gulp back the lump growing in my throat. "... not having *her* here. I can't believe she left us for Daddy's new family."

Momma's smile slips to a frown.

I force a beaming grin. "But you, me, and Ben are still together."

We open bins of lights and holiday decorations. I help Momma untangle the strings as she places them in neat rows. A pine scent fills the room as we layer the garland and hang the ornaments and tinsel on the blue spruce. As the tree shimmers in red, gold, and silver, Momma's happiness returns, and she retells her memories of the chilly winters of her youth.

"Millie, when the snow falls, Central Park turns white, and the sled hill glistens as a magical wonderland."

Our town stops everything when the first flakes hit the ground. I close my eyes for two heartbeats and pretend to understand how a city can do anything with so much snow. Still in awe, I ask, "Does the sled go fast?"

She claps her hands. "Yes, as fast as Santa's sleigh."

"Did it snow there like it did here last winter when ice froze on everything? I remember how the trees sparkled in the sunlight, and the next day everything melted."

"Not quite. Nobody wants to play on ice unless you're at the skating rink." She wears a brief smile, then the creases between her eyebrows deepen. An indentation circles her ring finger from sixteen years of wearing a wedding band. I guess by having the ring off she showed Daddy there would be no second chance. She presses two fingers to her temple. "So stressful today with Britney moving to your Daddy's."

"Momma, why did Britney *choose* to move in with Daddy's new family over ours? Was it because they live in a bigger house and she... she doesn't have to share a room with me."

"Sweetie, Britney will always love you. Sharing a room with you isn't why she left us. You know how she loves to shop and be with her friends. And Daddy doesn't hold to curfews."

As I drape the red tree skirt around the stand, Momma rubs a finger between her eyes.

"Now, where was I in the telling?" Her hands flap up as though surprised. "At Rockefeller Center, the golden angels hold their horns as though they're trumpeting in the glory of the season." Momma gets the stepladder and places the angel tree topper on the highest branch.

"We'll have to visit Grammy's this winter, and I'll take you to the park. We can skate, and sled in Central Park, and shop at the big department stores." Her voice grows more excited as she continues. "Grammy used to take me when I was your age. We would fantasize about where to wear all those fancy party clothes on display."

"That sounds like fun, Momma. But didn't Grammy move to Florida?"

"You're right. My memory." She touches her head with both hands. They burst away, and then she waves her fingers like fireworks falling. "What would I do without you?"

On the television, the commentator reminds viewers that the network changed the one-hour broadcast to two. One more hour until the dark corner of the family room glows in soft, twinkling lights.

"Momma, I've been extra good this year. What if Santa catches me awake late? He'll put me on the naughty list and won't bring me that cool tablet I asked for. You know, the one that erases just with a couple shakes."

"I'm sure you'll be fine."

I stare at the television. *I hope so.*

The minute hand creeps, tick by painful tick, toward nine o'clock. Different singers and dancers entertain on the show as Momma rearranges some decorations I hung to higher branches.

She gives me strict instructions. "Millie, it's almost time. Get your brother. He's in one of his cranky moods since your sister left. You don't take *no* for an answer, you hear?"

"Yes, Momma." My sigh empties all the air from my lungs, much like what happens when Ben gets to talking about video games. I push open his bedroom door. The walls are bare. The bookcase is empty. The bedding is gone. All the belongings from my room are in the middle of the floor.

"*Momma!*"

I don't hear Momma's footsteps racing toward me, but I hear Ben's snickers come through the wall. Two heartbeats later, I'm running back to Momma. Between hiccupped cries, I say, "Ben t–took my room. That's Britney's room, too. What if she wants to come back? He can't just take it. C–can he?"

Momma's eyes narrow, and the perpetual smile she wears disappears into a tight-lipped, on-a-mission face. "Benedict Andrew Buchanan, get out here this very second."

When Momma uses our full names, she's not happy. Giddiness sweeps through me. *I'm getting my room back.*

I stand beside her in the same posture–with hands on hips.

"You're in trouble now, Benedict," I say his name hitting all the syllables.

He sticks out his tongue at me. His hair clipped on the sides and long on top, makes him look like the troll doll tossed on the floor with the rest of my stuff.

"Benedict Andrew, I've had about enough of your attitude today. Why did you take Millie's room?"

"I have three reasons," he says, then gives me a smug smile. He counts on his fingers with each fact. "First, I'm the next oldest. Second, Millie isn't sharing the big bedroom anymore since Britney went to live with Dad."

She turns to me. "He does have a point, Millie. Ben, asking me first would have shown maturity. Those were two . . . what is the third?"

He stands in front of me and bends to face level. In a rush he finishes, "And third, I don't have to behave, 'cause there's no such thing as Santa Claus."

Tears well in my eyes. "Liar! There is *so* a Santa Claus."

Turning to Momma, I want her to disagree with him. I want to hear that he lied. That there *is* a Santa Claus. That the kids in my second-grade class who say there isn't a Santa are wrong, too.

She doesn't disagree with him at all.

"Millie, go watch television." Instead of sitting on the couch, I sneak around the corner, listening and watching.

Momma presses a hand to her temple. "Boy, you just tipped this headache into a migraine." She grabs Ben's earlobe and marches him to the newly claimed bedroom. He's half-walking, half-hopping to keep up with her.

"I don't care," Ben says with a sneer in his voice. "Next year, when I'm old enough, I'm moving in with Dad, too."

"You listen to me, young man. Until you move to your daddy's house, I make the rules. You hear me? And you *will* behave . . ."

I go and sit cross-legged on the couch. The television picture wavers through my tears. I lost my sister and my room. And Santa isn't *real*? This is the worst day ever.

When Momma returns, her face is pale, and wrinkles crease between her eyebrows. "Millie, let me know when I have one minute left to plug in the lights. I need to lie down."

The countdown clock reads six minutes. The commentator announces, "Mayor Bill de Blasio and Santa are here to press the button and turn on the five miles of multi-colored lights on this magnificent Norway spruce."

Santa must be real. He's standing right there.

Wiping my tears away with my sleeve, I stare at the television. A scary monster with fur covering his body stands behind the Mayor and Santa.

Do they know the monster is there?

Horns branch high on top of its head, bigger than any reindeer's rack. His devil-mask has a tongue that sticks out longer than a panting dog on a hot summer day. On his back is a large basket, and he holds a bundle of twigs in a thick fist, swatting at whatever is beneath the basket's cover. Every time he moves, big bells connected to his belt clang.

The commentator backs away two quick steps as the devil monster looms closer. "Who do we have here, Santa?" he asks in a hesitant voice.

Santa moves to the microphone and tugs the monster's arm to stand by his side. "Ho, ho, ho. My friend, this is Father Krampus. You might not be familiar with him, but he's a big part of the Krampusnacht Festival celebrated in some European countries every December fifth. This year, Father Krampus and I are teaming up to help conserve fossil fuels. Do you know what those are?"

Some in the audience surrounding the makeshift stage react.

"I see heads nodding–good. Instead of leaving a lump of coal in bad boys' and girls' stockings, because we need to conserve coal, Father Krampus will—"

Father Krampus smacks the twigs against his leg and answers in a growl, "—teach them to behave."

I shake with a startle and sink deeper into the sofa.

Krampus's eyes pierce through the television as though he can see me. A shiver runs down my spine. I don't want to be on *his* naughty list.

The countdown blips on the screen, and the commentator continues to talk over the ticking clock. "One minute until Bill de Blasio, the one-hundred-and-ninth mayor of New York City, and Santa Claus press that button on the eighty-seventh Rockefeller Center Tree Lighting. This incredible, seventy-seven-foot-tall, forty-six-foot-wide, twelve-ton Norway spruce, cut from the yard of Florida, New York, resident Carol Schultz..."

"Momma. Momma, they're starting."

No answer comes from her room.

I kneel on the couch, lean against the back, and look for her down the hallway. My, I mean Ben's, and Momma's doors are both closed. "Momma, it's time," I shout.

She opens the bedroom door. "Millie, you'll have to light the tree for me. The lights will hurt my eyes with this migraine." She retreats into the dark room and closes the door.

He must have given her a really bad headache for Momma to miss her Christmas tradition.

"Ten, nine, eight, seven..."

I scurry off the couch to crawl beneath the branches and fish the plug from under the red skirt. Pine sap oozes from the pegs holding the trunk straight. The sharp needles scratch my neck and arms and tangle in my hair.

The commentator raises his arms to encourage the crowd to cheer. "Three, two, one. Mayor de Blasio and Santa, press that button."

I plug the cord into the socket and, at the same time, Christmas lights turn on in my house and on TV. The Rockefeller Center tree illuminates the night sky bigger than the brightest moon. Here ours flickers on and off like it's covered with twinkling stars. *Magical.*

Momma is right. It's as though I'm the one who lit the tree in Manhattan. Tingles race up and down my body. *Now* I understand why Momma loves this tradition.

The crowd's cheers drown out the announcer. I turn off the show. The soft, flickering bulbs cast shadows on the family room walls. Sleep pulls at me and my bed isn't made yet.

I head to the refrigerator for my late-night snack. Momma insists on us each eating an apple a day before bedtime. Since Ben isn't going to eat his, I add his slices to mine and take the plate to my new room.

I stand in the doorway staring at the empty bookshelf, dresser, and small bed and bedside table against the far wall. The only thing Ben didn't take was his stinky boy smell. My stomach growls, and I munch on the apples to figure out what to do first.

What would Britney do first? She always kept our room tidy. But she isn't here to clean up after me anymore.

Why did she have to leave? I kick the heap. *Ben just isn't fair.*

I yank out the sheets, blanket, and pillow to make the bed. Dragging my stuffed animals to the shelves, I all but fill them. My sneakers and dress shoes go on the bottom shelf, and I pick up armfuls of clothes and stuff them into drawers.

There are only a couple of coloring books, a box of crayons, and my library book left where the pile once stood. These I plop into the nightstand drawer. Sorting through the mess took more time than I wanted. At least the room has everything off the floor, and I won't trip in the dark. *Britney would be so proud of me.*

I slip into bed and sleep tugs my eyes closed. Bells clanging outside wake me. Am I dreaming? Is that Santa?

Ben said Santa isn't real. But that Santa on television had a real white beard, not like the Santa's helpers at the mall.

The noise grows louder. Something scrapes the walls in the hallway. When the doorknob turns, I pull the covers up to my nose. I whisper, "Santa?"

The door opens and the monster with the devil mask ducks through the doorway. My breath hitches, blood pounds in my ears, and hot tingles race up and down my limbs. His fur smells like a wet dog, his horns mark the ceiling, and he slouches to stand inside the tiny room. I yank the comforter up higher and hold my breath, hoping he'll leave.

Whimpers sound from the basket he carries. Oh my gosh, what's in there? Are those bad kids in his basket? I want to call out to Momma, but then he'll find me.

I chance a peek. A swat from the twigs he carries silences the cries from the basket.

In a gruff voice, the monster calls, "Benedict, wakey, wakey. You've been a naughty boy. You're coming with me." He rips the comforter off the bed with one pull. His horns gouge the ceiling when he jolts back. "You're not Benedict."

Cowering against the wall, I plead, "Father Krampus, please . . . I've been good. I promise."

The monster spots the apples on the nightstand and glances between me, the plate, and back again.

He looks hungry. It's better that he eats my snack than eats me. "D-do you want some apple?" I ask.

"Millicent, thank you for sharing." His voice is deep and rumbles like the sound of thunder.

I open my eyes wide. "You know my name."

He removes the basket harness and sits on the floor. The bells clang and then deaden on the carpet. He harrumphs. "Of course I do. But this is a surprise. You are not on Father Christmas's naughty list."

"Wait . . . so there is a Santa Claus?" Relief floods through me.

"Father Christmas is known by many names, but yes, Millicent, he is as real as I am sitting before you."

Sitting on the bed and leaning against the wall, I study him. He's more of a goat man than a devil monster. "But you're scary."

He waves a hand from head to toe. "I must be to scare those naughty children into being good."

"Oh, okay. That makes total sense." I leaned back against the wall, more relaxed. Then the basket shakes. Another whimper escapes. I shrink against the wall. "What's in your bag?"

Krampus pats the top of the covered lump. "Some children misbehave more than others. The very naughty ones come with me."

I pull my legs tight and wrap my arms around them. Maybe he's not as nice as I thought. "Do you live in the North Pole, too?"

"Not that far north, Millicent. The alpine mountains are my home."

He straps the basket onto his back. "I must go. Father Christmas has one night to deliver gifts, and I have just one day to teach the naughty a lesson." He stands to leave. "Thank you for the apple slices, Millicent."

As he ducks through the doorway, I say, "Oh, Father Krampus?"

The goat-man stops.

"Ben's room is the next door on the left."

Pearl Harbor Day
December 7th

Creating A Memory With Gram

Debra H. Goldstein

A striped bikini was the last thing Sally threw into her suitcase before zipping it. Hawaii! She couldn't believe Gram and Granddad, before he died three months ago, had, out of the clear blue offered—no make that *insisted*—that Sally accompany them to Hawaii as an early Christmas present. They pointed out that next year, as a first-year English teacher, her ability to travel would be tied to her school's vacation schedule.

Sally hadn't thought twice before yelling, "Yes!" After watching *South Pacific, Blue Hawaii,* and *From Here to Eternity* with Gram, she'd developed a dream to visit Hawaii's pristine beaches, islands, and volcanic mountains. A college film class piqued her interest further when she learned that movies of all genres, including *Raiders of the Lost Ark, Honeymoon in Vegas, Planet of the Apes,* and *Jurassic Park,* were also filmed there. And now, on December 5, Gram and she were only minutes from landing in Oahu.

She glanced again at the open page in the guidebook lying on her tray table and then at her phone. "Gram, we're landing on time. We'll have at least two hours of daylight to hit the beach."

"I promise you'll see plenty of beaches while we're in Hawaii, but not tonight. By the time we get out of the airport and to the hotel, it's going to be later than you think. Remember, I'm not as young as you. Traveling this far takes a lot out of these old bones."

"You're the youngest seventy-five-year-old I know."

"That's because I'm probably one of the few you know." Gram chuckled, but then got serious. "Granddad, may he rest in peace, and I made this trip so many times that I can assure you jet lag will creep up on both of us. That's why I made us a dinner reservation in our hotel's restaurant, which, by the way, is very good. Then, we'll call it a night. Tomorrow is going to be a busy day."

Sally couldn't prevent her mouth from puckering into a pout.

"You know," Gram said, "the first time your grandfather and I came to Hawaii was on our honeymoon. He made the same plans for our first full day as I've made for us for tomorrow, but he scheduled nothing for the night of our arrival. Annoyed with him, I booked us a late romantic dinner at one of the island's finest restaurants. Dinner started well, but we both almost fell asleep before they brought us our entrees. We ended up taking our dessert back to our hotel."

Gram averted her face from Sally and made a noise like she was clearing her throat. When she finally turned her head back, Sally gently wiped away the tear that sat on Gram's cheek. As selfishly excited as she'd been that Gram hadn't canceled their trip after Granddad's death, she hadn't considered how hard it would be for Gram to visit Hawaii without him.

"I miss him, too," Sally said.

With Granddad being twenty years older than Gram, it was not unexpected that he died first. The emotions Gram must be feeling, knowing that after almost fifty years Granddad and she would never be together again, hit Sally. Although Sally couldn't change reality during this trip for her grandmother, she vowed to be more conscious of anything that might trigger painful memories.

Gram hugged Sally. Then, perhaps taking Sally's lingering silence as her still being disappointed, Gram smiled and said, "Don't worry honey, during the next ten days, you'll spend plenty of time on Hawaiian beaches. Except for tonight's dinner, the only plans I've made are tomorrow's Pearl Harbor memorial tour, reservations for a night and day near Haena Beach on Kauai, where *South Pacific* was filmed, and arranging for a driver to take us on the Road to Hana on Maui. The rest of our trip, you're free to sightsee, sunbathe, snorkel, or do whatever you want."

"I can't say touring a memorial excites me, but I'm definitely up for the beach."

Sally knew she'd said something wrong when Gram's smile changed to a frown.

"The USS Arizona Memorial is why we're on this plane. Why we're making this trip."

CREATING A MEMORY WITH GRAM

Not even five minutes after promising herself to be careful about things that might distress Gram, she'd blown it. Sally bit her lip. "I'm sorry if I upset you."

Gram patted Sally's arm. "It's okay. Granddad and I never made it clear to you that the most important part of this trip is our visit to the memorial."

"Why is that?"

"Because, as a journalist, your grandfather lived by the power of the written word. Sometimes, though, he felt seeing and touching was better for instilling truths in others. To him, it was a matter of L'dor V'dor—handing down values and traditions from generation to generation. That's what he wanted to do with you on this trip."

"Really?"

"You remember Granddad had a much older brother who enlisted in the Navy?"

"Yes. Granddad said when things were tough for the family, his brother went into the military to help support his younger sisters and him, but his brother was killed in World War II."

"Not exactly."

"What do you mean?"

"In October 1941, while the world was in a turmoil, your grandfather's brother, Bill, joined the Navy as a seaman recruit. After he finished his training, Bill was promoted to being a full-fledged seaman and assigned to the USS Arizona."

"1941?" The connection suddenly made sense. "Are you saying he was on the USS Arizona when Japan bombed Pearl Harbor?"

"That's right. Bill was one of the 1177 crew members killed on December 7, 1941, the day President Franklin Roosevelt later called 'a date which will live in infamy.' The United States didn't enter the war until December 8, so technically, your great-uncle died before we were part of World War II."

"I knew Granddad was a World War II history buff," Sally said, "but I never realized Great-Uncle Bill died the day before America joined the war."

"For your great-aunts and Granddad, losing their brother was devastating. Later, Granddad obsessed about learning everything he could about World War II, especially the bombings that started the war and ended it."

Sally shuddered. "I get goosebumps thinking about the pictures I've seen of the aftermath of the bombing of Hiroshima."

"Those pictures bothered Granddad, too. He researched the impact both bombings had on humanity, but something about Pearl Harbor ate at him."

"Losing his brother?"

"It was more than just that," Gram said. "Granddad went out of his way to delve into the events of that day and the ones that followed. He interviewed people who lost loved ones, made personal connections with members of the Pearl Harbor Survivors Association, and wrote articles detailing their stories hoping the survivors and the dead wouldn't be forgotten."

"Is that why you two visited Hawaii every five years? I always thought your trips were like a renewal of your vows and honeymoon."

Gram smiled. "They were that, too. But his educational mission took on a new life when a recent president, during a private tour of the USS Arizona memorial, expressed the fact that he didn't have a clue as to its significance. Your grandfather felt that if that president was ignorant, what did that say about the general population? That's why Granddad thought it important for us to bring you to Pearl Harbor to experience National Pearl Harbor Remembrance Day."

"As a way of teaching me?"

"And, he hoped, others through you." Gram paused to bring her seat upright for landing. "Pearl Harbor Day was first recognized as a holiday in 1994. Flags are flown at half-staff until sunset, but it's not a federal holiday where they close government offices, so a lot of people don't even know it exists. Because of their ignorance, your grandfather worried that future generations, not understanding the horror of Pearl Harbor and World War II, would repeat history. He wanted you to have the tools necessary to educate your future students and the children who will come after them."

"But we're touring the memorial on December sixth?"

"Only because with all the other events being held, they don't run the Navy Boat or give the tour on Pearl Harbor Day. We have tickets to the activities on December seventh if you want to go. That's up to you."

The next morning, they were on the first Navy boat leaving the Visitor Center for the USS Arizona Memorial. Sally listened as a voice came over a speaker explaining that they would be visiting a 184-foot-long structure, built to span the middle portion of the sunken battleship. Upon docking, Gram pointed over the rail at the water. "You can still see the oil residue from the Arizona."

CREATING A MEMORY WITH GRAM

She led the way into the entry room. "It doesn't take long to go through the monument," Gram said, ushering Sally into the next room. "This is the assembly room. They hold ceremonies and do general observation from here. The next room, the shrine room, is the one that's important for you to see. Come on."

Entering the room Gram was so eager to get to, Sally pulled up short before a marble wall covered with names. It took her a moment to find her voice. "There are so many of them."

"All of the eleven-hundred seventy-seven names are on that wall. To your grandfather, each name represents an equally significant life. Look over here." Sally's gaze followed to where her grandmother pointed. "There's your great-uncle's name."

Gram's hand found Sally's. For a moment, they simply stood there in silence. Finally, Sally spoke. "The beach can wait. I'd like to use those tickets you got to be part of tomorrow's Remembrance Day."

"Granddad would be so proud of you." Gram hesitated and then waved her hand toward the wall. "Being here for this last time, I'm at one with your grandfather."

"Don't talk like that, Gram. You'll come back again."

"Honey, we can't ignore the passage of time. I'm no spring chicken."

"You're as young as you feel."

"And that's pretty crickety. No, this will be my final trip to Hawaii for National Pearl Harbor Day."

"But, with or without my bathing suit, it won't be mine."

Hanukkah
25th Day of Kislev

Latkes and Sour Cream

Peter J Barbour

"When can we light the candles?" six-year-old Sammy asked his mother. He danced in place while she glided through the kitchen putting the final touches on the holiday meal. *Maybe Momma will let me light the first candle.* He continued to spin.

"Once the sun goes down," his mother said as she chopped onions and grated potatoes to be pressed into pancakes, called l*atkes.*

"Be patient," she added in a kind supportive voice.

"Can't we light them now? When will Aunt Nancy be here?"

"Soon, I hope," Mother muttered under her breath. "I just hope she remembers the jelly donuts."

Aunts, uncles, and cousins arrived. Some carried extra folding chairs to be set about the dining room table, so everyone had a seat. Along with his older brothers, Ross and Max, Sammy collected their share of gold foil-wrapped chocolate coins at the door, Hanukkah *gelt*. *Sweet and yummy.* He liked chocolate, but he loved raspberry jelly donuts even more.

The aroma of potatoes and onions frying in hot oil mixed with the fragrance of roasting vegetables and beef brisket wafted through the house. Family filled the living room and spilled into the kitchen.

Where is Aunt Nancy? She was Sammy's favorite aunt and frequently late.

Aunt Nancy told me she would bring a special gift. But, who's it for?

Sammy wended his way through the crowd into the kitchen and pulled at his mother's shirt sleeve. "Can we light the candles now?"

"Has the sun set? Is Aunt Nancy here?" Mother replied. Sammy frowned.

He made his way to the living room and peered out the window. The sun had almost set. He could see the moon, but darkness hadn't fallen yet.

Across the street Aunt Nancy got out of her car. She carried a rectangular box in her right hand and a larger square box positioned under her left arm.

A smile spread over Sammy's face. He waved his arms and spun around. He guessed the smaller container held jelly donuts, and he hoped the other box held a present. Too small to be a bicycle or a keyboard, too large to be a Play Station or Xbox.

It seemed like ages until Aunt Nancy made it to the front door. He greeted her with a long hug. She kissed his cheek as he took in the familiar smell of her perfume.

"What's in the boxes?" Cousin Fred called from across the room as she entered the house. Aunt Nancy just smiled, her eyes twinkling. She shook her head, shrugged her shoulders, wagged her finger, and said nothing as she disappeared into a back room away from the noise and commotion and shut the door. Sammy wanted to follow her down the hall. *Can I get a peek into the box?* But he stopped. Sammy kept an eye on Aunt Nancy. He caught her checking on the box twice. Once, she disappeared outside.

Evening arrived. "Come gather around," Father announced. "It is time to light the candles." First, he lit the *Shamash*, the helper candle, which would be used to light the others. Everyone joined in as Father chanted in Hebrew the three prayers for the first day of Hanukkah. Then, he continued, "The first prayer is the commandment to light the Hanukkah lights. The second offers thanks for the miracles that God performed for our ancestors, and the third gives thanks to God for sustaining us and allowing us to reach this season. It is the first night of Hanukkah, and only one other candle will be lit."

Mother took the kindled *Shamash* from Father. "Sammy, come here." She guided his hand with hers, and they lit the first candle together. Sammy took in the smell of melting wax as he puffed out his chest and squared his shoulders, then hid behind his mother as everyone clapped.

"Come, let's eat," Mother said. She served the meal with the help of Sammy's aunts. They placed the beef brisket, carrots, asparagus, Aunt Janet's salad, *Challah* (a braided bread), and *latkes* with a choice of toppings including home-made applesauce, honey, sour cream, and capers, on the table that stretched from the dining room into the living room. Sammy's father helped him to a *latka* covered by plenty of applesauce to start.

For dessert, mother put out fruit and pastries including rugalach and Nanna's coffee cake. Aunt Nancy brought out the raspberry jelly donuts, always a big hit. Sammy ate his donut slowly, savoring each bite as the sweet sticky filling oozed onto his fingers and his face. The food was gone. Everyone helped clear the table, but father elected to postpone his dishwashing duties until later.

After the table was cleared, the grownups still sat around the dinner table, drinking tea and coffee, and talking. Sammy found his cousins Danny and Becky and his brothers Ross and Max in a corner of the room playing with a *dreidel*, a four-sided top. A pile of filbert nuts lay on the table where they took turns spinning the top. Grandpa wandered to a chair where the children played. He watched them take a couple of turns before interrupting the game as he always did each year.

"Can someone tell me what the Hebrew letters on the sides of the *dreidel* stand for?" Grandpa said.

Sammy looked around. *Who will say something first?*

"Sure," Max said. "I'll explain. You spin the *dreidel*. When it stops, one of the four letters faces up. *Nun, Gimmel, Hay,* or *Shin. Nun* stands for *Nichts*, none. You can't take any nuts from the pot. If it comes up *Gimmel,* or *Ganz,* you win all the nuts. *Hay* is for *Halb,* which means half, so you take half the pot, and if it comes up *Shin,* for *Stell,* you must put a filbert back in. The person with the most nuts in the end wins." Sammy nodded his head.

"Yes, that certainly works for your game," Grandpa said, "but these letters also stand for something else, *Nes Gadol Hayah Sham,* which translates to 'a great miracle happened there.' So, who can tell me what the miracle was?" Sammy listened, his eyes wide open.

Becky raised her hand. "The Maccabees defeated the Greeks and made our Temple holy again in Jerusalem," she said. "The sacred light above the Torah was kept burning for eight days with oil that should only have lasted one day."

"Correct," Grandpa said. "Thus, we celebrate the festival of lights for eight days and eat foods cooked in oil, like the *latkes* and donuts."

"Children come here," Aunt Nancy called out and waved her arm to signal them. "It is time to give out gifts," she said. "I have something for everyone." She handed each child, including Sammy, an envelope containing money, real gelt, a dollar for each year of age. "I'm sure your parents may have something more for each of you as well."

She turned to Sammy. He held his breath, eyes focused on his aunt. The box she'd hidden in the back room sat on the floor beside her within arm's reach. Sammy stood still and didn't grab. Patience, his mother taught him.

Max, Ross, Dan, Fred, and Becky chanted, "What's in the box? What's in the box?"

"Open it," Aunt Nancy said. Sammy giggled as he stepped forward and lifted the flap. A head popped up, soft and furry, with large brown eyes, a fuzzy black face, and floppy ears. Her body was tan and black with large white paws. "She's twelve weeks old," Aunt Nancy said as she picked up the puppy and handed her to Sammy. "I house trained her. She's very smart." The puppy wiggled, wagged her tail, and licked Sammy's face. Sammy was so happy he started to cry.

"You and your brothers will need to care for her," Aunt Nancy said. "She'll need a name."

"Latka!" Sammy blurted.

With sheepish eyes, he looked at Max and Ross for approval, then at his aunt. "Will Momma and Daddy let us keep her?" Sammy asked, his voice trembled.

"I already took care of that," she responded with a reassuring smile.

Everyone wanted a turn holding the puppy. They stroked her and took her into the yard to play. When they brought the puppy in, Aunt Nancy placed a water dish next to one filled with the kibble that she retrieved from her car. Father set up a crate with a soft towel for bedding in the kitchen.

The hour grew late. The candles in the menorah had long since burned out. Parents gathered their kids. It was time for everyone to go home.

Sammy helped settle the puppy onto her bed and kissed her head. "Goodnight, Latka. I'm so glad you're part of our family," he said as he turned and headed to his room.

Before getting into bed, Sammy wrote in his diary: *Best Hanaka ever.* And as he went to sleep, he thought about how he would spend his Hanukkah money on dog toys.

Christmas
December 25th

High Tech

Dianna Sinovic

Thirty minutes to early dismissal on this Christmas Eve. Hope adjusts her headset and takes a breath. Thirty minutes *if* whatever call she's on is completed by the top of the hour. If not, then she stays—politely, with no urging anyone along—until the problem is solved.

The call center room is nearly empty, with only four others on her inbound team there for the day. The rest are working from home. Hope is glad she's at the office. To be at her apartment, sitting at her kitchen table with her laptop open, would push her to tears. She'd sent Farley away three days ago.

"It's me, not you," she said, knowing the words were trite but having no way else to explain the staleness she felt between them.

He'd begged her to reconsider, which made the severing worse.

Now, Hope is thinking she's made a mistake. Christmas will be lonely this year; her parents are celebrating the holiday in France with her younger sister, married to a Britany man.

Her set lights up: a call. With a flick of a switch, she is on.

"Good afternoon. Tech Solutions, Hope speaking. What issue can I help you resolve?"

The call screen identifies the number. By the area code, she guesses Cleveland.

"Hope, you say?" The voice is male, forceful but thinning. She guesses mid-sixties. White hair, pale blue eyes, six feet, slight paunch. It's a game she plays, never seeing the people she speaks with day after day. It helps her focus on the call, to imagine how they look. It must help because she gets a solid five stars most times. Her supervisor has told her she's among the best.

That's not saying much, since call center work wasn't what she planned on doing for long. Four years and three months later, she's still there.

Someday she will get her charter pilot's license. Ferry rock stars and business moguls around the world. She has more than four hundred hours left to log, and some days—like today, feeling hopeless—she thinks the goal lies beyond her reach.

"Whom do I have the pleasure of speaking with this afternoon?" Her words are a blend of respect and efficiency, friendliness tempered with don't-fuck-with-me steel.

"It's Christmas Eve," the man says. "I was surprised someone answered. Thought you might be from India, but you sound American."

"That I am," she confirms. "And we are open for about twenty-five more minutes, then the answering service takes over. What problem are you having that I can help with, Mister . . . ?"

Glancing out the window visible across several cubicles, she watches snowflakes drift down. They are large and thick. *A wet drive home.*

"My grandson promised to come by to help me, but he's late. When I tried to install the update, nothing happened. The circle is just spinning . . ." His words are edged in worry. Then he adds, "Cam."

"Excuse me?"

The man laughs. "Cam—that's my name. Cameron Wells. You can call me Cam."

Hope pictures pistons and shafts and other automotive parts, not the man on the other end of the line. And the tires of her coupe slipping on snow-slicked pavement. Twenty more minutes. With a shake of her head, she pulls herself back to the call.

"I can remote into your computer, if you're okay with that," she says.

"Come again?" Cam sounds puzzled.

She tries a different explanation. "I can take over your computer from here and help you with the install."

He doesn't respond.

"Mr. Wells?"

"I was just wondering if that was safe," he finally says. "My grandson should be here any minute."

You called me, she thinks. "Yes, it's safe. I'm here to help you, sir. Do you want to proceed?"

He sighs. "Teddy probably forgot. Not the first time, you know. Promises big and seldom delivers. A lot like his mother."

HIGH TECH

With a wave, Sarah passes by Hope's cubicle on her way out. "Merry Christmas!"

Hope waves back. At this rate, she'll be on the phone until half past four. A slice of kuchen sits to her right, its lemon scent tempting her. Nicole, who loves to bake, brought the holiday cake to share with the meager in-office crew. Nibbling at the slice, Hope tries to sweeten her soured spirits.

"Sorry, sir," she says.

"Oh, go ahead," Cam says, muttering, "And a fine Christmas this will be."

With a few simple instructions to Cam, Hope establishes the connection and sees his desktop wallpaper: A woman maybe a bit older than she, a wide smile and short cinnamon curls. She's standing on a strand of beach in a two-piece swimsuit, hamming for the camera.

I'd like her. "Nice photo," Hope says. She's seen the best and the worst of desktops and always braces herself for the latter. Often a porno shot, or, in one especially gut-wrenching moment, a torture photo. Once Hope grasped what she was looking at, she cut off the call, badly shaken.

"Connie, my wife," Cam says. "Many long years ago."

Hope looks for the program that needs updating, and Cam continues to talk.

"We were happy in those days. Young and in love."

With a few clicks, Hope sees the issue. "I'm going to uninstall the program and then reinstall. That should solve the problem."

"But Connie grew tired of me. She said she had other things to do in her life and I was holding her back." His tone is wistful.

The uninstall is progressing slowly, and Hope keeps the conversation going. "I'm so sorry." She thinks: *You still haven't moved on—if that old photo is still the center of your universe.*

"And you, my dear," Cam says, "you sound young and full of vigor. Do you have someone special in your life?" He coughs slightly. "I don't mean to pry."

Hope knows she's not supposed to antagonize the caller, but she can't help it, not on this afternoon, when she has the chance to leave early. The old guy is getting on her nerves. "Did you ever move on?"

"What do you mean, dear?"

The dear, especially.

"From Connie. She's still on your desktop all these years later. Was she right about you?" Grimacing at what she's said, glad he can't see her, she adds, "That came out more harshly than I wanted. I apologize."

The uninstall completes, and Hope starts the reinstallation of the program.

"You ask an astute question, which shows me that you are fully engaged, a credit to your job," Cam says. He doesn't sound angry. "Not something that I can say about many young people I encounter these days, my grandson among them."

Surprised at his compliment, Hope says nothing, watching the program progress bar as it inches along.

"I married Dorie about three years later and we had a family—two girls and a boy. I had a successful career as a middle manager, white collar world. Dorie passed away five years ago. I loved her, and she was a fine woman, but Connie was the one who took my breath away, who every day gave me a reason to live."

Michael and Jeremy walk out of the call center together, saluting Hope farewell. She is alone, and it's five after the hour. The progress bar is at ninety-five percent, and suddenly Hope doesn't want this call to end. Farley's devastated look will haunt her once she hangs up.

"Did you ever see her again? Did she regret what she'd done?"

Cam laughs. "I sense you are wondering yourself if you'll regret what you have done."

Her mouth drops open. "How did you know?"

"Call it the wisdom of the aged," he says. "That tinge of guilt in your words. Were you kind to him?" He pauses. "Or, should I add, to her, when you let them go?"

"Him." She also pauses, her eyes smarting. "Yes and no. I tried, but he seemed deeply hurt." Hope imagines Farley's desktop, *her* photo on it, while he talks with some IT pro fifty years from now. "It was for the best."

"It always is," Cam says, gently, "no matter the pain."

Hope tracks Cam's computer as it finishes the installation, and when the program relaunches, there is no longer an endlessly spinning circle. Her work complete, she disconnects from his system, yet still she wants to linger with this stranger from Cleveland.

"You're all set, Mister Wells," she says. "The program is up and running. Is there anything else I can help you with today? If you celebrate, have a Merry Christmas."

HIGH TECH

"Thank you, Miss Hope. I will. Don't forget about faith and charity," he says. "They're just as important."

She ends the call with a groan: such a tired cliché; she's heard it a million times if she's heard it once.

Hanging up her headset, Hope shuts down her computer. It's now twenty past the hour. She straightens her desk and picks up the plate of kuchen. She dumps the remainder of the cake in the trash and washes the plate in the office kitchen. When she returns to her desk for her purse, a small, wrapped package sits next to her keyboard. It wasn't there a moment ago. Or was it?

She picks it up. The tissue paper wrapping is red and green; the package itself feels thin and rectangular. Her name is on the card, so it's definitely for her. The handwriting is one she knows well.

"Farley?" Hope looks around the room, but she is the only one there.

She hesitates. To open the gift might have consequences she won't like. But leaving it unopened seems wrong. Farley meant well, whatever his faults.

Carefully detaching the tape, she removes the holiday tissue to reveal a slender white box. A wallet? A journal? She can't guess.

Inside, she finds a photo of herself, the day they hiked the Delaware Water Gap. She stands on a boulder on Mount Tammany, overlooking the Delaware River far below. She's smiling, hamming for the camera, her shoulder-length hair tucked under a broad-brimmed hat.

On the back, Farley has written: *Remember me when you're sky high.*

Nestled beneath the photo is a money order that will buy her at least ten hours of flight time.

"Love and joy come to you, Farley," she whispers.

A Winter Wonderland . . . Well Sort Of

Jeff Baird

Four days before Christmas in 1995, a light, barely discernable flurry of snowflakes fell from the sky. Not much, but enough for the school where I worked to be canceled, raising my hopes for a white Christmas—the first since Patti and I were married.

Our two-year-old son, Riley, sat on the seat in front of the bay window in our living room, his hands and face pushed up against the windowpane, with the glow of our Christmas tree in the reflection. All the Christmas presents wrapped with ribbons and bows were neatly piled under the tree. Ninety percent of the presents were for Riley, and the remaining ten percent for Patti and me. As far as I could tell, I only had two presents, but both of them were quite large.

On either side of Riley were our trusted Irish Setters, Emerald and Shamrock, with tails whapping side to side. All three of them wanted to go out and romp in our big yard, but Riley was ill and confined to the house. Although Riley's fever was finally abating, he still suffered from other symptoms of his stomach bug, especially explosive diarrhea that could turn our beautiful little redhead into a red-and-brown, Picasso-inspired disaster.

The doctor assured us that his diarrhea would subside after a few days if we kept him clean and dry and controlled his fever. Sure, that was easy for him to say.

Patti and I took turns looking after the little tyke, which seemed a losing battle against the ever-present brown stain, as if he were an on-demand poop machine. Trudging up and down the basement stairs to run his clothes through the washer and dryer became a daily—and nightly—struggle. We finally developed a cleaning assembly line that even Henry Ford would have admired.

To complicate matters, the dogs had to be watched as well. Every time Riley would let loose, they would come running to investigate. Luckily, we had a fenced-in backyard and could keep the dogs outside much of the day until Mother Nature worked against us. The temperatures dropped, and the winds picked up. The once misty snowflakes fattened and began accumulating on the grass.

Between diaper changes and corralling the dogs, Patti and I monitored the storm. By Friday, December twenty-second, the flakes increased in speed and density as the day progressed. It soon became clear that the predictions were correct. We were in for a full-fledged blizzard. The radio told us we already had up to six inches of snow in some parts of our area and we should watch out for additional drifting snow.

"Patti, I'm going to run to the store before everything shuts down. What do we need?"

"Here, I've made a list," she said. "We have a turkey in the freezer that I plan to use for Christmas dinner, but we need milk, bread, butter, and dog food. In fact, let's double up on all of those. And, whatever you do, get as many disposable diapers as possible. We're almost out."

I thought about checking the driving conditions with the local weather station but didn't waste the time. Whatever the forecast, it wasn't getting any better. I had a sturdy, four-wheel-drive Ford Bronco that routinely got me through various weather-related problems. Yet, the sooner I got out there and back again, the better. Especially since our home was on a hill, on the crest of a steep ridge, on a dead-end road.

I knew there was a problem when I tried to back out of our driveway. I had failed to notice the sheet of black ice covered by the thickening snow. Within seconds, the console warning light registered slippery road conditions. I tried to stop slowly, but soon, the inevitable panic took over, and I frantically pumped the brakes to stop. Nope, not going to happen. The Bronco slipped and slid, finally stopping in a drainage ditch at the bottom of the drive, where I lost a battle with a large evergreen. I got out of the car unharmed, but my transportation was less fortunate.

After inspecting the situation, I realized there was no way I could get my car out of the ditch without a tow truck. My options had narrowed to one: walking back up to the house. That proved treacherous, as I had to either stomp through snow-covered grass or go up a driveway that had yet to be treated for black ice. Considering my way down, I picked the grass.

It took me what seemed like an hour to walk back up, falling multiple times. When I came in from the garage with no bags or supplies, my wife gave me a quizzical look.

"Do you need help with the groceries?"

"Well, I have something to show you first." I turned to where the car was resting in the ditch.

"Oh my God, what happened? Are you okay? Is the car okay? Did you make it to the store? How are we going to get the supplies up here?"

After playing twenty questions, I responded that yes, I was okay. The Bronco, not so much. No, I don't think we have to worry about getting the groceries up here because no, I didn't even make it out of the driveway.

We stared at each other, trying to consider our next move. Finally, I said, "Well, it looks like 'Miller Time.'" We walked into the kitchen, broke open a couple bottles of beer, sat down, and let the fireplace glow and the loving nudges of Shamrock and Emerald momentarily take our minds off things.

I realized our problems weren't solved by ignoring them, so I decided we needed a plan. "The plows won't be able to make it up Mount Everest to clear the roads until the storm stops, let alone get a tow truck here to pull my car out of the ditch. We might have to hunker down and make do with what we have on hand."

Patti nodded. Looking out the window, all we saw was a whiteout. Then we heard Riley stirring from his nap. He was cranky when he first woke up, poor little guy. If I had a wet, stinky diaper and the remnants of a fever and body aches, I'd be cranky, too. We got up and followed our hounds into Riley's room and investigated the by-now not-so-foreign scents.

Patti said, "I'm going to take care of Riley and then take some of the dirty clothes and bedding downstairs and do some laundry."

"Okay," I said. "I'm going to go out in the backyard and start shoveling to make sure that there's a path for the dogs to go out and take care of their business. Then I'll go out front and try to clear the driveway so that we can get your car out when this is over."

After about two hours' worth of scraping, salting, and shoveling, I had cleared at least ten inches of snow from our driveway. I was cold, hungry, and exhausted. I went inside, brushed myself off, hung up my wet winter gear, and grabbed a cup of coffee in my favorite Scooby-Doo mug. I could hear Patti talking to Riley in the basement as I eased into my recliner. In front of the fireplace in the pine-scented room, listening to Nat King Cole sing "The Christmas Song" on the stereo, with my beautiful Irish setters at my feet, warm and comfy while the snow whipped about outside, I felt as if I had stumbled into a Norman Rockwell Christmas scene.

Then I heard a loud *clunk*.

At first, I thought it might have been something from outside, like a humongous icicle hanging off the roof that had fallen onto the patio. But the clunk was soon followed by noises from downstairs.

Stomp. "Freakin A—, you gotta be shittin' me." *Stomp, stomp, stomp.* Patti swooped up the stairs, carrying Riley, with a frantic look on her face.

"What happened?" I asked.

"You're not going to freaking believe it. The main water pipe leading into the basement just cracked wide open, and water is pouring in everywhere. You gotta get down there and turn the valve off."

I rushed down the stairs into the utility room and reached the water turn-off valve. After a few turns, I closed it down and surveyed the damage to our finished basement. There was water everywhere. At least two inches of water covered our nice, carpeted basement floor. Somehow, some liquid detergent must have spilled into the water in the laundry room. A white foamy mixture bubbled up and seeped throughout the room. Not only was I getting soaked, I was sudsy. The irony of the situation soon dawned on me. Whiteout conditions were making a winter wonderland both inside and outside.

I tried to regain my composure, went upstairs, and refilled my coffee mug. I swear I heard Scooby Doo yelping at me, seeing an evil villain sneaking up behind me. *Ruh Rho.* He was right. Sick kid, blizzard, roads closed, disabled car, limited supplies, diarrhea, no water, trapped. Ho, Ho, Ho.

Patti entered the room after changing herself and Riley into dry clothes. Between my sudsy clothes and the look on my face, I knew she could tell I was scared.

"Were you able to turn off the water? How much damage did it do? What are we going to do if we don't have water?"

I didn't know which question to answer first, and I didn't want to scare her, especially since she held our son in her arms.

"Yes, the water's off. It's hard to tell what damage was done. The white foamy detergent is preventing much of an inspection." I feared she was about to cry. "On the positive side," I offered, "if Riley poops again, we can use the new family room aquatic center to clean him off."

We sat on the basement steps and took stock of our situation. We weren't sure whether we should laugh or cry.

The outside temperature continued to drop, and the wind howled. It was too late to call a plumber to come out—even if they would brave the storm. We tried to get some sleep to help us get through the next day, but eerie sounds, thuds, and thumps made sleep nearly impossible.

Saturday morning, December twenty-third, arrived, with snow still falling. Being the early riser of the family, I was the one who let the dogs out. I opened the kitchen door to the garage, which led to the backyard, and quietly praised myself for shoveling a pathway out. Well, so much for patting myself on the back. The area that I had cleared was filled with at least a foot of snow. They didn't mind a bit. They ran and frolicked and barked at the still falling snow. I left them to their fun.

I scooped up a clean bucket of snow and went back into the kitchen to boil it up for coffee, all the while keeping an eye out the back window. But something didn't look right. What was that dark shadow in the backyard? It was hard to tell with the drifting snow. I rushed back out and discovered a utility pole was leaning against a tree. Wires danced every which way.

I called for the dogs. "Shamrock, Emerald. Come. Come here, boys. Good boys."

I was afraid that the wires might be electrified and dangerous if the pups touched them. Then I noticed that our backyard spotlight was still on. How could that be? Regardless, I didn't want to take any chances and got the dogs into the house.

Patti came into the kitchen and frowned. "Is something *else* wrong? Did we get more water into the basement?" she asked.

I motioned for her to come to the window and pointed. "That's what's wrong."

Her eyes widened. "Is that what I think it is? But how can that be? We still have power."

I was thinking the same thing until it suddenly dawned on me. I reached over to the kitchen wall phone and hesitantly lifted the receiver. The line was dead.

We looked at each other, and Patti put my thoughts into words. "No way to call a plumber now. Yep, we're screwed."

"Yeah, I guess you're right. Let's devise some emergency plans in case we're snowbound for a long time."

A WINTER WONDERLAND... WELL SORT OF

After a quick check of supplies, we began to compare notes. "Are you kidding me? We're already out of diapers?" I wailed with frustration.

"Not quite. I found a few in a diaper bag, but yeah, we're nearly out."

I felt like a bad parent. "I should have bought some sooner. I never thought it could get this bad."

"Don't worry. We'll figure this out," Patti said. I couldn't see how, but I hoped she was right.

"Okay, what do we do?" I asked. "Where do we go from here?"

Patti replied, "Let's take stock of our supplies and figure out how long they should last." Then I saw an idea light up her eyes. "Didn't Grandma give us a goody bag for Christmas? Let's open it up and see what's inside."

Under normal circumstances, I don't think seeing a pack of diapers and wipes would make anyone that excited, but *score!*

Thanks to the snow, we still had a plentiful supply of extremely cold water. But, by day three of the blizzard, we were getting close to not having much in the house to eat except a slowly thawing turkey. That paled in comparison to the fact that Rley was still using diapers at an alarming rate. Despite Grandma's largess, we would soon run out again.

"We could borrow an idea from *Gone With the Wind*," Patti suggested. "But instead of using curtains, we can use old sheets and T-shirts on the little guy."

But with no good way to wash them, I knew even these wouldn't work for long.

"That's a good stopgap," I said, "but I have another idea. I was hoping I wouldn't have to do this, but I don't see any other way. I don't think our roads will be cleared until after Christmas. The only thing I can think of is to . . ." I pointed to the big presents under the tree.

Patti stifled a squeal.

"Those are cross-country skis, aren't they?"

She looked up at me, blinking. "Surprise!" she said, a silly grin on her face.

"Thanks. They're just what I needed." I said with a chuckle. "I'm sure all the grocery chains are closed, but maybe the Oneida Market is open. The owner lives above it, right?"

Patti nodded. "I think so. So even if it isn't open, you might be able to get him to open up for you when you get there."

"I've got that big backpack Mom gave me last Christmas, so I can ski down, pack it as full as I can, and bring back essential supplies."

Patti looked worried. "Seriously, you're going to head out in this blizzard? You've never even used those skis before. You'll break your neck."

"If you have any better suggestions, I'm listening."

"I don't know. I don't like the idea of you going out in the storm like this."

"Well, I'm not thrilled at the idea either, but I can't see that we've got many choices."

Patti didn't look convinced.

"It'll be okay," I said, brooking no resistance. "I'll get up at sunrise tomorrow and start skiing down the hill. Getting into town shouldn't be a big deal since it's only a fifteen-minute drive in good weather. And it's all downhill." I was more worried about getting back up the hill, especially carrying whatever groceries I could scrounge up, but hoped there would be emergency vehicles in town that could help me out.

The next morning, Christmas Eve day, I bundled up in several layers. As I expected, there was not a soul on any of the roads They were all covered with unplowed snow—by now, two feet deep. It was reasonably easy going down the mountain. I followed the streets as much as possible, thinking it would be the safest way down. I pushed myself to get to the market as soon as I could, knowing the trip back would take me a lot longer. I was making decent time until I hit an unseen drainage ditch and fell head over heels.

Stunned, I took stock of my situation. I was uninjured, so I righted myself and inched my way back to the road. I needed to slow down, pay more attention, and not repeat my previous misadventure. If I wasn't more careful, I might not make it there at all.

The snow continued to come down in large white clumps, crusting over my wool cap and sunglasses. Often, the snow was so thick that I needed to wipe it away using my hand, which was tethered to one of my ski poles. Talk about awkward movements while skiing downhill. Bumps and divots threw me off balance, necessitating more stops to collect myself.

Finally, the town below came into view and offered me a glimmer of hope of reaching my goal. I had yet to see any vehicles on the road and knew I might need help to complete my mission. I was reminded of King Arthur's quest for the Holy Grail and felt a kindred spirit. Where was Sir Lancelot when you needed him?

At last, the Oneida Market appeared; thankfully, it was open. I slushed up to the entranceway, unclipped my skis, and gingerly walked into the store in my ski shoes. Ski boots are not meant to be flexible, so as I walked up to the counter, clippity clopping, I must have appeared like a drunken alien. *Take me to your leader.*

"Hi, sir. Pardon my appearance. I just skied down Avalanche Ridge because my family is desperate for some supplies. Sure hope you can help me out."

"Wow, you came down the mountain? I don't imagine that was fun. What can I do for you?"

"Well, most importantly, I need diapers. Please tell me you have some."

"You're in luck, buddy. We just got a shipment in before all this snow hit, so no one has been around to buy them up. You can have as many as you want."

I did some quick calculations on the volume of the supplies that we needed. Damn, I wished I had paid more attention in geometry class.

"If you don't mind, could I get my backpack out and do some exploratory packing to see what and how much of these items will fit?"

"Well, yeah, it doesn't look like I'm going to get many customers today, anyway. Honestly, I don't know why I bothered opening."

"I'm sure glad you did," I said.

Hoping that price gouging wasn't going to be a factor, I toted up how much I could afford. But for what we needed most, I was prepared to pay whatever price was necessary.

He got out a couple of toddler-sized packs and laid them out on the counter. I started packing them. Ten, twenty, thirty. Okay. Then I ran through my mental checklist of other needed supplies, including cereal, batteries, veggies, and Pedialyte. Finally, I grabbed a few more diapers and crammed them in one at a time. I was able to load seven more into the pack.

"Do you suppose I could borrow your phone to see if I can get someone to help us?"

"Sure, no problem. Give it a try, but I gotta tell you that the lines have been down all morning. We either get a busy signal or we get some stupid message about the call can't be completed. But you're welcome to try."

I dialed 911, and just as he'd said, there was a busy signal.

"Okay, well, I can't wait any longer. I've got a long way back up the mountain, so I'm gonna get going. I can't thank you enough for everything that you've done for us. What do I owe you?"

"No, don't worry about it. Consider it my Christmas present to you and your family. Good luck and Merry Christmas.'

"Thanks again; after all of this craziness is over with, I'll stop back and let you know how things turned out. Merry Christmas."

I stepped out into the storm, loaded to the gills with my treasures. Looking about, I again tried to find an emergency vehicle that could give me a hand. But the streets were still deserted. By then, it was afternoon, and I had a long journey ahead of me. I knew I'd better get my rear in gear if I was going to get uphill while it was still light out.

It was easygoing at first, as long as I stayed on the relatively flat streets of the town. When I got to the turn-off to start up the hill, though, I realized the enormity of the task in front of me. Like the little engine in the story, *I think I can, I think I can*. I thought I was in decent shape, however the terrain and a full backpack soon overtaxed my athletic ability. I stopped to catch my breath and realized I hadn't yet gone a quarter of the way up the hill.

I began to picture the scene from *The Shining* where Jack Nicholson is chasing the little boy out in the snowstorm on the mountain ski resort Timberline Lodge, gets exhausted, and essentially ends up collapsing and ultimately freezing.

I heaved and grunted up the hill, breathing extremely hard. With the slushing of the skis and poles, I noticed nothing else. Then, bright lights shone behind me through the darkening afternoon, casting an eerie shadow on the snowy landscape before me. It was surreal. Was I hallucinating? I stopped and looked around. Finally, I heard an engine revving and saw lights flashing on and off. *Oh my God are you kidding me?* A big four-wheel-drive truck. Was I ever glad to see them. I stopped and pulled off to the side of the road as the guardian angel inched his way up to me and rolled down his window. An older-looking gentleman called out to me, asking if I needed any help.

"Absolutely," I said, relief flooding through me. "My kid is sick, my car is in a ditch, and I have a broken water line. I've gotta get this stuff home as soon as possible."

"No problem. Where do you live?"

I told him.

"Oh yeah, I know right where that is. I can take you there."

I used the points of my ski poles to unclip my shoes from the skis and threw my gear into the open truck bed. Then I loaded my bag into the truck and slowly eased my way into the cab.

"I can't thank you enough for this. I was starting to worry about what I would do if I didn't get there before dark."

"Don't worry. I've seen stranger things happen in this backcountry, especially during a storm. I can't believe you skied all the way down and were halfway up the mountain when I almost ran into you."

"You saved my life, mister. I can't thank you enough."

We started driving, and I could tell the traction on the roads, while not perfect, was reasonable with a little bit of slip-and-slide fishtail as we started up the remainder of my route. We were going ten times faster than I could have made it on skis. I began to relax when we rounded a bend, and I could see the last street leading up to my house. "There it is. I can see it," I blurted out.

I'd startled the driver. He didn't quite make the turn. Instead, we slid on the frozen road into a corner snowdrift. Not again. I felt so bad.

"Oh no, I'm so sorry. I didn't mean to scare you. I'm so sorry. Do you think you'll be able to get out?"

"Not sure," he said, pulling his red coat closer around him. "I'm gonna get out and look things over." He unhooked the seat belt and struggled to get his ample belly out of the way of the steering wheel. Once outside, he walked around the truck but was having a hard time with all the accumulated snow. Finally, he came back into the cab. His snowy white beard was dripping wet.

He rocked the truck back and forth with four-wheel drive, inching slowly forward and backward to free us from the snowbank. We made progress, but it was incremental at best.

The man put it in park and turned to me. "Listen, don't worry about me. You have a sick baby up there, and you'll get home faster if you ski up from here. I'll be fine. It'll just take me a while to get going again."

"Are you sure? Please let me help you. At least let me pay you for your time and trouble."

"No, really, buddy, none of that's necessary. I'm just glad I came along when I did."

"Can you give me your name and phone number so I can contact you later and properly thank you?"

"My name is Nick, and I live north of here, but there aren't any phone lines up there. I'm just happy to help you folks have a merry Christmas."

I got out of the truck, got my skis and poles out of the back, and strapped them back on. Nick pushed the backpack over to me and I slung it on my back.

"Thanks again," I said, wishing I could do more to express my gratitude. "And Merry Christmas."

Nick just laughed. "Now, get out of here and go take care of that little boy who I'm sure is waiting for his daddy."

The sun had set, but I knew exactly where I was: less than half a mile from home. I also had a renewed vigor so that half mile went by quickly.

I turned onto my street and went up the block until I was at the end of my driveway. All the outdoor lights were on, and the Christmas tree lit up. Riley, Patti, Emerald, and Shamrock were peering out the bay window. Riley saw me first and began jumping up and down, which caused the dogs to start running around, chasing their tails. Patti opened the front door and out rushed both dogs, who bounded through the snow and jumped up on me at the base of the driveway.

I looked up and realized that the snow had finally stopped falling. The clouds parted and the cheeriest stars twinkled above. Off in the distance, I heard the toot of a truck horn, and I swear I heard the sound of jingle bells. *Nah, it couldn't be.* But you know what? Even if it wasn't, Nick was my Christmas angel. I would be home with the people I loved most, and we would all be safe, warm, and happy together.

Despite having no water, no phone, and with a car in a ditch, I couldn't have felt more grateful to be in this winter wonderland.

Flue Shot

Jerome W. McFadden

Dispatch: *Car 502, what is your 10-20?*
Car 502: *Williams and 24th.*
Dispatch: *Female at 4038 Walnut Avenue reported standing in her front yard, acting hysterical, waving and screaming at passing cars.*
Car 502: *We are five blocks over. Should be there in four minutes. Woman is in the front yard standing in the snow?*
Dispatch: *Reports say the woman is in her nightgown waving frantically at all passing cars.*
Car 502: *In her nightgown? We can be there in two minutes.*
Dispatch: *Please confirm your comment was due to the apparent emergency situation, not the nightgown.*
Car 502: (said with sounds of laughter) *10-4.*
Dispatch: *Report when on site.*
Car 502: *Turning corner now. Woman out front waving arms, apparently relieved to see us.*
Dispatch: *When situation settled please report why she did not use 911. Also advise if you need backup.*
Car 502: *We are exiting car now, switching to body phones . . . walking woman into home. Will advise if backup needed.*
Dispatch: *502, 10-1. Receiving you poorly.*
Car 502: *Wait one. Fiddling with phones.*
(Long moment of silence)
Car 502: *Dispatch, confirm you are receiving.*
Dispatch: *10-2. Now receiving loud and clear.*
Car 502: *Following woman into house now. Asking her to quiet down, to put on robe, and explain.*
Dispatch: *Copy.*

Car 502: *Uh . . . somebody apparently caught in house chimney.*

Dispatch: *Uh . . . Christmas Eve and somebody's caught in the house chimney? Is this for real?*

Car 502: *We are not making this up and woman quite frantic. PC Smith returning outdoors to look on the roof for reindeer and sled. Will report.*

Dispatch: *Uh . . . right. Copy.*

(Long silence)

Car 502: *PC Smith reporting no reindeer or sled on the roof. But there is a long ladder on side of house leading to the roof. Woman reports the vic in the chimney is her husband . . . trying to entertain the kids.*

Dispatch: *PC Smith going up on roof to examine chimney?*

Car 502: *Negative. Ladder slippery and roof covered with snow.*

Dispatch: *Are you requesting firetruck and EMS back-up?*

Car 502: *Firetruck definitely. Will advise on EMS.*

Dispatch: *10-4.*

(Moment of silence)

Dispatch: *Have advised both. On the way. Fire wants to know if vic went in head first or feet first?*

Car 502: *Is that important?*

Dispatch: *Vic may have tripped when close to chimney and went in head first instead of feet first. Apparently it will require an entirely different operation for retrieval.*

Car 502: *Cannot ascertain from inside house. Wife and children do not know and voice coming down chimney not intelligible.*

Dispatch: *Fire team will bring equipment needed for either situation.*

Car 502: *Copy that. PC Smith now back inside looking up inside chimney with flashlight . . . Unfortunately a very large bag appears to be stuck, apparently blocking view of interior.*

Dispatch: *Did you ask the wife why she did not use 911 call as soon as chimney's blockage noted?*

Car 502: *Wife said she could not remember the phone number for 911 call.*

(Moment of silence)

Dispatch: *Uh . . . right. . . . Please confirm when fire team and EMS on site.*

Car 502: *Both arriving now. 10-6. Standby.*

(Long silence)

Car 502: *Fire team now on roof. Two went up on their own ladder.*

Dispatch: *EMS?*

Car 502: *One inside waiting. Other on the roof watching. Fire team inside house now pulling large bag down chimney. . . . Whoops. . . . Bag apparently ripped. Toys tumbled down from chimney. PC Smith and I are pulling the kids back.*

(Screaming kids and angry shouts from mother in background)

Car 502: *Fire team reports vic hanging upside down in chimney. He apparently slipped or tripped on chimney top and fell head first. Stuck about halfway down.*

Dispatch: *Fire team can handle?*

Car 502: *Fire team inside has pulled bag and remaining toys down. Santa Claus hat came with it. They are trying to pull vic to floor, but he is shouting for them to ease off.*

Dispatch: *EMS?*

Car 502: *One inside waiting. Other on roof watching.*

Dispatch: *Any resolution on why vic is stuck?*

Car 502: *Vic appears to be too big for chimney.*

Dispatch: *Define big.*

Car 502: (Silence, then a whisper): *Fat. Really, really fat.*

Dispatch: *Copy.*

Car 502: *Fire team now on roof using poles to push against vic's feet. Inside fire team trying to reach his hands to yank him down. Vic's clothes apparently catching on pieces of inside bricks.*

Dispatch: *I hear swearing and yelling. They have a problem?*

Car 502: *Swearing is from vic. Yelling is from kids fighting over the toys and mother screaming at them to get out of the way.*

Dispatch: *Car 502, 10-4.*

(A long wait filled with shouting and arguments, with wife yelling at children to get out of the room, with vic and the firemen arguing on progress or lack of it)

Dispatch: *Status report, please.*

Car 502: *Fire team has instructed vic to use his hands to try to crawl down, but vic is complaining that all movement is ripping his costume, and his white gloves are getting dirty. Fire team considering to hose him down. Meanwhile, EMS stuffing the hearth with pillows and pads to soften landing.*

Dispatch: *Can't somebody just stand in the chimney to reach up and pull him down?*

Car 502: *Negative. He is above reaching height and below pushing depth.*
Dispatch: (A sigh) *Keep me informed on progress.*
Car 502: *Oops. New situation. Oldest son came in with a heavy rope. Fire team throwing the rope up to vic for him to hold onto so they can pull him down.*
Dispatch: *Smart kid. Apparently he does not take after his father.*
Car 502: *Smartest person in the room.*
Dispatch: *Roger that.*
Car 502: *It's working. Oh, holy Jesus, here he comes.*
(Loud screaming, crashing and swearing)
Dispatch: *Advise situation, please.*
(More crashing and swearing)
Dispatch: (in concerned voice) *Advise situation, please.*
Car 502: *Santa has landed but now yelling at fire team about damage to his Santa suit and gloves and the broken toys . . . threatening to sue. EMS trying to get him to settle down and take off the Santa suit so they can assess possible wounds. Meanwhile the kids are back, screaming about the toys. Apparently they are not the toys they wanted.*
Dispatch: *Tell EMS to stuff the angry Santa into the wagon and take him to the ER for examination and tell Santa he can contact his lawyer when the holidays are over and the lawyers are back to work. And you two file a report and get back on the beat. The night's not over.*
Car 502: *Roger that. Can't wait for New Year's Eve.*
Dispatch: *And a jolly good night was had by all.*

Oh! Christmas Tree

Rhonda Zangwill
First Place Winner, 2024 BWR Short Story Award

'Twas the night before Christmas and all through the . . . wait, no, this is not a sweet little story about sleeping mice and snuggly children. I don't have children, or mice, and I didn't have them then either.

What I did have was Marty, my third AIDS client and first woman. I was her "buddy." Literally. Their Buddy Program was the signature service of the Gay Men's Health Crisis, GMHC, maybe the largest AIDS organization in the country. Buddies were advocates and allies, companions, and comrades.

My first client, Martin, was a social worker and blackjack enthusiast. He had optimistic post-it notes stuck all over his house: "Today is *your* day" "Be the Change." Andrew, my second client, was obsessed with ocean liners and made a killer pie crust. Really, it won awards.

Andrew and Martin both died within six months of my meeting them.

But not Marty. We were together for six years. Years. Marty completely skewed the usual GMHC demographic. Straight white female, and long-ago wife and mother. And a long-term survivor. Despite having an endless number of infections, diseases and conditions, she always rallied. And had done so since her AIDS diagnosis when she was 35, five years before we met. In those horrifying days, AIDS was, almost without exception, a death sentence. Marty was a medical miracle, one for the journals.

In her pre-AIDS life, Marty was a nurse, and she affected a kind of fatalistic irony when discussing the body. "I think I have a touch of lupus," she might say. Or with a half-grin, "Guess what, they told me I have 'vegetation of the heart.'" She delivered her medical bulletins from the comfort of her well-worn Barcalounger while casually gesturing with her cigarette and sipping a chocolate Ensure. Curled at her feet was her cat, Reuben, named for the sandwich. "Who ever heard of a cat who loved pastrami?" she would joke.

We had a nice rhythm, Marty and me. I'd often arrive just in time for *Jeopardy,* and we'd play along. She always won. Or we'd take walks. In the later years, I learned how to maneuver her wheelchair. But mostly we hung out. We'd have tea and I'd settle in for her stories: her childhood in Nigeria with parents who were diplomats. Later this changed to missionaries. Her career as an infusion specialist with a six-figure salary. Still, on our first day she casually mentioned being in debt for six million bucks. Later this changed to eleven million. One day the debt evaporated, thanks to an admirer who then made her executor of his estate. Was any of this true? Does it matter? Marty's boundless capacity for drama coupled with that self-deprecating humor was part of her charm. Maybe this helped her cope with unending medical traumas and personal tragedies. Maybe it was a survival instinct. Once she told me she ran into an acquaintance from her old life:

"Marty," said the friend. "You're still alive!"

"It's a matter of minutes," she said. "Maybe seconds."

Marty's ongoing health crises often meant my tangling with the health care bureaucracy, navigating an alphabet soup of agencies to make sure she got her benefits and visiting and running interference for her in the hospital. And even though she often joked that she was still alive "thanks to my last T-cell kicking in," Marty's many afflictions were very serious and often landed her in the hospital, sometimes for weeks at a time.

On that night before Christmas in 1995, that was where she was, in the ICU on a ventilator. And word was she probably wasn't going to make it. But I did not focus on Marty's possibly imminent demise. We had been through this before, more than once, and the Marty I knew somehow always pulled through. Was I in denial? Maybe, but I had no time for that. For Marty, I just knew that every poke and prick would pale in comparison to her rage at missing Christmas—the holiday she looked forward to all year.

I was well versed in Marty's holiday rituals. It was all about the *tree*.

Every year, Marty would have a massive fir tree carried to her tiny studio apartment. She would spend days decorating it but always banished me from the house while this was going on so she could orchestrate a dramatic reveal. And she never disappointed. Marty's dazzling trees put the Nutcracker to shame. Plus, we had eggnog.

The idea of Marty spending Christmas in a hospital gown with nothing but tubing and IVs and machinery devastated me. I flew down my five flights of stairs, propelled by the fervent hope that the tree seller on First Avenue would still be there on Christmas Eve. I skidded around the corner as he was rolling up the last of his twine. But not a tree was in sight.

I took a deep breath. "Please-I-need-a-tree-for-my-friend-she's-in-the-hospital-I-just-found-out-and-it's-all-the-way-out-in-Queens-Jackson-Heights-Hospital-it's-a-terrible-place-and-it's-Christmas-and-well-she-waits-all-year-for-Christmas-I-mean-for-the-tree-and-you-wouldn't-believe-she's-got-all-these-ornaments-one-of-them-even-plays-'Jingle-Bells'-she's-got-to-have-her-tree-it's-Christmas-for-Godsake-or-at-least-I-don't-know-maybe-well-maybe-some-tinsel . . ."

I ran out of steam.

The tree seller was just staring at me, a crazy babbler. New York City was full of them. He said nothing but went into his makeshift shed and came out with his arms full of pine needles. He took what looked like a big branch and stuck it into one of those red metal stands. It wobbled a bit, then stood upright and suddenly he was holding a tiny little tree, two, maybe two and half feet tall. "Merry Christmas" he said. Then he turned out the lights on the shed.

My little tree and I got on the L train to Eighth. From there it was the E to Roosevelt Avenue and then the bus. The whole thing took almost an hour. I had made this trip to Jackson Heights to see Marty many times in the past, but this was the first time I got a seat, start to finish. So I was feeling practically festive. And festooned. Around my neck was a bunch of silver tinsel, also a gift from the tree man.

There are strict visiting hours in the ICU, but that night – not a Scrooge in sight. Plus, by then I was a familiar face to the staff. Not that they could really see my face, since it was all but obscured by the tree as I clomped down the halls, shedding needles all the way. To my surprise and relief, I saw that Marty was sort of awake and even a bit propped up in bed when I got there. She was all tethered up to a bank of blinking beeping machinery. Of course she couldn't talk, not with that breathing tube they had shoved down her throat. But she did have a blackboard in her lap and some colored chalk.

Her tiny room was crowded even though officially the ICU allowed only two visitors at a time. I guess Christmas Eve loosened things up a bit. Not to be morbid, but I think the staff wasn't going to turn anyone away. Not when they thought that this was IT for Marty. Her last hurrah. Also standing vigil was her friend Mary, weepy and kind of gulpy, and John, Marty's other friend, fingering his rosary.

I was so focused on squeezing into the room that I didn't really notice that I was getting pretty perforated by all those pine needles. Maybe even a little bloody. Thankfully John came to the rescue. He cut his praying short and took charge, setting up that tree on the only available surface, on top of the ventilator. Then he gently relieved me of the tinsel and expertly wove it through the branches. While searching in my bag for some Band-Aids, I found Marty's special glittery origami angel that I'd been carrying around for her. Up it went, thanks to John, right on top of the tree, catching the light from the fluorescents. News traveled fast. Suddenly the doorway was filled with people – nurses, aides, maybe even a doc or two, all straining to get a peek.

By now Marty's eyes were wide open. She was blinking at me like mad and with her one good hand, the one without bruises and protruding IV needles, she started scratching out big hearts and xxx's and ooo's all over the blackboard in lime green chalk. She was so excited that her wiggling feet kicked off those thin hospital blankets and her painted toenails, one foot green, the other red, added another festive touch.

Of course, just a few days later, Marty limped back to life. Some thought it was the angel. My money was on the piney scent. Clears the lungs. Not that *that* mattered. Once the tubes came out, I knew she'd be sneaking out to the courtyard to catch a smoke. Nurses—her sisters-in-spirit—were her loyal accomplices, generous with the Marlboros that filled their pockets. But if anyone did object, I could easily imagine her argument:

"Save your shocked outrage. Of all the things vying to kill me, cigarettes are way down on the list. C'mon now, find me a pack of matches."

When next I saw Marty, she was back in the Barcalounger, hooked up to her usual IV of TPN, a nutritional supplement. Usually her dining table was filled with gauze and tape and antiseptic sprays but that day — no. Instead there was my little tree in all its spindly glory. Decorated! Tiny spinning ballerinas, little bears that blew bubbles, even the oversized plastic M&M's. And of course the tinsel and that crowning angel. I was thrilled —and shocked.

"Marty! What did you . . . How could you possibly . . ."

Marty grinned, took a long drag and settled in.

"Did you really think I could leave my little Charlie Brown tree to wither and die in the ICU? Are you kidding? After you dragged it all the way out to goddam Jackson Frights?"

I had to admit that Marty did have a point.

"Anyway, maybe a few days later, after your pilgrimage, they decided it was time. To tell the truth, I didn't really think I'd be discharged so soon, but welcome to health care in America. I guess once my crack team saw that I could breathe without their intervention, Wham! Up and out!"

Marty rarely had anything good to say about her care. She switched doctors all the time, mostly because she didn't agree with their ideas for treatment. She was always telling me about how dismissive so-called specialists were and, true to her profession, how nurses really ran the show.

"Well," she continued, "after they told me I was free to go, I had to find a way to bring my little tree with me. I knew it was too prickly to sit on my lap when they were wheeling me out. I looked around for some orderlies, but of course, not one to be found. But if there's one thing I know, it's my way around the hospital bureaucracy. The most important thing is that there's not much a little bribery can't get you."

Marty told me that she found the perfect co-conspirator in Shana, the sixteen-year-old volunteer reader for the blind. For just a pack of cigarettes and the promise of a six-pack, she got Shana to commandeer a gurney.

"That Shana," Marty said, "she laid my little tree onto that gurney as if it were her own sweet grandmother. Together we lashed it down with IV tubing. Then she lined up a bunch of red and green Jell-O cups kind of like an honor guard for the tree. She plopped the angel in my lap, made herself a crown of tinsel and then used some extra tubing to tie us all together. Shana! What Christmas spirit!"

While reciting her holiday saga, Marty's TV was on in the background, like always. When she finished, I heard that familiar theme song. I patted the angel as I walked over to the stove to make us some tea.

It was time for *Jeopardy*.

The Catcher

Kidd Wadsworth

I've had the same two dreams, maybe a hundred times, night after night for months now. First one, then the other, always in the same order.

In the first dream, I'm in a circus. I don't mean that to sound bizarre, like everyone around me is a freak; that's not it at all. I'm happy there, wildly happy. What I notice most is that everything around me is filled with color: the huge tent is red and orange, the signs saying, "ticket booth" "hot dogs" and "clowns only" are painted in purples, pinks and blues, and the people sitting in the stands are gayly dressed in bright orange shirts, or green pants, or polka dot ties. Everyone is waving at me: the ringmaster in his coal black suit and shiny black top hat, the elephant trainer in his khakis, and, of course, Brighter, the clown, who I know from his ear-splitting whistle, is my friend. His face is so familiar, but I can't place it. "Jump," he shouts. The sweet scent of cotton candy wafts by my nose, and the music, it's the happiest music—with a melody that dances from note to note—greets me. I'm grinning ear to ear because I belong. I am one of them.

I'm a trapeze artist. I remember really loving my skimpy costume. I'm barely covered in emerald-green sequins. I'm wearing a feather on my head and sparkly light-weight green boots. I look ravishing. I mean, *really*.

I'm standing on a small platform at the top of a hundred-foot ladder. And everyone is waiting for me to swing out into the air and let go.

I know I can do it. My legs are strong; my grip is strong.

It's a simple trick. Swing out, pump the swing with my legs. Swing back—higher now. Swing forward again, let go, roll into a ball, tumble . . . once, twice, unfold and catch the waiting hands.

I look at the man, my partner, who I know will not fail me, swinging from the bar. He is already hanging upside down, his huge hands waiting to catch me.

I want to jump. I know I'll be all right.

Then the second dream begins and the scene shifts. I'm in my apartment: soft carpet, big bed, kitchen cabinets filled with food, but everything—my couch, my bedspread—is devoid of color as if I'm standing on the set of a black-and-white TV show. I think, maybe the power is out. Then I look out the window at the beautiful world. The new grass is almost lime green. Blossoms in every shade of pink weigh down the branches of hundreds of cherry trees, while bright yellow daffodils bloom in random clumps, and azalea bushes, fully pregnant with buds, tremble.

The birds are chirping.

I want to open the door. I want to go out into the beautiful world, but there's a man out there, waiting for me with a knife. The minute I step out the door, I know he's going to kill me. My heart pounds in my chest as I reach for the doorknob.

And here's the scariest part. The man, waiting for me with the knife, is the same man. He's the catcher on the trapeze. He's my partner—my friend.

And then I wake to the loathsome music of my cell phone alarm.

I told my mother about the first dream. Yeah, that was a mistake.

Every time she calls, she repeats the same refrain, over and over. "It means you're supposed to take the job. You're afraid because it's a leap, but don't worry. Your new boss is the man who will catch you."

"I don't think so, Mom." I don't want that guy's hands anywhere near me.

She insists. "It's more money. That job is everything you've always wanted. It means security. Security is important, sweetie."

Almost I tell her about the second dream, but I don't. I don't want another interpretation I won't agree with and can't get her to shut up about. *Will she please let it go?* Somehow, I don't think working incredibly long hours in a small, cramped office with a man who keeps trying to look down the front of my blouse is in any way equivalent to flying through the air.

There's a third dream. But it isn't a dream at all. I mean it is a dream. I dream it at night, when I'm asleep, every year at Christmas—since Mike died. But it's more than a dream; it's a recollection, a memory. You see, it actually happened. Mike and I are in bed planning our wedding. I bought this book, *Creating the Wedding of Your Dreams*. It was more of a workbook, and I'm dutifully going through every worksheet. Paper is everywhere. When the dream opens, I'm trying to pick a menu that doesn't involve chicken in any form. Ultimately, I have our reception catered from

Mike's favorite Mexican place. Tamales are the best wedding food ever. Mike leans over, crunching the papers, and kisses me. "Why do you love me?" he whispers, as if anyone could possibly not love Mike. My answer jumps out of my mouth. I don't even think before I reply, and the reply is a surprise to me. It's like someone else, someone that lives inside of me is speaking, but immediately I know the answer is absolutely the truth. I say, "Because I like who I am when I'm with you."

*

It's December fifteenth. Time to decorate. Wow, is this fun. Can you hear the sarcasm in my voice?

Memories flood my mind. I try to close my eyes to shut them out, but I can't.

"Ho, ho, ho, and where's my hot toddy." Mike shouts as he stumbles—nope, not the most graceful man. His job is to gather all the boxes of ornaments and lights. Mine is the juicing of lemons and then the screaming of, "I forgot to buy bourbon."

By the time I return from the store, he has the tree up, Christmas music playing, and strings of lights spread out on the floor. "Did you buy replacement bulbs?"

Yeah, you guessed it. The answer to that question is, "no."

*

I turn on the gas fireplace in my cozy living room. I push down other memories. *Don't go there.*

Christmas in a trailer park is not exactly the stuff of a Hallmark movie. Dad headed out when I was four. He took the money in the joint bank account with him. Mom became a check-out clerk at the grocery store and took out a fifteen-year mortgage on a $35,000 used trailer. We lived from mortgage payment to mortgage payment. Her wedding ring was the first thing she pawned. Every year a Christmas present would arrive for me in the mail—from Dad. It was always beautifully wrapped. And every year I'd hope. One year, he bought me a tennis racket. Did he think the trailer park had tennis courts? Or that I was on the tennis team? The next Christmas he bought me purple hair sheen. Dyed hair wasn't allowed at my school. Every Christmas, it was the same. A gift would arrive, I'd get all excited, and then I'd open it. The truth was that my dad didn't know me. He never called. He never visited. He gave me a gift every year and then never thought about me again. I was used to it. I told myself I'd adjusted.

Mike and I met in February and married in May. When he handed me my first Christmas present, I froze.

He was all excited, dancing around the room. "I know you are going to love this."

But what if I didn't? What if Mike didn't really know me? We'd married so quickly. Maybe next year, or the year after, he'd say, "It was fun," wave goodbye, and I'd be left sitting on the couch in a trailer crying, wondering how I was going to make the next mortgage payment. I put the present on the mantle.

"Julie?"

"I'll open it later."

"What's going on, Babe?" He took me in his arms; I pulled away.

"It's better this way. What we have is so special, I don't want to damage it. I mean, what if you got me a tennis racket?"

"A tennis racket? Why would I get you a tennis racket?"

For the next fifteen minutes I tried to make him understand. "I can't open it. I just can't. It will be wrong, and then . . ." I backed up; went into the kitchen. He stormed out. Of course, he came back. He held me; I sobbed. He never mentioned the gift again. It sat on the mantle until we took down the Christmas decorations. Without a word, he packed the present away in a box with our stockings.

The next Christmas, I felt even worse. Mike held out his gift to me. When I didn't take it, couldn't look at him, he put it on the mantle beside the first present.

He adapted. About a week later, by some strange coincidence, a new mixer showed up in the kitchen. He'd gotten a candy apple red one, to match the color I put on the walls. Yup, I have one bright kitchen. A month later, a cup holder appeared in my car. Although a portion of it fit inside my car's regular cup holder, the top part expanded to fit even my giant coffee mug.

Our third Christmas he'd said, "Someday you'll trust me. Someday, you'll open the gifts." Then he put his present on the mantle.

But that someday didn't come. Mike was killed in an automobile accident a week before his twenty-eighth birthday.

So, here I am on December fifteenth, drinking my hot toddy. I get the Christmas ornament box down off the top shelf of the closet. Wow, is it heavy. I put the three gifts on the mantle, the first one is the smallest. It's wrapped in gold foil paper with a white ribbon, its bow a dove. The second, is huge, maybe eighteen inches long and twelve inches wide. Wrapped in green and white striped paper, it looks like a mint candy cane. Mike went for classic for the third present. It's wrapped in red and white Merry Christmas paper and is adorned with three large red bows. It's the size of a standard clothing box from a department store, the kind used to wrap a man's dress shirt.

I know the third box is empty. Why, would Mike keep getting me presents he knew I'd never open. But the first two . . .

It's late and I'm incredibly tired. I'm looking forward to sleep. I want to dream about Mike, asking me, "Why do you love me?" I close my eyes. I'm in the circus . . .

*

The next day, work goes long. It always goes long. I drag myself home at seven p.m. Madge—she lives across the hall—must have heard me fumbling for my keys. I get the door unlocked. She pushes it open and walks in—in front of me.

Her blond hair is cut short, layered, a thousand perfect curls framing her flawless face. She is tall and slender to my barely five-foot-two. I tend toward voluptuous. I'm forever buying new bras hoping I'll find one that's comfortable and renders me professionally jiggle-free.

She eyes the three presents on the mantle. "Those again." Her disdain isn't veiled. "Really?" She gives me the look. "Either shit or get off the pot."

I truly detest her potty mouth, but I don't roll my eyes; I don't sigh; I don't react. I put down my briefcase and the two bulging nine-by-twelve manilla envelopes I've brought home. Of course, my boss, Junior, I think he should be called Junior Delinquent, wants them done ASAP. I hate those initials. *ASAP. ASAP. ASAP.* Everything is ASAP.

"Earth to Julie. Earth to Julie."

I come back to a conversation I don't want to have.

"Obviously, you don't want to talk about," she points to the gifts, Mike's gifts, the unopened gifts, the unopened dreams, in three perfectly wrapped boxes, "but it's time," she says, taking the first one, with the dove-for-a-bow off the mantle. Like it's hers to do with as she pleases, she plucks off the bow and casually tosses the dove onto the floor.

"Stop." I scream at her and grab *my* present from her hands.

"All right. All right." She shrugs as if I am the one acting crazy.

"No, it's not all right. Get out." Honestly, I don't know where those words are coming from. I'm usually a polite person, but I am shaking—

THE CATCHER 139

inside and out. I feel like a timer is counting down in my stomach and when it goes off, if she's still here, I'm going to hit her.

She walks toward the door. My breathing slows. Thank goodness she's leaving. Then, she turns into the kitchen. That does it. I put Mike's present back on the mantle, pick up the Henderson Curtains' manilla envelope—it's the bigger of the two—and head to the kitchen. Her butt is sticking out of my refrigerator.

Whack.

"What the fuck?" She stands up.

"Get out of my house." I jump up—yes, I'm so short I have to jump—and smash the envelope down onto those perfectly dyed curls. *"Get out!"* Gripping the envelope in two hands, I pummel her with whacks.

The tall twit decides to defend herself.

I escalate the conflict. I am standing by the sink. So, I turn on the water, grab the sprayer, point it at her nose, and—

She runs out—cussing.

I lock the door behind her, and then just as my heart rate is returning to normal, rush back into the kitchen. When I've saved Henderson Curtains from the approaching tsunami—and my boss, Junior, from another blow up—I collapse onto the couch. The dove is on the carpet. I pick it up and put it back on the present. At least it wasn't injured.

I know this sounds stupid, but I start bawling, not crying, or even sobbing, this is shoulders shaking, can't stop, flat out, eyes gushing water, bawling.

When it is over, I crawl—I can't walk—to the bedroom and somehow get in bed. Still in my clothes I sleep straight through the alarm. The sun is high in the sky when I finally wake. I take my temperature, but I don't have a fever. I ignore the phone. Three times Junior calls. Puffy grotesque eyes look back at me from the mirror. Everything aches, my joints, my arms, my shoulders, my head—wow, does my head hurt. Someone pounds on the door. I peer through the peep hole to see blond curls. Nope, I don't unlock the door.

"Hey, are you all right?"

"Yes." I scream. "Go away."

Thank God she leaves.

I spend the day ignoring my phone and watching TV. Junior calls twelve more times. I have an enchilada TV dinner for breakfast, and a frozen pizza for lunch. Dinner is a wedge of frozen apple pie topped with rocky road. Life is looking up when I decide to watch this sappy movie. You know the type where the hero and heroine at first don't even like each other and then they do and it's glorious. I make myself a hot toddy and gaze up at the presents.

I tell myself that I don't have to open them. This is my life. I get to make my own decisions.

I pick the first one up. I know from experience that it doesn't rattle. It is small, square, about five inches on a side, barely big enough for the dove. I try to remind myself that Mike had been human, not a Hollywood hero crafted out of a highly paid writer's imagination, guaranteed to make me cry at the end of the movie.

I place the dove on the mantle. I turn the present over; play with the tape a bit.

What could be this light?

This is the first present, so I know the box isn't empty.

The paper gives way under my prodding fingernail, a tiny rip, but it's enough. The paper slips off revealing a white box. Jewelry?

I open the lid. Inside is a slip of paper and a business card. I look at the business card first.

Best Friends.

I easily recognize Mike's handwriting on the note. "Babe, remember in September when you stopped in front of the pet store window, and I could barely drag you away? Well, I thought perhaps you might like a dog. If you do, call Best Friends and ask for Jim. He runs a rescue operation and has a huge selection. Pick out any dog you'd like. He's expecting you. I've already paid him. Merry Christmas."

A dog?

Between this present and now I'd had two more Christmases with Mike and two without—four years.

I glance at the clock: 9:30 p.m. No one will be there. I pick up my phone and enter the number.

"Hello, this is Jim."

*

That night I don't dream.

The next morning, I call my oh-so-wonderful-boss, Junior.

"Sir, I'm ill."

He's in a bad mood. You know, the same mood he's in every day. "You'd better get your ass into the office right now."

THE CATCHER

"Sir, my head is pounding. I can't think."

"I don't give a damn."

"Look, I'll take the days as vacation days."

"You're pushing me. You know I hate it when you push me."

I want to say, "If I don't push you, nothing gets done, unless, of course, I do it." But I don't say that, instead I say, "Sir, I have ten vacation days left."

Click.

I breathe. Slowly, over the next hour the headache fades. When I can raise my head off the couch, I glance at the clock. Jim said he'd be in all afternoon.

*

He introduces me to basset hounds and sheep dogs, rottweilers and Pomeranians. Across the huge play field a dog is running toward me. He has floppy ears and blond curls all over his body.

"That's a miniature golden doodle," Jim says.

"A what?"

"A cross between a minature golden retriever and a miniature poodle. He's three years old and house trained. You won't find a better friend."

"How much is he?"

Jim holds up his hands, clearly refusing my money. "Your husband paid me, what, four years ago? If anything, I owe you the interest on his money." He opens the gate and picks up my new best friend.

As I get in my car, the dog in a carrier in the backseat, Jim asks, "What are you going to name him?"

My mind drifts back to the man in my dream hanging upside down on the trapeze. I know this dog is not that man, but somehow the catcher helped me open Mike's present. He gave me the courage. I swivel around and look at my excited new friend in the back seat. "Catcher," I say.

*

Madge, my neighbor, is waiting at my door.

"You got a dog?" she scoffs. "He'll ruin the furniture."

A kind of peace fills me. I'm quiet inside. I pick up Catcher. He's growling at her. "You know," my voice is barely above a whisper, "I don't think I want you to stop by anymore."

"What?" She doesn't look hurt. She looks baffled. "*You're* dumping *me?*"

Catcher bares his teeth.

I open the door, walk in, and shut her out. I put him down on the floor, where he stands for a moment gazing up at me; then he barks.

"Yes," I say, "you're right. Good riddance."

*

Three days pass before I even glance at the remaining two presents. I mean, the first gift was so incredibly wonderful . . . The second can't possibly be as meaningful.

Mom stops by. I'm surprised by Catcher's reaction. He doesn't bark, he doesn't growl. He sniffs her feet, wags his tale and yelps.

"Oh, sweetie," she says, "he's wonderful."

A slight problem occurs when she tries to hand me my Christmas present. Catcher seems to think it's for him. But after some disappointed yelping and Mom's promise to bring him something next time, he forgives her and rolls over, begging for Mom to rub his tummy.

As Mom hands the gift to me, she says, "I hope it fits—I think."

She looks far older than her fifty-four years. Her hair has gone gray. Lines mark her face. She is painfully skinny. I always make pasta when she stops by. I want her to gain weight, but she doesn't eat much. She's trained herself to leave the food for me.

Mom's presents are always humorous. Our first Christmas without Dad, and without money, she gave me a box of brownie mix. Sitting, snuggled together on the couch, eating hot, gooey brownies and watching *How the Grinch Stole Christmas* is one of my best memories. The next year I was having trouble at school with Suzie Trample, the local bully. She was a full head taller than me. Mom bought me a small water pistol. We filled it with diluted deer-off. Does that stuff ever stink. I carefully concealed my "weapon" under my sweatshirt. I made sure I shot her in the face. I got expelled, but it was worth it.

I rip open the wrapping paper. Inside is a—I start to laugh. I'm sitting at the kitchen table. I literally fall out of my chair and onto the floor.

She's laughing, too. "I found it at a thrift shop." She pulls me up. "Try it on."

"I can't. I mean, *Mom*."

"It's just us here. Go. Go."

I take the present into my bedroom, and, after a few deep breaths, I put on the emerald-green, sequined, one-piece, low-cut, extremely low-cut, leotard. My breasts are threatening to spill out of the bodice. Way more than half of my bottom is sticking out the back. Talk about leaving very little to the imagination.

Flinging my arms into the air, I emerge from the bedroom. "Tah-dah."

Mom claps. "Bravo. Bravo."

Catcher is barking and running around the room. He jumps up on the couch and down again, goes into the kitchen and comes back out, and runs around me in circles. I know he doesn't know why Mom is clapping, but he's all for a celebration.

After Mom and I finally manage to calm Catcher down, I change into sweats to fix dinner, which is shrimp scampi and more of the frozen apple pie topped with rocky road. We talk past eleven.

"I should go," Mom says. "I know you have work tomorrow."

Shaking my head, I reach out and touch her arm. "I took some vacation."

Her eyes open wide in shock. "Junior let you have vacation?"

I grin. "I didn't give him much choice."

"Sweetie—"

I know what she is going to say, so I interrupt. "I already turned down the other job."

Her head droops. "You need security."

When she is sound asleep in my king-size bed, I put back on the emerald-green leotard and take down the second gift. Catcher comes to sit beside me on the couch. I'm so proud of him, for welcoming Mom. And when Mom lay down on the bed, he totally stopped yelping. I give him extra scratching.

I run my fingers lightly over the second present. "It's okay," I say to Catcher. "I know this gift can never be as wonderful as you." My fingers are shaking. "I'm prepared," I tell him. He licks my face. When still I hesitate, he licks it again.

I slide my fingernail under the tape. Effortlessly the paper falls away.

I can't breathe. I'm so dizzy . . .

When I come to, Mom is calling my name. "Julie. Julie." Somewhere, a dog is barking. "Sweetie, are you okay?"

I look up into her worried face. "Mom, I opened the second gift. Mike got me watercolors."

"You fainted over watercolors?"

*

Long after Mom returns to bed, and Catcher settles down in his doggy bed, I sit at the kitchen table, experimenting with washes, trying out all of the brushes Mike purchased, and finally paint flowers. I've forgotten the joy of seeing nature bloom beneath my brush.

"You have such an eye for color," Mike often said.

Then I notice that's there something else in the box. In the bottom are four pieces of paper stapled together. Mike had printed out the course requirements for an art degree at Pitt. I glance up at the closed bedroom door.

"I'm sorry, Mike," I whisper into the quiet room. "I can't do it. I don't have the money and Mom . . ." Slowly, I put the lid back on the palette. "She cried when I got a credit card, even though I promised to pay the full balance every month. The mortgage on the trailer, it was all she ever thought about. If I take out a loan, I think it will kill her."

*

On Christmas eve, I make a ham and a pecan pie. Mom whips up some of her famous candied sweet potatoes.

"Mom," I say, sitting back and patting my stomach, "after this meal, I don't think I'll fit into that trapeze outfit."

She laughs. "Who cares?""

After dinner, we sit on the couch. She's sitting near the end, I'm reclining my head on her chest, and Catcher is on top of me, getting his tummy scratched.

"I never liked Madge," she says.

I grin. "You know, I didn't either."

She laughs.

"Why was I ever friends with her?" I ask.

Mom caresses my hair. "She moved in, two days after Mike died."

Mom leaves on Saturday, the day after Christmas.

That night, I dream again. I close my eyes and smell the cotton candy. I'm climbing the ladder. I love being so high above the crowd. Below I hear Brighter the clown's whistle. I look down. This time I recognize him.

Like I've been hit by lightning, I shock awake, sitting up in bed. "He's Mike."

I jump from the bed, pacing. Intending to get a drink of water, I walk to the bathroom, only to see the trapeze leotard hanging from a hook on the back of the door.

"All right," I shout.

Catcher whimpers from his bed.

"Sorry, boy. I'm not shouting at you; I'm shouting at me. I guess Christmas isn't quite over. It's time."

Now dressed in green sequins, with purposeful steps and my head held high—yeah, I'm faking it—I go into the living room and take the last present off the mantle. I'm trying not to give myself time to think. Still, my hand pauses above the wrapping paper.

"Jump," I shout and rip open the paper.

Inside the box is a fancy folder with the word 'Prudential' on the outside.

"What?"

Taped to the folder is a note. "I will never willingly leave you. Never. But if something should happen, this will help ensure that you will never be left as your mother was. The policy is completely paid."

For hours I sit on the floor and cry. Not because I have the money to go to college, to become an artist, but because Mike had truly known me. He was the best gift he ever gave me.

*

Sometime around three in the morning, I stumble back to bed.

And the dreams came, only this time the second one is first. I'm standing in my dark, colorless apartment. It's stuffy as if the windows haven't been opened in years—two years. I turn the knob and walk outside. The man is there waiting for me with the knife. I stand in front of him, my arms at my sides, my eyes closed, waiting for him to plunge the knife into my chest. Instead, I hear a strange clanking sound.

Opening my eyes, I look down to see him kneeling at my feet, using the knife to pry off the chains hobbling me. When they fall off, I leave my old life behind. I let it die. Shaking with excitement, I run toward the music and the red and orange tent. With every step, my clothes change until I'm wearing the skimpy, emerald-green leotard. My breasts are jiggling; I am wildly on display. Joy fills me.

With my bottom hanging out of the back of my costume, I climb the ladder. Below me Brighter/Mike whistles. When I reach the top, I clasp the bar and jump.

I swing out pumping my legs. I swing back—higher now. As I swing forward, I let go, rolling once, twice . . . unfold and hold out my hands.

And he catches me.

And I know who he is.

He is God. He is Mom and Mike, the people who love me.

And he is *me*.

Dad left, and I survived. Mike died, and I survived. I have no doubt that this will not be the last time I lose someone I love. But now I know that I am strong enough, talented enough, disciplined enough to survive—and not only survive but prosper. I will live and love again. I have only to trust myself.

I can catch me.

Just Ask Santa

Bettie Nebergall
Second Place Winner, 2024 BWR Short Story Award

Somehow, mothers of small boys react instantly to the moment of eerie silence which precedes disaster. As an unmarried aunt, I lack that particular "Spidey-sense." My sister Susie was already up and running when I registered the crashing sounds.

I raced past my team of volunteers preparing the Altamonte Mall's North Pole for a Secret Santa visit. Uninterrupted by catastrophe, they continued to set up snack tables, photo stations, and wheelchair accessible walkways for the families of local Wounded Warriors.

"Mom, it's Santa! Come quick. I think we killed him!" Timmy, my seven-year-old nephew, barreled into his mother's knees.

Susie examined Timmy for injury while I scanned our Christmas Village. Erect candy canes lined the walkway to St. Nick's snow-crusted throne, and the mechanical reindeer lifted and lowered their heads, undisturbed.

The calamity lay behind them. At the bottom of the escalator, a large pair of shiny black boots protruded from an avalanche of torn and jumbled packages still shuddering from impact.

Two of Timmy's friends dug through the heap, pausing only to evaluate the most intriguing treasures. I pitched in and rolled away the heavy box pressing Santa's head onto the floor. Kneeling to block him from view, I quickly reapplied his wig and beard, then straightened his jacket. Twice.

Tomorrow morning, Santa planned to glide down the moving staircase with enormous bags of toys. He would mingle and greet the families as two brawny elves delivered the donations to each child. Clearly, the rehearsal didn't go well.

Holding half-open presents, Timmy's buddies stared at Santa's inert form. Redheaded Jason stood alone, dazed, and shamefaced. "Is he dead?"

"He must be." Mason, scruffy, blond, and so frightened his freckles glowed like stoplights, pointed at the body. "He's not crying."

"We didn't mean to do it, Auntie Mel," said Timmy. "Jason just wanted to talk to him."

Susie settled her son with his fellow culprits as I lifted Santa's beard and found a pulse in his muscular neck.

"It's all right, kids, he's alive." I stifled a sigh. *I wouldn't mind a little mouth-to-mouth with this guy.* Deep brown hair, chiseled jaw, wide, intelligent forehead. An altogether different Spidey-sense tingled my insides.

His eyes flickered open, focused on me, and glazed over as he lost consciousness again. My heart skipped a beat. This gorgeous man, in one moment of lucidity, whispered: "Angel."

"Hallucinations," I muttered. "Possible concussion." *Angel, hah.* I held no illusions. Flyaway brown hair, minimal makeup. Everyone called me Mel, never Melissa. Gal pal. Little sister. Always a bridesmaid, never a lover.

Santa moaned. A goose egg dominated his brow and swelling distorted half his face. Gently, I ran my fingers through thick side-swept hair beneath his wig, discovered no bumps or cuts, and moved my attention to his left hand, happy to find no impediments there, either. "Does anyone know his name?"

The boys looked at me like I was crazy. "Santa," they caroled in unison, voices full of derision. "Dummy," went unsaid.

Susie turned on them. "What happened? Start at the beginning."

Jason hung his head. "It's all my fault. For Christmas, I want my parents back together. I ran down the *sascalater* to ask Santa, but I couldn't stop, and we crashed into the pile at the bottom. I didn't mean to hurt him." He snuffled and wiped his tears on his sleeve. "He'll never help me now."

I refocused on my patient and noted rapid eye movement beneath his long-lashed lids. His sculpted chest rose and fell in perfect rhythm. While I may lack many of my sister's extra senses, I can tell a possum player from a mile away. I was a kid once. I pinched him.

With amazing reflexes for a "dead" man, Santa snatched my hand and rubbed his thumb across my knuckles, hesitating on my empty ring finger. A corner of his generous mouth twitched, one wicked emerald eye opened—the other had swollen shut—and he grinned.

"Oh, sweetheart, that little stunt's gonna cost you. Bounced you right to the top of my Naughty List." The soft Carolina accent in his baritone voice rippled over my skin.

Before I could formulate an appropriate reply, volunteers surrounded us, full of questions and advice. Mothers corralled and soothed children, others began rescuing presents. A mall security guard appeared, point man for the pair of EMTs jogging toward us. In spite of Santa's protests, they braced his neck and strapped him to a backboard, checked his vitals, and lifted him to a gurney.

"Help me out here, darlin'!" He turned pleading eyes to me. Well, one pleading eye. "Tell 'em I'm fine."

"Apologies, folks, mall policy." The guard took charge. "Florida Hospital is right next door. He's headed to the ER. We need a medical release for liability insurance."

Santa growled. "I'm not going to sue! It was an accident."

"Wait! My sister's going with you." Susie pulled me to the EMTs and blocked their progress.

She passed me my purse and used her "Because-I-Say-So" voice. "Follow them and get copies of the paperwork. Bring back the suit."

"Oh, Nick, I'm so sad about this." She patted Santa's shoulder. "I'll arrange a substitute for tomorrow. You just focus on getting better."

Seriously? A Santa named Nick? I rushed to my car. *Is this a joke, or a wish coming true?* In the hospital lobby, stoked on bitter coffee, I replayed his words until a nurse wheeled him into the room. The green scrubs matched his sparkling eyes. Even bruised and battered, the man made my knees weak. I wobbled across to him.

"There's my angel," Nick beamed. I wanted to tease him, but he looked so weary my smart remarks died unspoken.

The nurse smiled, so I addressed her. "I'm Melissa Jacobs. How's our patient doing?"

Before she could speak, Nick handed me a folder full of paperwork. "Proof of my good health, with copies for you and the mall." Hefting the bulky plastic hospital tote made him wince. "Your Santa suit."

"They kept you quite a while. Are you really okay?"

The nurse shook her head and flashed her eyes sideways. The we-women-know-better smirk. "Honey, your man's a hot mess. Covered in contusions and one cracked rib. We taped it, stuck ice packs on him, and loaded him up with Tylenol. Good news is no concussion, no broken bones. Bad news is he's benched for the rest of the season."

She bent over him and got right in his face. "No driving for three days, and no rooftops or chimneys, you hear me?" She hooted with laughter and rolled him outside to the pickup circle.

He started to stand, but she stiff-armed him and spoke to me. "Rules is rules. He stays in the chair while on hospital property. Go on now and get the car." She giggled. "I can't wait to see them reindeer."

My passenger seat retracted far enough to accommodate his long legs, and we pulled away with a hearty good night.

He groaned. "I survived Iraq with fewer injuries."

"Santa should get hazard pay. Do you want something to eat before I take you home?"

"Miss Melissa, I'm too tired to eat, but thanks for everything you're done. For this trip, I'm staying down the road at the Hilton."

"Good choice." I turned right onto Altamonte Drive and slowed for the succession of stoplights.

"Yeah. I'm holding candidate interviews on Monday. My company teaches advanced communication skills. It's a lucrative field for veterans, and critical in today's Army."

He shifted in the seat and rebalanced. "I flew in from Raleigh a few days early to connect with the guys from my old unit and they needed a Santa the kids wouldn't recognize."

"I'm so sorry your reunion turned out this way." In light traffic, we glided past the mall.

"Stop, Lissa! My rental car's in the parking lot. I'd be real grateful if you'd drop me off and I'll manage from there."

"Oh, no. You heard the nurse. 'Rules is rules.' No driving for three days."

"Angel, I need my car." His voice firmed up, hinting at the commander he'd once been. "I have to be there tomorrow."

"No way, Susie will have a sub—"

"I'm committed to my men. We saved each other's lives countless times and vowed to always be there when needed. It's getting harder to get everyone together. I don't want to lose touch. Also, I need to talk with Jason."

"Jason?" My breath caught. I couldn't let him punish the boy. "He's in trouble enough."

He reached across the console and gently touched my arm. "I want to help with his Christmas wish."

The streetlights illuminated his injured face. "But Nick, you can't fix the divorce."

"True, but I can help him understand it's not his fault."

My heart melted. "Are you some kind of shrink?"

"No, but I've been in his shoes." His grin skewed down. *How could one man be so sexy, wise, and kind? Am I dreaming?* "Jason feels responsible for the split. He's a sweet kid going through a tough time, and I want to help, too. I'll be your shuttle service."

"That's an offer I won't refuse." He reached for me again, groaned, and dropped his hand to the console. "When I opened my eyes and saw you kneeling above me, lights twinkling around you, I thought you were an angel. You've proved me right every minute since. Melissa, please let me take you to dinner tomorrow."

My tummy shimmied, but not from hunger. "Sounds delightful."

The Hilton appeared much sooner than I liked, and we fell silent as I parked under the elegant portico. As office manager for a diverse team of professionals, I knew how to navigate among conflicting personalities, unrelated specialties, and difficult clients. Yet I felt as awkward as a girl on her doorstep after a first date.

He fumbled the recessed handle, and I hopped out, rounded the hood, and yanked his door open so fast he almost toppled out. Thankfully, only the tension broke.

"Whoa, Nick, you're completely jammed in there. Can you swivel around and put your feet on the ground?" I gritted my teeth to stop babbling. Counted to ten as he maneuvered into position. He staggered and swayed into me.

I looped my arm around his waist. "Let me walk you to the elevator." He smelled of eucalyptus rub but felt solid as an oak. *Oh, mama.*

He gripped my shoulder; I held him against my side, and we shuffled through the lobby. He leaned against the wall beside the elevators. "I hate to see the evening end."

"Me too, but you need rest." I stepped aside, but he turned to me and took my hands. I ached to touch his poor face. I wanted to soothe him. For starters.

He smoothed a wisp off my forehead and tucked it behind my ear. "Melissa, we have a real connection. Please tell me you sense it, too."

I nearly swooned. He'd said my name, the whole thing. Three times. My inner princess blinked awake. Lissa. Angel. Girly names! My vision blurred. Snowflakes? Sugarplums? I stretched up and kissed him. In confirmation, bells jingled, and Bing Crosby crooned overhead.

Nick ignored the elevator's arrival. His big hands stroked my shoulders and pulled me closer. "A series of final sessions will keep me here next week, and I want to spend as much time as possible with you."

At warp speed, I mentally assessed my schedule, shuffling appointments, and delegating meetings as my heart stuttered Mel-lis-sa, Mel-lis-sa, Mel-lis-sa.

Unaware of my turmoil, Nick continued, "I need to scout the metro area." His breath tickled my ear. "And determine if Orlando makes a good base for me." He nuzzled my neck. "I'll need a guide."

I could no longer suppress a giddy smile. "We have a lot of territory to explore." Bells jingled; Bing crooned. "I'll clear my calendar and gas up the sleigh."

The Tour

Ralph Hieb

The dark gray cylinder slid gracefully through the cosmos to its destination planet. The non-reflective shell hid the portholes that allowed occupants to see outside instead of using their viewing screens.

Inside, the passengers watched the planet they passed fade from sight as another came into view. It was blue, with a haze of white covering sections of the aqua waters. Some others watched their viewing screens while younglings spun in circles on the cushioned, reclining seats.

A voice interrupted the silence.

"Hello again, everyone," Maura said into the sound amplifier. "I am happy to introduce you to the third planet in this minor solar system." Looking at the happy spacecraft full of over fifty passengers, she smiled as their antennae shook with excitement. "Captain Ophelia has assured me this will be an uneventful visit since the surface of this planet, which the inhabitants call 'Earth,' is mostly water.

"A quick question for our younger visitors," Maura continued. "Who can tell me the main difference between their species and ours?"

Several younger ones raised their three-fingered hands in response to the question.

Smiling Maura picked the purple youngling first.

"I know," she answered. "They don't have antennae."

"That is a very good answer, but not the greatest difference."

Maura picked another youngling, who also got the answer wrong, and then another and another.

"Well, it seems as if I'm the only one who knows the answer." Looking around she smiled, the correct answer is that the inhabitants of this planet are carbon based while we are silicon based. But since we had so many good answers, I have containers of Skalids for everyone."

"Our flight attendant, Alina," Maura said, indicating the young female, standing next to her, "will be happy to get you refreshments to enjoy as we pass the northern axis." Alina gave a shy wave to their guests.

"Even though much of the surface is currently covered in visible masses of condensed water vapors, you can see on the viewing screens that this is a relatively new planet, rich in plant and animal life, with a warm-blooded, sentient land species known as humans." She tried not to sound bored with the prepared script. "You are taking this trip at a good time because at this time in their orbit, the humans celebrate what they call 'the holiday season.'"

"What's special about it?" asked a youngling who had not fully developed antennae.

"Well," Maura answered, "this is a time when they meet with their families to eat and drink together and repeat holiday traditions."

"Why don't they meet with their families more often?" the youngling asked.

"Some do, but during this time, a larger portion of the population makes an effort to reunite with those for whom they have special ties of affection. We are approaching the northernmost axis of the planet, and you can see some very bright lights of different colors in the atmosphere. This is similar to the light shows we observed on other worlds. We believe that the colored lights that inhabitants use to decorate their homes are an attempt to duplicate the lights in the sky. They also enjoy the custom of giving gifts to friends and family during this season. They believe in a mythical human who is immortal and lives at the northernmost part of the planet. He dresses in red and flies around the entire globe in one night to distribute gifts. This being uses a vehicle called a sleigh that is pulled by several animals known as flying rain-deer. If you look at your viewing screens, you will see an image of the being in his sleigh drawn by these animals." She hesitated for a moment before continuing. "Most creatures in this area are warm-blooded but have adapted to the colder temperatures which are typical of the region of the planet now below us."

All orbs turned toward the portholes when the ship lurched. Maura grabbed hold of a nearby seat to steady herself. "What was that?" She looked at Alina, who had fallen and was sitting on the deck, looking confused.

THE TOUR

"Is everyone okay?" Alina asked, as she headed for the control area.

A few passengers rubbed their frontal ridges while others stuck out their tongues, to see if they bit them. Everyone seemed okay.

The voice of Captain Ophelia came over the sound system. "All crew members report to the control area."

"Be right back," Maura said to the crowd, holding up two digits. Then, gesturing to Alina to follow her, she continued to the front of the craft.

As they neared the control area, the craft lurched again as if they had struck a heavy object. "What's happening?" Alina's hoarse voice rasped, they stepped through the hatch into the closed cabin where Racine, the pilot, sat at the controls with Captain Ophelia bent over her, looking at the screen.

"We have hit some kind of electron force. Its source could be their star." Racine wrinkled her nasal sensor and sniffed, a green shimmer of sweat covering her face. "And there is more." Her face folded into a frown. "Our invisibility shields are down." She frantically turned dials and adjusted levers trying to regain the shields.

"Are we visible to the inhabitants?" Ophelia asked. She had captained hundreds of tours. Maura felt certain she would have a plan for just such an event.

Straightening her back ridges, the captain barked, "Get us to the far side of their moon."

"If I do, they can observe us with their sensors," Racine answered. "This planet has a history of trying to eliminate anything they perceive as a threat."

"And anything unknown is a threat to them," Alina said.

"It will soon be light enough that they will be able to see us without help from detection equipment," Racine added.

"Then raise the force field and dive into the ocean," Ophelia ordered. Turning to Maura and Alina, she added, "You two get back and ready the passengers for an under-ocean adventure."

Maura and Alina glanced at each other as they left the control area.

"Just pretend it's just a normal part of the tour," Maura whispered, seeing fear in Alina's orbs. "We can't let on that there's anything wrong or we'll have a full-blown panic."

Alina nodded and swallowed hard. Straightening her shoulders, she preceded Maura into the cabin.

Maura picked up the microphone. "Attention please, ladies and gentlemen. Our captain has determined that we can add a very special treat to the regular tour. We are going to explore below the surface of one of this planet's seas. We will get to see some creatures that approximate some found on our world, and some like you have never seen. So, keep your orbs focused out the portholes as we descend."

Maura crossed her fingers at Alina for good luck. Alina braced herself as the ship levelled on top of the water and then slid below the surface.

"We are down to about three thousand semi-sectors," Maura estimated, quietly.

"The force field is holding," Alina whispered back. "No sounds are emitting from the hull indicating stress."

"Miss Maura?" It was the same curious youngling. "It's getting cold in here. My antennae are shivering. Can you do something about it?"

"I'll talk to the captain," Maura said and walked toward the front.

On the way, several other passengers asked if she could adjust the temperature before they began to freeze.

"Captain," Maura said once she reached the control area, "several of the tourists are requesting that the cabin temp be warmed a bit."

"Can't do it, Maura," Ophelia said. "We need the power to repair the shields.

"But—" Maura began. The look from the captain stopped her.

"I'll see what can be done," Captain Ophelia said.

Racine sniffed. "Captain, we need to surface so that I can repair the damage from the impact."

"Why can't you repair it here?" Ophelia asked.

"This ship was meant to work in a vacuum and can only spend short periods in a dense environment. I have no idea how much damage the liquid will do to the circuits and cables. We don't have enough power to sit here much longer."

The captain hissed through clenched teeth, her orbs turning a dark gray. "Then surface now. This part of the planet has very few of the humans who might see us, and their star will soon be on the other side of the planet."

Racine sniffed. "We can start now, but the trip to the surface will take longer than it took to submerge. And I will need to shut off all excess power, including dimming lights."

THE TOUR

"Maura, help Alina console the passengers about the cold. Tell them we are working on the problem," Ophelia commanded.

Maura nodded and left the cabin.

"Maura," one of the passengers called. "Why have the lights dimmed?"

Maura knew she had to think fast. "We have dimmed the lights so that it will not get overly bright in here and frighten the creatures of the deep." That sounded good to her sound sensors. Then she got another idea. "Please watch out of the windows and I am sure you will see several types of cold-blooded species. For this reason, we cannot raise our ambient temperature. It might have an ill effect on these species. We are slowly surfacing, and as we rise the temperature will also rise."

"The passengers are watching to see if they can spot any of the water creatures, and Alina is passing out refreshments," Maura reported back to Ophelia.

"Very good. At this rate we should only be visible for a short period until it is dark enough to repair damage," Ophelia murmured.

The ship lurched and the captain barked to Racine, "Steady, slow it down. Why are we rising so fast?"

"I wish I could say that I'm using its thrusters controlling the rise to the surface, but the ship is doing it on its own," Racine replied.

"I haven't ordered you to put it on automatic control," Ophelia roared.

"I know," Racine said, cowering from the noise. "It's not on automatic, but it's acting on its own."

As the ship broke the surface of the water, Maura saw a white streak in the sky. "What is that?" she said, pointing her digits at the light.

*

Returning to the cabin, Maura thought she detected a sound overhead. She tilted her head to listen. Something was moving along the craft's hull.

Heading into the control area Maura heard Racine screech, "Captain! Look at the instruments."

Ophelia scanned the control panel. Every instrument read within normal parameters, and the energy storage indicators read full. The two officers stared at their screens. Then looked at each other with oral cavities agape.

"What in the worlds?" Racine whispered.

"Turn on the invisibility units. Let's get off of this planet fast," Ophelia ordered.

The passengers slowly roused themselves from a trancelike state to find brightly wrapped gifts strewn throughout the vessel. Younglings discovered each package had one of their names attached. After looking at their parents for permission, they unwrapped them to find toys and games inside. Their excited cheers filled the cabin.

"Look Maura," a youngling said, holding a toy dinosaur. "Isn't this a likeness of one of the creatures that once inhabited this planet millions of orbits ago?"

Answering questions from passengers, Maura confessed that she could not explain where the presents came from. Then she noticed Alina's odd expression. "What is it, Alina?" she asked.

"I was looking out of the cabin window, thankful that we got free, when I saw the most peculiar thing," Alina said.

Maura asked, "What did you see?"

"You're not going to believe this, but I swear it was a human in a sleigh. And it flew through the air pulled by eight rain-deers."

Millie's Christmas Wine

D. T. Krippene

Chuck Schmidt belched in three octaves on the patio of his Florida condominium while watching an egret fish in the pond. Ever since he and Millie moved to the place a few years ago, the community's name, Cottages at the Lake, still irked him.

"I've seen bigger bodies of water from overflowing septic tanks," he grumbled, swirling the dregs of his near-empty beer. "Wisconsin had weather and a real Christmas, not pink and turquoise lights on palm trees."

Day drinking used to be limited to weekend sports, or hunting and fishing trips. He hadn't hunted since selling his beer distributorship in Oshkosh. When the last of his fishing buddies died back home, he didn't give a damn anymore.

The cell phone chirped in his pants pocket. He wriggled it free and answered without checking caller identification. "Yep."

"Mr. Schmidt. It's Sandra. Do you have a minute?"

"Ah—that's a no." Chuck hung up, turned it to silent mode, and set the phone on the patio tabletop.

The receptionist for the management group that ran the place, Sandra, fielded calls for the young stuffed-shirt condo manager transplanted from New York City. She was okay, but her jerk of a boss stipulated that she act as the front line of communication for the homeowners.

"If he wants something from me, he can call me direct like a man," he said to the egret. He debated the options of having another beer during lunch or skipping it altogether in favor of an early nap before the cocktail hour that started around four.

The cell jiggled on the table. The caller ID announced his daughter, Jennifer. With Millie gone, Jenny was the only one left of his sparse relatives and the only reason he didn't pack up and move back to Wisconsin.

"Hey, sweetie," he answered, followed by a squeaky burp.

"Dad, it isn't even lunchtime. Sandra just called and said you hung up on her."

Chuck did the obligatory eye roll. "Surely you have better things to do than scold your old man in his not-so-golden years." At first, he thought she'd disconnected in the following silent moments.

She prefaced with a loud exhale. "She didn't get your RSVP for the annual Holiday Dinner Ball at the clubhouse next week."

Chuck grunted. "Didn't send it last year. Nobody seemed to care then."

"Well, so soon after . . ." A gargled throat clearing followed. ". . . Mom died . . . they probably assumed you didn't feel very festive."

A sharp stab of buried grief rose inside him, always there to remind him Millie had been gone eighteen months. "I'm still not feeling very *festive*. You can RSVP a big fat no for me."

"It's a little different this holiday. The organizing committee wants to dedicate the event to Mom's memory. Honor her legacy in the community. The organizers asked if I'd help choose the holiday wine selection on Friday. They hoped I could talk you into joining me at the tasting."

The only positive aspect about moving to Florida, besides decent onsite care for Millie, was Jenny living nearby in Bonita Springs. Millie used to be one of the few high-ranking oenophiles in the country, and she passed her love of wine to Jenny, who took it to the top level by achieving the Master of Wine title.

"I'm a former beer salesman. I know jack-squat about wine."

"Come on, Dad. You pretended to be not into it, but you learned a lot from her, and you know it."

True. Millie had insisted he participate when she returned with homework from global events. He loved to make Millie laugh when he offered his own wine reviews. *Redolent of Reunite. Velvety like a freshly cracked Old Style. Notes of Walleye. Essence of winter fishing shanty. Hints of overcooked bratwurst.* And his favorite, *this is good shit.*

"Can't imagine anyone would reject anything you'd recommend." he said. "But I suppose the caviar bunch on the board feels it their sacred duty to bless the selection. Are all eight of them attending?"

The shuffling of papers on the receiver took a few seconds. "Only two board members: Mrs. Elizabeth Anderson and Ms. Clairissa Ottoman. Everyone else is tied up."

MILLIE'S CHRISTMAS WINE

Chuck groaned inwardly. *The board busybody, who prides herself on meddling in everyone's business, and the community floozy, who trolls resident wealthy widowers for expensive dinner dates.*

"Oh, and a Mr. Robert Weaver," Jessica added.

"Weaver? Geez Louise. If God's gift to the management group is coming, you can count me out."

Jenny went silent, but Chuck heard the subtle hitch in her breathing, not of exasperation but sadness at the disconnected, curmudgeonly father he'd become.

"You . . . really want me there?" he asked.

"You don't have to do anything but join in the tasting. Stephano will be there to assist."

He'd only met Stephano Marchessi once in passing. Chuck thought of him as okay, despite hailing from a century-old Italian winery, and certainly better than the turd ball Jenny divorced several years ago. Even though she claimed to be married to her work, a father could still hope Santa might find his daughter a decent life partner.

"Fine. I'll be there." When Jenny didn't answer, he added, "I promise."

The egret flew off when Chuck's joints cracked while rising from the chair. The beer had him craving a real bratwurst from Sheboygan, not the salty, tasteless version made at the local grocery. Instead, he settled on another beer for lunch.

*

A woman with a turban of blue hair filled the entrance of the ballroom doorway. Chuck blinked at her multicolored sweater studded with red beads and a necklace of colored flashing bulbs.

"Charles," she greeted with gravel-voiced cheeriness. "How wonderful you could attend. It's been forever since we've seen you."

He'd long given up on the biddies who patrolled the community and continued calling him *Charles* like he was some uppity New Englander. Chuck eyed the fake mistletoe dangling above the woman's head with suspicion. "Is my daughter here yet, Betty?"

"It's Beth for Elizabeth," she corrected. "She's setting up in the back."

Betty stepped aside with barely enough space to scootch past without Chuck getting tangled in her blinking mini-traffic lights.

"Oh. I almost forgot your badge." She took her sweet time attaching a black-enameled nametag with "H. Charles Schmidt" to his dandruff-sprinkled midnight-blue blazer. Betty patted the pin. "There you go. You never told me what the "H" stood for."

Horace was his grandmother's idea, in honor of a great-uncle who was an avid fisherman and died of sepsis from being bitten by a toothy northern pike. Over the years, he'd been tempted more than once to say his first name was *Hellno*. Millie had threatened to leave him if he ever did.

Jenny called to him from a table of wine bottles and a stack of unopened cases. "Dad, over here."

He ambled over with hands in his pockets, glancing at stacked chairs and folding tables waiting for setup. Stephano looked every bit the dashing Continental in his starched shirt, yellow tie, and snappy slim-fit suit with the subtle sheen of expensive fabric.

"Stephano," Chuck greeted. He examined the badge on his lapel that ended with initials and couldn't resist asking. "I keep forgetting what W.I.A. stands for. Wine Imbibers of America?"

Jenny squinted at her father as a warning.

Stephano took it in stride with a smile and heavy sing-song accent. "Wine Insegnante Association." He shook hands with Chuck. "I never had a chance to know Millicent very well, but she was an icon in the industry. We all miss her terribly. It is an honor to work with her daughter."

Her daughter? Guess I know where I stand in the hierarchy.

"May I offer you a Pellegrino before we begin?" Stephano asked.

"Got any Bud Light?"

"Shall we find your station, Dad?" Jenny pulled on his arm to coax him toward a long table with four place settings. "Here you go." She leaned close with a frown and whispered. "Behave."

Chuck almost quipped, "Why start now?" Instead, he took in the ballroom's festooned walls of silver wreaths and the ceiling-tall fake Christmas tree loaded with glittering balls and tinsel. The overbearing pine aroma sprayed from a can and cinnamon-scented oil votives made his nose itch.

It brought back the memory of meeting Millie's parents for the first time in Connecticut. They eschewed real Christmas trees, claiming it risked ruining their expensive carpet with needles and sticky sap. After he and Millie married, she grew to love the tradition of fresh-cut fir and pine trees, often using the scent in her wine reviews. *Suggestive of freshly cut spruce.* What the Westport native saw in a lower-income Wisconsin beer distributor who took her to a place with winters rivaling the North Pole always baffled him.

Chuck glanced up when Clare Ottoman sashayed into the room wearing a tight-fitting green pantsuit and jangling a cluster of bangle bracelets. Pearls strategically dangled in the cleft of her half-exposed breasts. For a widow, Clare still turned a head or two at her age. *Not exactly the grandmotherly look Norman Rockwell painted in his vintage holiday paintings.*

And wouldn't you know it? The Big Apple-bred condominium manager, Robert Weaver, settled into the chair on Chuck's right.

The man nodded. "Charles."

"Bob."

The man despised the less refined version of his first name almost as much as he hated saying "Chuck."

"Shall we begin?" Jenny announced.

Stephano poured while Jenny described it. "A Sauvignon Blanc from a small winery called 'Cracked Corn Creek' in the famed region of Marlboro, Australia. This vibrant white offers a laser beam of citrus and berries. It has a whiff of beeswax and accents of litsea oil and passion fruit, ending with a chalkiness on the long finish."

Jenny had certainly acquired Millie's poetic license. *Beeswax?*

Betty swished the wine like mouthwash and hummed to herself. Clare inhaled through her lips to aerate the sample on her tongue, sounding like an adolescent slurping the last dregs from a soda can with a straw. Bob had his nose deeply inserted in the glass as if attempting to use it as a neti pot.

Chuck raised his hand. "What's litsea oil?"

Stephano answered when Jenny's mouth flattened to a thin line. "It is an essential oil used in massage therapy for those suffering from coughs and cold symptoms. It has a citrusy smell like lemongrass."

"The oil also dampens negative emotions and improves mental clarity," Jenny added.

Ouch.

Stephano circled back with a red wine labeled "Mamma's Big Table."

"The next selection is from the Willamette Valley," Jenny continued. "This tightly focused pinot noir is richly refined with zesty raspberry, baking spices, and tea leaves, ending with hints of forest floor persistent of slightly burly tannins."

Mamma must have overindulged with her creation to come up with that label. Chuck mentally ranked the wine with his usual three-worded review for mediocre samples. *It doesn't suck.*

"A Cote du Rhone from Chateau Xavier," Jenny recited when Stephano poured a third sample. "You'll find it's densely coiled, simmering with layers of smoked duck and unripe persimmon. Built around a spine of toasted iron, it finishes very lengthy with a dash of dusted pepper."

Bob swirled the red wine to scrutinize traces of syrupy residue on the glass called *legs*. The evaporation of alcohol affected the surface area of the liquid. More legs, more alcohol. Unless drinking fortified wines, Millie considered it a pretentious test and the mark of an amateur.

Chuck tossed back an uncultured swig and pinched his lips at fun memories with a French simile he'd tease Millie with. *Honey, where's that Coat du Ruin bottle from Chateau Migraine?*

Once, he invented an alternate label for a Bordeaux from *Chateau Vespaciennes,* the French word for water closet. He got her belly laughing when he used a poorly written book opener to describe it. *It was dark and stormy wine, where the legs were many and fat, until the sheepherders, deprived of beer, broke into violent fighting, agitated by the scanty flame of lamps burning on last year's over-fermented Vin de Pays bilge.*

Jenny winked when she poured a garnet wine into a fresh glass and placed it before her father. The label was wrapped to cover the brand.

"We thought it would be a bit fun with this unique vintage," Stephano announced. "After tasting it, we'd like to know your impression before revealing the label."

Chuck did the obligatory swirl, gently poked his nostrils below the glass rim, inhaled, and immediately froze to the heady earthiness of fruit and leather he hadn't experienced since Millie died.

"Perhaps Mr. Schmidt would describe it for us first," said Stephano.

Obviously, a setup, Chuck wouldn't have minded so much if it didn't churn the well of perpetual hurt burbling in his soul. His silence had everyone glancing at each other with concern.

Jenny placed a hand on his shoulder. "Maybe we should take a recess and break for lunch."

Chuck waved his hand. "No. It's all right. You must have gone to a lot of trouble, and I don't want to spoil it."

He straightened his posture to steel himself. "It's a Chateauneuf du Pape. Millie's favorite during the holidays. She called it our Christmas wine. We drank it every year. Not a particularly popular wine, it's a grenache-heavy blend that pairs well with hearty Christmas food like beef roasts and ham, even bratwurst." He exhaled a deep sigh. "Millie sometimes opened a bottle after I returned from a deer hunting trip. A perfect vintage, she claimed, for the hunter home from the forest."

Chuck gently tore off the paper taped over the label. He swallowed to clear the forming thickness in his throat. "Same small winery. It's been hard to find for a bunch of years. Millie was lucky to snag a few bottles before they stopped shipping it to the U.S."

It took sheer willpower to stay composed. "Might have one bottle left. But with Millie gone, I can't imagine drinking it without her."

He patted Jenny's hand that rested on his shoulder. "You have lyrical insight with your wine reviews. You got that from your mother. But to me, it was never about *hints* of certain fruits or whiffs of beeswax."

Never one for literary embellishments, words long suppressed behind the wall of Wisconsin gruffness flowed from a hidden place in his heart as if written in a book.

"This wine will always remind me of the taste of dark chocolate on her lips when she kissed me. The playful rub of her fingers against the stubble of my week-old beard when she ordered me to shower after coming home with strong whiffs of my latest fishing trip."

Everyone chuckled—even Bob.

"Just tasting it . . ." Chuck took a deep breath to keep the sorrow from overflowing the banks. "It brings back memories of her fairy-like laughter when I joked about her craft and the softness of her summer dress lilted with the freshness of a lake breeze."

He stared at hands clutched in his lap when his voice quivered. "Most of all, the lingering warmth of her perfumed lotion when she slept against my shoulder on a cold winter night."

Chuck looked at his daughter who did her darndest not to bawl. "I'm forever grateful to see her spirit in you, honoring the craft she dearly loved."

The only sound for what seemed hours long was the mosquito-like buzz of a Christmas tree bulb about to short out. He ran fingers through his hair when Betty's nose-blowing honked him back to reality.

"Well, look at me, all sappy and Longfellow-ish," Chuck half-joked.

Claire dabbed her face to catch several layers of mascara dripping on her cheeks. Bob's posture sagged. Eventually, with nervous, light laughter all around, Chuck's fellow tasters rose from their seats to engage in awkward conversation.

Stephano winked at Jenny and gently placed an unopened case of Millie's Christmas wine near Chuck's setting. "As you suggested, we will adjourn for lunch before sampling the other wines."

Jenny dragged a chair alongside her father and grasped his arm like the little girl she once was.

"I know you're doing this in your mom's memory," Chuck said quietly. "It's a very nice sentiment, but this wine is wasted on the hoity-toity palates around here."

"It's not for the party." Jenny kissed her father on the cheek. "Merry Christmas, Dad."

Chuck did a doubletake. "You can't be serious. How did you..."

"It took a little digging, but I do have connections." She waggled her eyebrows. "And the condo board asked if I'd attend the event to handle requests from residents who wish to add to their private collections."

Chuck figured the invite was also part of the conspiracy to lure him out. "I don't know. Women outnumber men two-to-one at these things. I have no desire to fend off widows plotting when to move in after I say hello."

"You can be my date."

"Stephano would make a better date than this grumpy old badger."

"I don't fraternize with my staff. Besides, I'm having Stephano do most of the work, so he'll be pretty busy." Jenny squeezed his arm. "I'll make sure the caterer stocks cold beer for you."

"Well then. Can't be leaving you to the fate of a wallflower." Chuck opened the case and cradled a bottle of the gifted wine. "Maybe afterward, we can retire to my 'Cottage on the Lake' so you don't have to drive home compromised. Open one of these and wish Merry Christmas to your mom in heaven."

Claire stopped by the table. "Thank you, Charles. That was wonderfully heartfelt." She pecked Chuck on the cheek and whispered in his ear. "Save a dance for me." She blew him a kiss from the door before disappearing.

Chuck rolled his eyes. "And your assignment, dearest daughter, if I agree to be your date, is to keep that woman ten feet away from me."

"I thought Ms. Ottoman only went for well-to-do gentlemen."

"Rumor has it when she gets a few nips in her, it's any port in a storm."

Jenny giggled. "Deal." She wrapped her arms around her father's neck. "And I'll take you up on the offer for an after-event tipple of yours and Mom's Christmas wine."

Harold and Hagemeier's Christmas Ale

Christopher D. Ochs

In the mountains far to the north, there's a little town called You Are Lost. It's in the middle of nowhere—forty miles to the east is the nearest ski lodge, forty miles to the west is the closest lake fit for ice fishing, and fifty miles in any direction might get you to the nearest burgh. A rather nondescript little town, there's little to recommend it, except perhaps Hagemeier's Bar & Grille.

Like its hometown, Hagemeier's, too, is a quiet, unassuming inn—that is, until the month of December rolls around. That's when Hagemeier whips up his Christmas Ale. His old family recipe has been a closely guarded secret for generations, and justifiably so. Anyone who has ever partaken of the bubbling brew would be willing to declare on a stack of Bibles and their mother's grave that it is more delicious than any potent potable they have ever tasted, and almost as addictive as crack cocaine.

At least that's what the tourists from New York City would say.

So, anyone could certainly understand how ol' Hagemeier's Christmas Ale commands the heady price of thirty dollars a pony glass.

Hagemeier is an astute businessman to boot. He will dole out free samples of the spiced draft —a dram here, a shot glass there—knowing full well that he'll sell a full glass or more after each sampling. However, shrewd as he was, Hagemeier was no Scrooge. Each Friday evening in December, Hagemeier held a contest. The person who told the best story would be awarded a portion of the Christmas Ale. And depending on how much Mr. H liked the story, the prize would be a pony glass, a chalice, or even a pitcher of the coveted concoction.

Now, in the town of You Are Lost, lived a down-on-his-luck gent named Howard. Howard loved Hagemeier's Christmas Ale as much as the next person, though he was as poor as the proverbial church mouse. But he certainly wouldn't let something as petty as money get in the way of his portion of Christmas Ale. For you see, Howard was crafty—perennially strapped for cash, but still crafty.

And he had a plan.

The first Friday of December, the citizens of You Are Lost crowded into every nook and cranny of Hagemeier's Bar & Grille for the opening contest and a chance to win a free glass of Christmas Ale. To be sure, there were quite a few contestants. But all the nondescript people of this nondescript little burgh told nondescript little stories. So it was no surprise that Harold won that night's contest handily with his story—a tale how Rudolph the red-nosed reindeer was not Santa's first choice—rather it centered on the misadventures of Randolph the blue-nosed baboon.

Well, Harold's story only received a few chuckles, but compared to all the others, it was still the best in the house.

"Not bad, Harold. Not bad," said Hagemeier as he handed Harold his prize of a pony glass of the hearty ale.

Harold gulped down the glass in the blink of an eye, and immediately wanted more.

"Now, now, Harold. You know the rules. You got your prize. Come up with a better story next week, and there'll be a full chalice of Christmas Ale for you."

Nothing could have motivated Harold more. And sure enough, come the next Friday, Harold was the first through the door at Hagemeier's Bar & Grille. Just as the previous week, after all the nondescript people told their nondescript stories, Harold rollicked the room with his story—a ribald yarn about how Frosty the Snowman ran a gambling racket, but the police could never catch him, because every time the heat was on, Frosty . . . *liquidated* his assets.

Hagemeier clapped Harold on the back, chortling "Now *that* was a good story," and served him a full chalice of the magical Christmas Ale. Harold quaffed the chalice in two long gulps, and of course wanted more.

"Now, now, Harold. You know the rules. You got your prize. Come up with your best story next week, and there'll be a full pitcher of Christmas Ale for you."

And sure enough, the last Friday before Christmas, Harold was practically breaking down the door to be let into Hagemeier's establishment. Harold sat impatiently, twitching in his seat as all his tired old neighbors told the same tired old stories, hardly able to wait to tell his own.

Now, I'm sure everyone has heard the silly story about why an angel is on top of the Christmas tree. You know, the one where an annoying angel pestered Santa so much, that when he demanded to know where to stick the Christmas tree, Santa shoved it up his... well, you know the rest. However, what you don't know about that story is that Harold was the person who came up with that story, and this night was the first time that story was ever told.

Well, as you might guess, when Harold finished, the whole tavern was howling with laughter, shaking the dust off of the rafters at Hagemeier's Bar & Grille. Mr. H himself laughed so hard, he was crying.

When he finally caught his breath, Hagemeier wiped the tears from his face and poured out Harold's reward.

"That was the best story I've ever heard. Here ya go, Harold. You certainly earned this!" and Hagemeier handed Harold a chalice of Christmas Ale.

Harold was dumbfounded. "What? A single glass? You said if my story won, I'd win a whole pitcher of Christmas Ale!"

"That's true," said Hagemeier. "But I'm sorry, Harold. Your story was too short."

"Sorry?" Harold shouted. "Sorry ain't enough. You yourself said a minute ago it was the best story you've ever heard. Why don't I get the pitcher?"

"I don't like repeating myself, Harold. It was too short."

Harold was red in the face. "Too short? What does that have to do with anything?"

"C'mon, Harold," Hagmeier said with feigned patience. "Everyone knows a pitcher is worth a thousand words."

The Goblin King's Music Box

A. E. Decker

The Goblin King glared from his iron-and-glass throne. This sat atop a platform that took many high, filigreed steps to reach, so by the time his glare fell on Jazmeen, shivering at the stairs' foot, it was a very heavy glare indeed.

"Search her," he said.

His voice didn't echo. The white walls of the enormous but narrow hall didn't dare to bounce it back. Two of the tall and terrible people ranged along the side of the blue carpet that divided the hall, unfurling and unfurling until it vanished in a distant pinprick, stepped forward. Their stiff silvery clothes whisked soundlessly over the marble floor as they grabbed Jazmeen by the shoulders and rooted through the pockets of her My Little Pony robe.

Trembling, Jazmeen hugged Panda-panda close. The plush kitty had a rip in one seam, and she'd gone all floppy in the middle from much snuggling, but she smelled of lavender, and that was very comforting at the moment.

Jazmeen's right pocket crinkled. "Contraband!" cried one of the terrible people, pulling out a handful of pick-n-mix.

"Bring it here," the Goblin King commanded, gesturing.

Forlornly, Jazmeen watched the terrible person climb the stairs to the Goblin King's throne. Those candies had been a special treat for babysitting her four-year-old brother, Chad. She'd hoped to make them last until Christmas. One peppermint slipped free and bounced down the steps. Its little pings seemed to annoy the rangy, white-haired guard leaning against the wall behind the king's throne. Opening an eye, he grunted.

The Goblin King snatched the pick-n-mix. "Any sign of my music box?" he asked, spilling the candy into a colorful pool on his lap and stirring it with a finger.

"No, your Majesty," the terrible person replied, bowing themself down the steps.

Angry color flooded the Goblin King's sharp gray cheeks. Tapping his throne's arm, he glowered at Jazmeen. His silk shirt shimmered in the fretful blue light that shone through the hall's translucent walls. A great plush cloak, richly and indescribably red, flowed from his shoulders, embroidered with gold stars and whirling comets. Jazmeen thought it looked warm. All she had on were her pajamas and robe. A chill breeze circled the hall, smelling of ice cream left too long in the freezer. Her bare feet kept trying to cringe away from the marble floor. She stacked one on top of the other.

"Where did you hide my music box?" thundered the Goblin King.

The boom of his voice yanked back Jazmeen's braids and rippled the ranks of stiffly dressed people like so many dominos.

"What music box?" Jazmeen whispered when it passed. Her scalp tingled. "I haven't seen a music box."

The Goblin King's finger paused mid-tap. "Then, what are you doing here?" he asked irritably.

Panda-panda sagged in Jazmeen's grip.

She hadn't asked to come to the Goblin King's throne room. She'd been brought here, sweeping and crashing through the night, bare feet dangling, carried by an owl—a great gray owl that had come bursting through her window when she'd gotten out of bed to see what was making the funny hoo-ah-yoo noises.

She wished she was there now, safe in her familiar room with her desk and chair, her white bookshelf, and her bedside table with its tasseled shade. She could be snuggled under her pink quilt and dreaming of Christmas instead of shivering under the glare of the Goblin King's cold gray eyes with slitted pupils like a cat's.

"I don't know why I'm here," she said, giving Panda-panda another squeeze. "May I go home?"

"Go home? After stealing my music box?" The Goblin King's thin lips bent into a sneer. He toyed with a butterscotch. "I think not."

"But I didn't—"

THE GOBLIN KING'S MUSIC BOX

"Perhaps you require stronger persuasion." The Goblin King snapped his fingers, and one of the terrible people stepped forward and yanked Panda-panda from Jazmeen's arms.

"No!" she cried, but they tossed Panda-panda all the way up the steps to the rangy guard, who caught her without blinking and yawned.

The Goblin King gave a cruel, cold smile. "Now, tell me where my music box is."

"I don't know." Jazmeen sniffled back tears. She glanced over her shoulder, hoping to see one sympathetic face, or a single pretty picture on one of the bleak walls, but the hall just stretched on and on, seemingly without end, and all the eyes stared pitilessly. The high ceiling slanted to a wicked peak and little knobs like spinal bones ran down its center. Shivering, she turned back to the Goblin King. "Can't you get another one?" she asked, switching the position of her feet.

"Another one?" The Goblin King's face flushed to match his cloak.

A hiss raked the endless hall. The stiffly dressed people murmured behind their hands, shooting glares at Jazmeen that prickled her back.

"Another one?" repeated the Goblin King. He stood, spilling candies off his lap. His shadow fell, black and chilling, over Jazmeen. "My music box is made from tigers' pearls and the shells of deep-sea unicorns. It's magical."

Magic... magic... magic... The word bounced furiously against the walls, threw a brief tantrum on the carpet, then rose up into the rafters to sulk.

Having no Panda-panda to hug, Jazmeen wrapped her arms about herself and shivered.

The Goblin King plunked back into his iron-and-glass throne. "When you turn my box's golden key, it plays a melody that makes all food taste irresistibly delicious."

He snapped his fingers and a table with three legs and a ridiculously long neck came hurrying up the aisle from somewhere in the unseeable distance. It carried a round silver tray heaped with goodies: flaky rolls, creamy cheese, iced cakes dusted with sugar sprinkles, and pink-cheeked peaches whose scent made Jazmeen's mouth water as it clattered by. Hurrying up the filigreed steps, the table presented its offerings to the Goblin King.

"May as well be eating stones since you stole my music box," he said, regarding them with indifferent loathing. Shooing the table away, he bent to pick up a taffy.

The table trotted past Jazmeen, wafting its peachy aroma. Swallowing, she looked up at the platform. Behind the king's throne, the rangy guard waltzed with Panda-panda. "Perhaps you'd be hungry if you waited a bit," she suggested.

Snorting, the Goblin King unwrapped the taffy. "As for my box's silver key—"

"It has two keys?" said Jazmeen, forgetting she was scared. She'd never heard of such a thing.

The Goblin King eyed her severely. "As you well know, little thief." He crumpled the wrapper. "The silver key's melody that grants deep sleep and sweet dreams, and it is that same tune that Lady Fizzibit heard you humming three nights ago."

Three nights ago?

Jazmeen clapped a hand to her mouth. Three nights ago, her little brother, Chad, kept jumping on his bed instead of sleeping in it. Mom got exasperated and Daddy started to shout, so Jazmeen crept into Chad's room and hummed to him. As she hummed, she grew drowsy. So did Chad. Mom had laughed the next morning to come in and find them both asleep, heads nestled on the same pillow.

"I don't know where I heard it," she said.

The Goblin King looked up. He'd stretched the taffy between his fingers, seemingly enthralled by its purple color. "A confession? Good. Return my music box by dawn, and I won't turn you into a woolly hedgehog."

"But I don't—"

"Do you know why most hedgehogs have prickers? It's because they're delicious. Without prickers, they'd get gobbled up in a trice." He brought out his cruel smile. "Perhaps the sight of you will stir my appetite."

"But—"

Lips smacked. All along the carpet, the terrible people rubbed their bellies, eyes glittering. Jazmeen looked from them to the guard and Panda-panda and the Goblin King, playing with the taffy again.

She swallowed hard. "All right," she said. What else could she do? "May I have Panda-panda back, please?"

"No." The Goblin King swiped Panda-panda from the rangy guard with purple-sticky fingers. "She'll be my hostage. If you don't return, I'll make her into a hat to keep the boojums from flying into my ears."

Jazmeen's eyes burned. She dug her nails into her palms. She *wouldn't* burst into tears in front of all these terrible people. "I need to go home so I can look for the box."

The Goblin King regarded her blankly.

"How do I get out of here?" She cringed from the ceiling, afraid the owl might swoop down and grab her again.

Shrugging, the Goblin King flung a leg over an arm of his throne. His wonderful thick cloak flowed down to touch the platform, bright as cherries, as rubies, as strawberry jam. "I don't know," he said, dandling Panda-panda on his knee. "Drift will show you."

"Drift?" she asked.

The rangy guard ambled down the stairs. "Heigh-ho. I'm Drift," he said, poking a thumb towards his chest.

"He'll keep an eye on you," said the Goblin King. "If you try to run, he'll swallow you whole. He turns into a white bear. Don't you, Drift?"

Drift smiled lazily. He had a droll mouth, amiable brown eyes, and seemed to grow taller with every step. "A little snip like you wouldn't even touch the sides of my throat."

Jazmeen shrank back, but he swiped her up easily and flung her over his shoulder. "Out," he said.

The hall blurred. The terrible peoples' faces went all smeary, as if melting. The last thing Jazmeen saw was the Goblin King offering Panda-panda a flower sculpted from the purple taffy.

Then, fresh, pine-scented air swept away the old-freezer smell. "Put me down!" shouted Jazmeen, pounding Drift's arm.

"Are you sure, Snip?" Turning his head, he offered a grin. His teeth were quite pointed. "The ground's cold."

It did look cold, thought Jazmeen, staring down from his shoulder. Bumpy, too, and covered in shivering, gray-green moss with a dollhouse sitting in the middle of it. No; a doll *castle*, made of glass or ice. Fireflies in striped waistcoats hovered about its spires, playing doleful tunes on tiny violins.

"Wait—is that the Goblin King's castle?" asked Jazmeen. Impossible! All those people couldn't possibly fit inside—it was no higher than Drift's knee.

Drift shrugged, jouncing Jazmeen. "He says it is, and I don't care enough to debate the issue. Heigh-ho!" Yawning, he stepped over the castle, swinging Jazmeen in a careless manner. Her squeal cut off when she landed on something soft and moving and warm. So *warm*.

It was rabbit, a brown rabbit as large as a carousel horse. It turned its head to look at her in a friendly sort of way, nose wrinkling up and down. A five-pointed patch of fur spread between its eyes, white as a marshmallow.

"Oh!" cried Jazmeen, burying her feet in the rabbit's warm brown sides. Reaching forward, she stroked it between its ears.

"That's Star-sniffer," said Drift, climbing onto the back of a larger black rabbit. "This is Inky. They'll take us where we need to go, wherever that is."

Home, thought Jazmeen. She wanted to go home. Drift was big, but Daddy would chase him away, and then her parents would hug her and scold her and tuck her in her warm bed.

And the owl would come for her again, maybe. At the very least, Panda-panda would be gone; made into a hat to cover the Goblin King's ears.

She just had to find the music box. Then the Goblin King would return Panda-panda and leave her alone. But where had she heard the sleepy tune? Not at school; everyone would've fallen asleep, even Mr. Freeman, her teacher, who *never* stopped talking. Yesterday had been the very last day before Christmas break, and he'd just kept droning until she'd thought he'd never—

Christmas!

"My swing set," she cried, remembering. Three days ago, she'd been outside, sitting on the swing and looking at their yard. Her family had never had a yard before. Until this summer, they'd lived in an apartment.

But now they had their own yard, with a garden for Mom and a wood behind it filled with wonderful twisty old trees and wild black raspberry bushes. Cardinals came to visit, and even the occasional deer. All that was needed to make it perfect was snow. A Christmas snow, deep enough for snowman-building. That's what Jazmeen had been thinking about as she looked at the yard and swung.

And then . . . and then she'd fallen asleep, right there in the swing. Mom had to send Chad out to wake her for dinner.

"I must have heard the sleepy tune while I was swinging," she told Drift.

"Mm?" he said. "Well, then, just whisper where you want to go in Star-sniffer's ear, and she'll jump over the moon."

"Over the moon?" Jazmeen looked up. It had been cloudy at home. Here the sky was clear and bright and slightly violet-tinted. A perfectly round moon hung in the sky like a dinner plate; huge and glowing and very, very high above her.

"Yes," said Drift. "We used to use cows, but they don't jump so well as rabbits." He scratched his jaw lazily.

Over the moon. *It's better than being carried by an owl,* Jazmeen tried to convince herself. At least she couldn't be simply . . . dropped. But her palms felt suddenly damp, and Star-sniffer's back uncomfortably slick.

Taking a firm grip on Star-sniffer's brown fur, Jazmeen leaned forward. "Take me to my swing set," she whispered into a long ear.

The wind whooshed. At first, it seemed gentle. Then, it yanked on her braids and roared in her ears. Her bottom slid a couple inches toward Star-sniffer's rump. The Goblin King's already tiny castle shrank to a glassy mote.

Closing her eyes, Jazmeen clung with all her seven-year-old strength to those two handfuls of fur.

A salty, butter-sour scent rose up. At the same time, Jazmeen's braids went weightless, floating above her head. Cautiously, she cracked open one eye.

She glided through a silken black sky, freckled with faint, silvery stars. Inky and Drift sailed a few feet behind her. Drift was yawning again. A pink comet shot past, somersaulting over its own toes. Something below her glowed.

It was the moon. Its face, pockmarked by craters, seemed to smile back at her. Kangaroo-like creatures with big, round ears and long, tufted tails bounded over its creamy yellow plains, nibbling at its cheese. They were so close that if she'd dared, she could've jumped off Star-sniffer's side and joined them.

What did moon cheese taste like?

Before she could quite work up the nerve, Star-sniffer cleared the moon. Beyond it, a tiny blue-and-green marble spun in a black void.

It started growing larger. Very quickly. The wind took hold of Jazmeen's braids again. She shut her eyes.

Crunch! Jazmeen almost shot off Star-sniffer's back, but her hands couldn't unclench fast enough, so she only rose up a couple inches before bouncing back down. In that time, she realized that she wasn't flying anymore. Also, it hadn't been a scary kind of crunch. More a crispy one; like Star-sniffer had landed on a bag of chips.

The air smelled familiar. Mud. Burning leaves. A hint of barbecued chicken.

She opened her eyes.

She was home, in her own yard, beside her swing set. The trees beyond the chain-link fence creaked in the chilly breeze. She'd never been out so late before. Her family's little blue house looked gray and powdery in the dim glow of the streetlamps out front. Its windows were glossy black sheets. Mom and Daddy must've gone to bed. If she shouted for them, would they hear her?

The frosty grass crunched again as Inky landed nearby. "Don't think it, Snip," said Drift, seeing the direction of her gaze. He slid off Inky's back and yawned. "I'll have to make an effort to stop you, and that'll annoy me. Heigh-ho, I'm tired! Yesterday, I was awake for five whole hours. It was most unkind of you to steal the music box."

"I didn't steal it," said Jazmeen, but Drift just sauntered to her swing set and began scratching his back against its angled pole.

Not knowing what else to do, Jazmeen sat on the swing. Its cold chains hurt her hands, but at least she could let her feet dangle instead of touching the icy ground. She began to swing slowly, as she had been doing three days ago. Where could the melody have come from? She'd been alone in the yard. The Jacksons next door had gone to visit family over the Christmas vacation. There was nothing nearby save the woods behind her, and the flowering quince bush by the fence.

Jazmeen stopped swinging. Now that she thought about it, she was almost certain that when she'd fallen asleep, her head had drooped to the left, in the direction of the quince bush.

She got off the swing.

"Did you remember where you hid the box, Snip?" asked Drift.

Ignoring him, she went to the bush. Daddy had dug it up when he installed the fence. He was going to put it out for the garbageman, but Mom told him to replant it because they grew pretty pink blossoms in the spring. Right now, it was just a tangled bundle of dark stems.

"Oh, a quince bush," said Drift, still rubbing against the swing set and making no effort to help at all. "I like quince tarts. Or I did before you stole the music box and made everything taste bland."

Jazmeen decided to ignore that, too. Minding the thorns, she poked through the bush, carefully untangling branches.

Gold flashed.

"Hey—"

That was all Jazmeen managed before an angrily buzzing thing shot from the bush and into her face. She stumbled back, tripped over Drift's foot, and landed hard on her palms.

"Back!" screamed the buzzing thing, whirling around Jazmeen's head. She couldn't tell if it was a little person or a large dragonfly. It was greenish and resembled something of both. Its wings were like a pair of curling brown leaves, and two long, feathery antennae topped its head.

"Back, or I hex you," it continued, swooping down to yank one of Jazmeen's braids. Its voice was a shrill whine, punctuated by clicks.

Drift stopped scratching. "What do you know? A fairy."

"A fairy?" said Jazmeen. This was a fairy? How disappointing! It didn't sparkle at all. She got up, swatting at the little creature. "Did you steal the Goblin King's music box?"

The fairy hovered defensively in front of the bush.

"We box need!" cried a second, shriller voice. Another fairy flew from the quince's branches. This one's head was covered in fuzzy spikes. It cradled a small bundle wrapped in dried rose petals.

Drift peeled himself off the swing set. "Thieving little beasts. Why are you awake at this time of year?" He ambled forward. "I'll swallow you, bush and all."

He'd almost reached the bush when it hit Jazmeen: *he actually means it.* "No!" she cried, throwing herself in his way. The fairies may have stolen the box, but she wasn't going to watch them get *eaten.* "They'll give it back. You'll give it back, won't you?" she asked the fairies over her shoulder.

"No!" shouted the fairy with the antennae.

"Can't," said the fairy with the soft spikes. "Dreadful cold metal bang-split our home. Daughter hurt bad. See?"

It flew forward, holding out the bundle it carried. Jazmeen looked. The petals wrapped another fairy, one no larger than her little finger. It was shivering. The edge of the brown wing sticking out from the petal-wrappings was as tattered as old cloth.

Oh. Oh, no. Suddenly, Jazmeen understood. Her hand flew to her mouth. This was a mama and daddy fairy, and the cold metal that had broken up their home and hurt their daughter—

Daddy's fence. The fence he'd decided to install after she'd gone wandering in the woods for hours and not heard Mom calling her in to supper.

"In spring, nectar we could gather," said the fairy with the antennae—the daddy fairy, Jazmeen guessed. He perched on a branch of the quince. "Now, only acorns. Bitter. Daughter no can eat without music to make them sweet. Can no sleep without box-song."

The tiny fairy opened her faceted eyes. They were the color of lilacs, Mom's favorite flower.

"Heigh-ho, this is boring me." Drift yawned, scratching against the swing set. "You don't want me to swallow them? I'll just pull the bush apart. You grab the box."

"No." Jazmeen kept herself between him and the bush. This was her fault. If she hadn't gone wandering in the woods, Daddy wouldn't have built the fence, and the little fairy wouldn't have gotten hurt.

Could she maybe go to the Goblin King and explain that the fairies needed to borrow his music box until spring? No—he wouldn't listen, and all the stiffly dressed people would just murmur and disapprove until she ended up getting blamed for ... for ...

Well, she didn't know for what. Littering his floor with candy wrappers, maybe—candies he'd stolen from her. Still stinging over the loss of her pick-n-mix, she thrust her hand into her pocket and discovered that one remained, wedged into its corner. She drew it out. A caramel with a sugar center—one of her favorites.

"Snip?" said Drift.

Jazmeen quickly stuffed the caramel back in her pocket before he could see it and take it. "Is there anything else that might help your daughter?" she asked the fairies.

They exchanged a glance. "Snow spider silk," said the mother fairy. "It be cool. Wrap wing, soothe daughter's pain. She sleep until spring. Mend."

"Snow spider silk?" Drift laughed. "Heigh-ho! May as well ask for black sunbeams, or rooster's eggs. The king's been wanting a snow spider silk cape for keeping cool in the summer, but no one's dared ascend to the clouds and gather any."

There were spiders living in the clouds? Cringing, Jazmeen glanced up at the thin film of clouds spread across the night sky. What if one dropped down? It was bad enough when one ran across the ceiling, all fast and creepy with too many legs.

The tiny fairy's lilac eyes closed. She shivered in her petal wrappings.

Jazmeen chewed her lip. Then, stiff grass crackling under her cold feet, she walked over to Star-sniffer.

Drift paused in his scratching. "Where are you going, Snip? Don't make me chase you."

Jazmeen climbed onto Star-sniffer's back. "Take me to the clouds," she whispered, wrapping her arms around the rabbit's neck.

"Snip!" shouted Drift, but Star-sniffer had already jumped.

It was worse than the journey over the moon. The wind howled instead of whooshing, biting at Jazmeen's ears. She kept her eyes open as Star-sniffer shot straight up into a cloud as soggy and heavy as a piece of wadded felt. Everything went gray. The cloud hugged her like a soaked blanket. She tried wiping her face, but her sleeve was as wet as her skin.

Her teeth had just begun chattering when Star-sniffer burst out of the damp grayness. Trailing a few clinging wisps, she sailed into a black diamond sky before descending in a gentle arc and landing with a series of bounces on the soft white surface below.

Jazmeen shook out her robe. All the moisture it had collected broke into powdery dust, like frost, and drifted to the ground so she was dry again. The land of the clouds was not what she'd imagined. It resembled a field dotted with crystalline stones and clusters of silvery, bell-shaped flowers. Feathery white grass covered the gently rolling hills. Star-sniffer tentatively stretched out her neck to nibble at it. After the first taste, her ears gave a delighted twist. She hunkered down for more serious grazing.

Giving her a pat, Jazmeen slid to the fluffy white ground, which was as bouncy and cool as cotton balls left in a refrigerator. She didn't see any spiders. Where did they live? And—

She gulped. How big were they? She hadn't asked, but if everyone was too scared to come to the clouds to collect their silk . . .

Maybe they were as big as a person. Or bigger. Perhaps they had long, clicking fangs and drooled poison. Maybe—

A bubble swelled in the ground to her left. An instant later, it burst, and Inky erupted from it, Drift clinging to his fur. Like Star-sniffer, Inky sailed a distance into the sky before landing in a series of springs.

Drift leapt off Inky's back. "You ran away," he said. The words emerged in a snarl. His face lengthened. He reached for Jazmeen with a clawed hand.

He *was* turning into a white bear! *You won't even touch the sides of my throat,* he'd said.

Shrieking, Jazmeen bolted. Maybe she only imagined his breath heating the back of her neck. She didn't dare turn and look. Bellflowers chimed as she brushed against them. Fists pumping at her sides, she bounded over the spongy ground, searching for a crack where she could wedge herself out of his reach.

A rock hidden by the feathery grass turned under her numb foot. Shrieking again, she tumbled, rolling over the soft surface until she fetched up with a bump against a faceted crystal rock.

Her legs were tangled in her robe. She couldn't run. Flinging her arm over her head, she closed her eyes so she wouldn't see Drift's jaws gaping to swallow her.

Christmas, she thought. *Snow. Daddy.*
Mommy! Mommy! Mommy! She wanted her mommy.

Drift whimpered.

Whimpered? Not... not growled, or snarled, or...

He did it again. Cautiously, Jazmeen cracked open an eye.

Drift was a bear. A huge white bear, with a shaggy coat and paws bigger than her head. He stood right over her, trembling until his fur rattled, brown eyes fixed on something behind her. From the way he whined, it had to be something dreadful.

Very slowly, Jazmeen turned.

A spider sat atop the crystal rock.

Jazmeen yelped, scooting back so fast she bumped up against Drift's front legs.

Spider. Spider, spider, spider. Spider!

The snow spider—it had to be a snow spider—looked at her with four enormous, glossy eyes set all in a row. Gray tufts stuck out from its head like whiskers, and its body was white and fuzzy. Two stubby limbs below its eyes twitched as it stared at Jazmeen. Was it thinking of pouncing on her? She shuddered. It was huge! As big as—

As—

Jazmeen folded her fingers into a fist and lifted it. It was the exact same size as the spider. Big, yes, for a spider, but not the monster she'd imagined.

Drift whined again. He was scared of the spider? What a coward! He could crush it with a flick of his paw.

So could she, she realized.

Inching forward, she raised her hand. The spider regarded her with those glossy eyes. She must've seemed almost mountain-sized to it—certainly bigger than Drift was in comparison to her—and yet it seemed more curious than scared. It certainly wasn't whining and shaking, like Drift was.

It really was very fuzzy. Jazmeen hesitated, then lowered her hand, ashamed of herself. This was the spider's home. What right did she have to come here and shriek at it and attempt to kill it? Especially when she wanted its silk.

Even so, she had to work up her nerve to reach out. "Please don't bite me," she whispered.

Pop! The snow spider jumped back just before she touched it. Jazmeen jumped, too, but she also had to laugh because the movement had been so sudden and silly, like a cap flying off a soda bottle.

"I won't hurt you," she said, crouching in front of the rock. The spider's little limbs twitched, but it didn't move closer. A strand of silk, glittering like Christmas tinsel, extended from its bottom to the rock. When she reached out again, it scuttled back.

How to make the snow spider trust her? She didn't have any bugs to offer it, if snow spiders ate bugs.

She had a caramel. She brought it out, unwrapped it, and balanced it on her fingertips. "Try this," she whispered, holding it forward.

The snow spider crept forward, fuzzy limbs working. The candy seemed to intrigue it. Behind her, Drift let out a moan.

All at once, the spider pounced. Jazmeen flinched as its legs tickled her skin. For an instant, she was certain it meant to bite her. Instead, it sank its fangs into the caramel's sugar center.

Jazmeen smiled. "I always eat the center first, too." Close up, the snow spider smelled of the candy canes they'd hung on their Christmas tree. It clung to her hand, contentedly sucking sugar, as she stood. "How much silk do we need?" she asked Drift.

He made a noise. Not a growl; something between a grunt and a mumble. She turned, and there he was, back in person shape, sitting on the ground and staring at her wide-eyed. "You tamed a snow spider," he said.

"Is this enough silk?" she asked, winding the strand around her finger.

"For what?"

"The fairies." Had he forgotten?

He shrugged.

Giving up on his help, Jazmeen started walking to where Star-sniffer and Inky were nibbling the feathery grass. "We'll let them decide how much they need."

"Yes, the king will be happy to get his cloak at last," said Drift.

Jazmeen stopped. "Cloak?" she asked.

Getting up, Drift stretched. "Yes, his cooling cloak. Or was it a jacket? Heigh-ho, I forget. I suppose he can have both now that you've tamed a snow spider."

"We have to take the snow spider to the fairies, so they can mend their daughter's wing," said Jazmeen.

Drift stared blankly at her.

"And then they'll return the king's music box?" she prompted.

"Oh, yes, the box." Drift took her arm. "I can fetch that. You take the snow spider to the king, like you promised."

Jazmeen stopped. Drift tried to pull her along, but she planted her feet.

She had *not* promised to take the snow spider to the Goblin King. And, she'd had just about enough of this silliness. When Drift tugged her arm again, she spun, thrusting the snow spider into his face. He yelped and stumbled back. Twisting free of his grip, Jazmeen ran to Star-sniffer and clambered onto her back.

"Take me to the quince bush," Jazmeen whispered in her ear.

Still chewing a mouthful of feathery grass, Star-sniffer jumped, coming down hard on her strong hind legs. The cloudy ground broke beneath them. For a moment, all was damp grayness again, but they passed swiftly through the moist layer into clear sky. Houses and streets spread out below them, tiny as a model train's neighborhood, and gleaming pink in the first flush of dawn.

Dawn? Oh, no! The Goblin King would turn Panda-panda into a hat if she didn't bring his box back soon.

But she didn't need to beg Star-sniffer to hurry. Already the tiny houses were swelling into their proper size. She could recognize her street, and the local park, and even make out her red swing set in the corner of her yard a few seconds before Star-sniffer landed beside it.

Jazmeen tumbled off Star-sniffer's back, carrying the snow-spider carefully. "Hello?" she called.

The fairies flew out of the quince bush. "You—with snow spider!" exclaimed the daddy fairy.

The snow spider dropped the caramel and spun in her palm, little limbs twitching. "It's okay," said Jazmeen, touching it to soothe it. Its fuzz felt as soft as plush laid over smooth glass, but her finger came away wet.

"Too warm here for snow spider," said the mama fairy. "They in sky belong."

THE GOBLIN KING'S MUSIC BOX

The snow spider spun again. Its four big, glossy eyes stared at her pleadingly. "I'm sorry!" cried Jazmeen. She'd never meant to hurt it. She placed it on the cool pebbles under the swing set, hoping that would help, but water kept dripping from the spider's body. "Hurry and collect the silk," she said.

The fairies flew to the spider's rear and began unwinding a thread of shimmering silk. Jazmeen looked towards the house. Had Daddy locked the back door? If he hadn't, perhaps she could run in and fetch ice cubes from the freezer.

The night air swished. A spot blacker than the now decidedly gray sky broke from the clouds and began descending. Inky, undoubtedly carrying Drift.

"Please, give me the box now," Jazmeen cried to the fairies.

They'd already managed to wind a thumbnail-sized ball of silk. Snipping it free of the snow spider's rear, they carried it to the quince bush and returned lugging the box between them, all pearly-gold and shimmering. Jazmeen took it and shoved it into her pocket.

Thump! Inky's landing shook the yard.

"Do you have enough silk?" asked Jazmeen.

The mama fairy nodded. "Two-three times enough. Much thanks."

Drift vaulted off Inky's back. Jazmeen didn't dare wait longer. Scooping up both the snow spider and the remains of the caramel, she deposited them on Star-sniffer's back. "Thanks," she told the snow spider, petting it a final time.

Frosty grass crunched under Drift's stride. Jazmeen leaned over Star-sniffer's head. "Return to the clouds," she whispered.

Drift's big hand fell on Jazmeen's shoulder, but he was too late. Star-sniffer jumped. Jazmeen watched the brown form with the small white one clinging to it rise up and up until they were lost in the clouds.

There'd be no one to whisper in Star-sniffer's ear and command her to return. She could wander the clouds' fields, nibbling the feathery grass, forever free.

"What a nuisance you are, Snip," growled Drift.

"I have the box," she said before he could threaten to swallow her, or even yawn again.

With a grunt, Drift tossed her across Inky's shoulders. "To the Goblin King's castle," he said, climbing up behind her.

The wind whooshed. Belly-down over Inky's neck, Jazmeen watched the moon sail by beneath her, glowing less brightly than before. Blue veins streaked its surface, and the cheese-smell rolling off it was stronger, with a hint of foot. Maybe it aged overnight. Whatever the reason, she didn't want to taste it anymore.

Inky passed over the moon and dropped beside the Goblin King's glassy castle. Jazmeen gratefully breathed the clearing's piney scent. The fireflies in waistcoats still circled the castle's walls, but they'd switched to playing accordions.

"Get in," said Drift, tipping back one of the castle's tower caps, which tilted like it was on hinges. Drift picked Jazmeen up and dropped her into the tubelike opening. She squeaked as she slid through, but found herself landing quite safely on the blue carpet at the foot of the Goblin King's throne a moment later.

"Oh, you're back," said the Goblin King, as if she were an uninvited guest. Panda-panda sat on his knee. Unwrapped pick-n-mix littered the platform. It appeared he'd sucked each once and tossed it away.

Drift landed with a soft thump behind Jazmeen. "She was no use at all, Your Majesty," he said, climbing up the stairs and yawning every step. "She ran away twice. She consorted with thieves. She tamed the snow spider as you commanded, and then deliberately lost it, along with a valuable riding rabbit. Furthermore, I suspect her of being very small, and therefore of little use. Heigh-ho!"

The stiffly dressed people murmured their outrage as Drift again slouched against the wall behind the Goblin King's throne. Clutching the arms of his throne, the Goblin King glowered at Jazmeen. A few of the stars embroidered on his splendidly red cloak winked angrily.

"I have your music box," said Jazmeen, pulling the awkward lump from her pocket. A knob on its lid, shaped like a rosebud, caught on a thread before she worked it free and held it out. She'd never really had a chance to look at it before. Its curving shape, like a cashew nut, fit smoothly in her paired palms. Even the walls' sulky bluish light couldn't dull its pearly-gold sheen, or the brightness of the spiral patterns on its sides picked out in pink and orange gemstones. Three keys stuck out of its back: one gold, one silver, and one glass.

The Goblin King's gaze passed coldly over the music box. "You think to bribe me?" he demanded. "Well, I won't forgive you for losing my snow spider. I command you to fetch it back before nightfall, or I'll turn you into a three-legged snake. Do you know why—"

THE GOBLIN KING'S MUSIC BOX

Jazmeen was staring at the box. Three keys. The Goblin King had only mentioned two. "What melody does the glass key play?" she asked.

A furrow appeared between the Goblin King's arched brows. "What? I don't know. Something boring. Don't interrupt me. I want you to go clean the beach. It's awful. Someone's left sand all over it."

As the Goblin King spoke, Jazmeen wound the glass key. When it could turn no further, she lifted the box's lid.

Music spilled out, the clearest music Jazmeen had ever heard. Each note chimed like it had been struck from a great crystal bell. The melody rushed into her ears and scrubbed out her head. Her thoughts tumbled into orderly lines.

"I didn't take your box," she said. "It wasn't my fault."

Nor was it her fault that Daddy had built the fence—nor his that the little fairy had gotten hurt. He couldn't have known about the quince bush. People made mistakes all the time. Wasn't it more important to fix them than to figure out who was to blame?

The melody kept playing, cascading along the long white hall, leaving a clean scent of limes and rainwater in its wake. Rubbing their eyes, the stiffly dressed people looked at each other in wonder. Up on the platform, the Goblin King hunched his shoulders and shook his head, but the music couldn't be dislodged so easily. Jazmeen could see it washing out his brain. Drift pushed off the wall, no longer yawning.

With a soft click, the clear notes faded, but the crisp, shining feeling they'd brought to the air lingered. The Goblin King sat straighter in his throne. "I haven't heard that tune in years," he murmured, massaging his brow.

"I can tell," Jazmeen replied.

The gold key made food tasty. The silver key made sleep come easily. The glass key made people *think*. The Goblin King and his court certainly hadn't been doing much of that recently!

The Goblin King looked from Panda-panda, balanced on the arm of his throne with a cup of tea between her paws, to the pick-n-mix scattered about the platform around his feet. "I've been rather ridiculous, haven't I?"

"Yes." Jazmeen set the music box on the steps. "You should turn the glass key more often." Then she reconsidered. "No. You should learn to think on your own because sometimes things get lost."

Drift came down the stairs. A new alertness banished the lazy vagueness from his face. "Sorry, Snip." He scratched behind his ear, stooped for the box, and turned it over in his hands. "I, um, I wouldn't really have swallowed you."

He probably would have—thoughtlessly. But he hadn't, and he really looked quite sorry and remorseful.

"Get some sleep," she told him. "And think it over when you wake up."

The corner of his lips lifted. She tried to smile back, but a sudden, overwhelming need to yawn gaped her mouth wide. "Can I have Panda-panda back, please?" she asked, covering it.

The Goblin King tossed Panda-panda down. Drift caught her and handed her to Jazmeen. She seemed less floppy about the middle than before and stuffing no longer poked from her torn seam.

Her yellow eyes sparkled when Jazmeen looked into them. But it was only the sparkle of glass. They didn't look back at Jazmeen, all black and glossy and alive with curiosity. She buried her nose in Panda-panda's plush fur. Lavender; homey and comforting.

But she missed the smell of candy canes.

She hugged Panda-panda anyway. "I'm ready to go home," she said. Past ready—it was becoming a struggle to keep her eyes open, and her feet were still cold. If she thought too hard about her warm bed, she'd cry, and even though the Goblin King seemed nicer now, she still didn't want to weep in front of him.

"Um," said The Goblin King. He fiddled with a fold of his robe. "Are you sure? You could stay and be Mistress of Spiders. You could have a medal, and a ceremonial robe, and cakes."

The table with the long, tippy neck came hurrying up the blue carpet again and stopped before Jazmeen with a bow that threatened to spill the goodies off its top. She couldn't help but look a little longingly at the cakes. Their creamy frosting had to be heaped at least three inches high.

"No, thank you," she said. "The snow spider wouldn't be happy living here, and I wouldn't either."

The Goblin King's face briefly darkened. His finger began to tap. Then, with a sigh, his shoulders slumped. "Very well." He beckoned the table forward and took a peach from its tray. He looked at the music box, and for a moment, Jazmeen thought he'd command Drift to turn the gold key.

Instead, he bit into the peach. "I suppose I should learn to eat without listening to the tune," he said through the mouthful.

Jazmeen nodded.

"It tastes better with music, though," he added.

Well, she supposed she shouldn't expect him to change instantly. She yawned again.

"Time to go, Snip." Drift lifted her. Cuddling Panda-panda, she wiggled her toes, half-wondering if they were still attached to her feet. The air whisked and cooled, exchanging its limy smell for one of pine.

She was outside again, she realized. With a small effort, she opened her eyes to a darkly pink sky. Inky waited patiently beside the Goblin King's castle, shooing away the drowsy fireflies with flicks of his long ears. Drift set her on his back.

"I didn't say goodbye," murmured Jazmeen, burrowing her feet into Inky's fur.

"We never say goodbye," said Drift. "Heigh-ho! Not unless we don't want to see a person again. Don't you want to see us again, Snip?"

Did she? The Goblin King had been rude and silly. He'd sent an owl to yank her out of bed and stolen her pick-n-mix. He could at least have given her a thank-you present after she found his box for him. And Drift had nearly *swallowed* her!

But . . .

Star-sniffer.

The big, glowing moon sailing beneath her.

The fairies, with their curled, brown wings.

The snow spider.

The snow spider.

Jazmeen's eyes fluttered closed. Her head was drooping. But she was pretty sure she whispered a reply.

She thought it might be "Yes."

*

Jazmeen sat up. Her pink quilt slid off her shoulders, revealing Panda-panda, snuggled by her hip. She looked around. All the familiar objects of her room sat just where they should: her desk with its chair, her white bookshelf, her bedside table with its tasseled shade. The curtains shielding her window tinted the hazy light shining through it pink, but didn't muffle the funny sound coming from its other side.

Jazmeen stiffened. She held her breath, listening, but it wasn't the *hoo-ah-yoo* noise from her maybe-dream. This was soft and feathery, like something was gently brushing against the glass.

Picking up Panda-panda, Jazmeen looked into her yellow eyes. "Should we go see what it is?" she asked.

Of course, Panda-panda didn't reply. Jazmeen fingered her mended seam. It *had* been torn, hadn't it?

The feathery sound stroked the window again. Jazmeen hesitated a moment longer, then threw off the covers.

Her feet touched her floor with a soft hush. Surprised, she glanced down.

She was wearing red socks—gloriously, indescribably red socks. Golden stars twinkled on her ankles and a comet sailed over her toes.

Her feet were warm. They stayed warm as she crossed to the window. They stayed warm when she pulled back her pink curtains and shrieked to see snow falling from the sky in lacy puffs. They stayed warm as she stood watching the snow collect on the trees' branches and turn her yard into a smooth, white sweep. Covered in tiny crystals, the quince bush resembled a bride's umbrella.

Curling her toes in her new, plush socks, Jazmeen hugged Panda-panda for pure joy. "A proper Christmas snow," she whispered.

She couldn't wait to go outside and play in it. But she wouldn't make a snowman after all.

She'd build a snow spider instead.

New Year's Eve
December 31st

The Star of the Party

Paula Gail Benson

To be an Eve on New Year's Eve is truly special. This year more than most.

Eve had just gotten out of her SUV with her wardrobe bag slung across one arm and her shoulder bag secured on the other. She looked up at the building. A green canopy made to resemble the fronds of a palm tree hung over the entrance of the Fountain of Youth Day Spa. An upgrade from Eve's previous visit to the spa when the business was under another name and management. Eve had received a flyer in the mail offering a discount on a new treatment: the Complete Body Holiday Party Prep. When she called to make an appointment, she was greeted warmly as a former client and told she needed to bring only her outfit, the salon would take care of the rest.

She had chosen a stunning dress. Rob wouldn't be able to resist her in it. Once she entered the room, his eyes would link with hers and he would be drawn to her side. Any thoughts about Brigette would be wiped from his mind.

Brigette. The hostess for the New Year's Eve party and the bane of Eve's existence.

All through school, jobs, marriages, and changes in social status—they had competed. Over grades, praise, cheerleader positions, roles in plays, pay raises, volunteer positions with the Junior League, and, of course, men.

But this time Brigette had gone too far.

After her nasty divorce, Eve sought out new experiences with potential for male companionship. Thinking she might travel, she enrolled in the Spanish conversation class at the local technical college. She dropped the course following the first class when she discovered it populated with balding, middle-aged, divorced men trolling for twenty somethings. Next, she switched to photography and found Rob—at least ten years younger, tall, wavy dark curls, a bewitching smile, and eyes that made you feel as if you could take a swim in their chocolate richness.

Rob was just the boost she needed. He became her photo buddy. They went on walks through the town, finding unique places to take shots, all the time discussing the future. Him talking about starting his own studio and her suggesting maybe she could be his partner. Financially and otherwise.

Then, one day, they sat having coffee at Starbucks when Brigette appeared in the doorway, backlit by the sun, as if a golden glow surrounded her body. Rob seemed transfixed by her image, stopping mid-sentence just to stare at her.

Brigitte rushed to their table, taking a moment to gush over Eve, before turning her full attention to Rob, who had stood and gestured toward an empty chair. Within moments, the two of them had huddled together, her head inches away from his, her rapt attentiveness focused upon him. His life story and skill as a photographer fascinated her. Almost as if she cast a spell over him, she had him agreeing to help her with a benefit. Her concentration enveloped him and suddenly she became his best bud, without him giving even a backward glance to Eve.

Well, Eve intended to fix that situation by stealing him back at Brigette's New Year's Eve party tonight. The flyer indicated that the Complete Body Holiday Party Prep Package offered by the Fountain of Youth Spa provided full body facials, hair styling, and nail and make-up treatments. "Walk in one age and leave as young as you want to be" was the Spa's advertised promise. She made an appointment for six p.m. The party began at nine p.m.

She entered the lobby and noticed another renovation by the current owners. Gone were all the products that customers were urged to purchase. Instead, the space was clear and clean with a fountain in the center. Beside the fountain was a table with cups.

"Won't you have a sip of one of our waters?" the woman sitting behind the registration desk asked. "Each spout of the fountain has a different variety."

Eve wrinkled her nose. "No, thank you."

The woman came from around the desk and reached for a cup. She considered the sprays coming from each spout, selected one, filled a cup, and held it out for Eve. "I know. It may seem a little unconventional, but I assure you it's very refreshing. We find it helps to get our customers in the mood for their services."

Eve took the cup and handed her wardrobe bag to the woman. She looked at the liquid and saw a citrus-looking pulp floating in swirls.

"Our own special blend," the woman said. "We believe it's best to start the rejuvenating process from within. Please try it and let me know what you think."

Reluctantly, Eve took a sip. The bitter pulp stuck on her tongue and in her throat.

"Interesting," she replied, putting the cup on the table. "But I prefer plain water."

"Of course." The woman reached for another cup and filled it from another spout of the fountain. She handed it to Eve.

Eve would have preferred not to drink, but the pulp had begun to feel irritating. She needed something to wash it down, so she took another cautious sip. This liquid tasted like water and helped her clear her mouth and throat.

The woman directed her to a room where she could disrobe. When the woman left, Eve noticed a vase in the corner, full of artistically arranged twigs. She recognized it as a remnant from the previous management—one Eve suggested the owner throw way. No woman coming for a moisturizing spa treatment wanted to see a dried-up bunch of twigs as part of the decor. Eve discarded her cup's remaining fluid into the twigs' container.

During Eve's nasty divorce, Brigette suggested they plan a spa day together. Once Rob entered the picture, Brigette made it clear that any double bookings would have Rob on the massage table next to her.

Eve smirked at the fluffy robe hanging from the hook on the back of the door. She took off her clothes and admired her sleek body in the full-length mirror.

Brigette, eat your heart out. And Rob, you can nibble on me.

Eve noticed the vase with the twigs reflected in the mirror. She glanced at it and, for a moment, thought she saw buds opening on the twigs. She turned to look at the vase directly and decided it had been a trick of the darkened lighting.

The massage table had been tightly wrapped, like swaddling for a baby. She gently slipped the top cover a few inches so she could slide between the sheets. The warming blanket made her feel safe, secure, and protected. This must be how it felt to be tucked into a crib.

The stylist entered. "My name is Linda," she said.

"Hello, Linda," Eve said dreamily. She had positioned herself facedown and tilted her head slightly to see the stylist. She had learned in Spanish class that "linda" meant "pretty." Surprisingly, this Linda was stocky and had a face that showed the ravages of acne, despite the woman's mature years.

Eve wondered why Linda wasn't beautiful. If by no other means, the fountain should have provided some rejuvenating factors. Eve felt justified in not relying on the waters.

"Have you had a spa treatment before?" Linda asked.

"Yes. Many times."

"Do you have any allergies I should be aware of?"

"None."

"Any expectations?"

Eve thought for a moment. "To be the star of the party. Smooth, sweet-smelling skin. Moist lips and no wrinkles. Tight around the chin and neck. I read that's what this treatment does."

Linda nodded while coating her hands with oil. Her hands felt soft and flexible as they kneaded Eve's shoulders. "The treatment can be very effective. How young do you want to look?"

"Like the youngest person in the room."

A small, sweet smile emerged on Linda's face. "I was hoping you might say that."

Linda explained every step of the process to Eve. The gentle massage seemed to lift the wrinkles from Eve's face. The alternately warm and cool towels tightened the skin beneath her chin.

The thorough and invigorating stroking of her flesh made Eve feel floaty, an out of body experience. She could sense herself shrinking beneath Linda's capable hands.

When Linda ran her fingers through Eve's hair and began to caress her scalp, Eve called a halt to the process.

"I need for my hair to look good. It almost feels like you're lifting it from my head."

"You're scheduled with the salon as soon as we finish. Relax."

Eve did. She gave herself over completely to Linda's ministrations. She felt herself falling asleep. When she woke, she heard Linda talking with someone else.

"I hope you're pleased with my work," Linda said.

"Absolutely," she heard Brigette reply. "Now, Eve, don't you worry. I'm picking up the tab, including a hefty tip for Linda."

Eve couldn't speak. She could think and hear, but her vision was blurry. She felt herself being lifted. How could Brigette manage that by herself?

Eve's eyes adjusted to the light. Brigette had Eve's garment bag across her arm while Linda held Eve up to a mirror.

"See your transformation for yourself, darling Eve," Brigette said.

Eve saw an infant in a diaper. Linda's finger traced a headband attached to the baby's head. In the center of the bow, it had a button with the date of the new year.

"Now you have your wish, Eve. You'll be the New Year's baby. And when you arrive at midnight, I'll be kissing Rob."

Eve heard a loud wail. She didn't realize it was coming from her mouth until Linda placed her in the arms of a very old man with a long white beard wearing a shimmering robe.

Ringing In the New Year

Peter J Barbour

I stared at Madison as she perused the menu. She turned to me, but I averted my eyes and suppressed a nervous laugh. *Try not to act silly. She'll be suspicious.*

The waitress arrived to take everyone's order. Ten of us sat around the table, old friends through high school, home from college, each with a date. One of my buddies, Mike, brought my younger sister, Sophie.

"Nice restaurant, Jonah," Madison said to me as she touched my arm. "I'm so glad I cut short my vacation in Miami with my parents so I could be with you."

"Only the best for tonight," I said. "Cloth napkins, and tablecloths, two forks, and flowers on the table. I just hope the service isn't too slow. After all, it is New Year's Eve."

"Are you in a hurry? We have the whole evening. I'm just happy to be here."

"No rush," I responded, but in truth, I couldn't wait until midnight. "Judging by the fragrances coming from the kitchen, the food should be good." I tilted my head back and took an exaggerated sniff. "Roasted rosemary, a hint of garlic, sautéed onions, and fresh bread." Sophie kicked me under the table, no doubt questioning my olfactory acumen and whether I had any idea what I was talking about.

Low lights, a wandering troubadour with his violin, table candles, and the tinkle of ice on glass by the bar created a sophisticated, cool, laid back, relaxed atmosphere. Except I wasn't relaxed.

"What are you going to order?" I asked Madison, struggling to speak in a comfortable, normal voice while hiding my excitement.

"I think I'll have the chicken Marsala, maybe over spinach instead of pasta."

"Okay," I said, still unsure what I wanted. My budget said hamburger, but this was a lobster night. *Just avoid anything with noodles and tomato sauce that I'll surely splatter all over my shirt.*

"I think I'll have the steak with peppercorns and wine gravy." Sophie kicked me again, possibly a reminder regarding my limited resources. I ignored her.

"Nice to include me, tonight." I overheard Sophie whisper to Mike. "I didn't want to miss this."

"I bet she turns him down," Mike whispered back. "I organized a betting pool, want in?" I couldn't make out her answer.

I reached into my pocket and ran my fingers over the smooth velvet surface of a small case. Checking on it had become an obsession. I feared the little box would poke a hole and fall out or jump out. The case held a ring. I planned to ask Madison to marry me at midnight.

Unable to control my exuberance, I shared my scheme with everyone. When I told Sophie, she insisted I offer Madison our grandmother's engagement ring.

"It's a simple, plain gold band, diamond set on top." she explained. "The stone isn't perfect, so what. I inherited it, which makes it an heirloom. I'd like you and Madison to have it."

An heirloom. I savored the thought. That made the ring special, sentimental. That's what counted. We took it to a jeweler who made it sparkle and shine.

*

Earlier that evening, before leaving for the restaurant, Sophie pulled me onto the balcony of our mother's apartment, where we were all staying. The early winter air was fresh, crisp, intermingled with the sweet aroma of burning wood wafting over the neighborhood from someone's fireplace.

While Madison was out of earshot in the bathroom preparing to go out, Sophie pulled me aside. "Do you think you ought to inform Madison about what you have in mind?" she whispered. "Please tell me you've already talked about marriage with Madison," she said when I remained silent.

"No, I hadn't thought to do that." I gave Sophie a puzzled look. *Why discuss that with Madison? She wouldn't reject my proposal, not in front of my friends. Would she?*

"You told everyone. You informed Mom. In fact, Mom has invited the family here for a New Year's Day dinner. I believe she expects you to make a formal announcement." Sophie rolled her eyes. "I hope she didn't share your intentions with the aunts in case, you know . . . Madison turns you down. You swore everybody to secrecy, right? And Madison hasn't a clue what you're up to?"

"Yes, all true," I said, then reflected for a moment; but I didn't see the problem. "I want to surprise her."

"I think a wise person only calls for a vote when they're sure of the result," Sophie said. She stared at me and scrunched her eyes. I think she was searching for the right words. "She's only a sophomore," Sophie continued. "You're going to grad school next fall. How are you going to live?" She shook her head. "Have you thought this through?"

"Of course," I said with confidence bordering on arrogance. Although I hadn't really considered all the ramifications. *Follow your heart, that's the ticket.* I just wanted to be with Madison and share my life with her.

Radiant as always, Madison appeared, and we left for the restaurant. I remained committed to my plan; my little sister had failed to deter me.

*

We finished our meal, and I managed to keep the gravy off my shirt. The evening was going well. I excused myself and headed to the bathroom. Once in a stall, I took out the case and opened it to be sure the ring was still inside.

The diamond winked at me as I exposed it to the light. I winked back. My hands shook as I held it. Fearing the disastrous consequence of a splash down in the toilet, I returned the ring to the case, restored the little box to the safety of my pocket, and made my way back to the table.

"I guess you liked your meal," Madison said as I sat. My plate was empty, wiped clean with the last of the bread. I ate so fast I almost forgot what I ordered.

"The steak was very good," I said. "Loved the peppercorns."

"My father says, you're a human garbage can. Step on your foot and your mouth opens." She glanced at me sideways with a little smirk, took my hand in hers, and squeezed. I melted as she smiled. *Oh boy, I can't wait to ask her father for his blessing.*

I checked the case, still safe in my pocket, no holes. I could hardly sit still. My heart pounded. Could Madison hear the thumping? *Remain cool.* Madison took her napkin from her lap, placed it on the table by her plate, and swept her hair back. Light shimmered off the golden brunette highlights. Her eyes sparkled.

Sophie and Mike rode with Madison and me to Jon's parents' home. I tried to enter the conversation without starting to giggle and laugh uncontrollably. I concentrated on my breathing. *She'll suspect something if I don't talk.*

"How was Florida?" I said. *How stupid.* I asked that earlier on the way home from the airport. My voice sounded several octaves higher than normal. I felt for the case. It hadn't left.

"Hot, I missed you. Miami was rough. I lay on the beach, swam, ate, slept, then repeated that sequence." I loved listening to her Long Island drawl.

Sophie piped up from the back. "Almost eleven. One more hour to go."

That did it. I almost wet myself. Could I wait until midnight?

Once we arrived at our destination, we settled in the den with its thick carpet, soft sofas, and plush chairs. Music played. The TV was on without sound as we waited for the magic moment when the clock struck twelve and the ball dropped. Madison and I danced. As I held her near, I inhaled the subtle bouquet of her perfume, sweet and inviting. Time slowed. *Will the new year ever arrive?*

At 11:55, I poured a glass of champagne for each of us. I removed the ring from the case, inspected it once more, and placed it in her flute. Once the ball dropped, we'd toast the new year, and she'd find the ring. I panicked. *What if she swallows it? I could put the ring in a piece of pastry, but what if she breaks a tooth? Stick with plan A and gamble that she'll only take a sip of the champagne.* I returned to Madison, bubbly in hand.

She took the glass but didn't seem to notice the ring sitting toward the bottom of the flute.

The ball started to drop. "Ten, nine, eight." Sophie turned to look at me instead of watching the ball. "Seven, six, five." Perspiration erupted across my forehead. "Four, three, two." Remain strong, focus. "One. Happy New Year!" We all shouted together, raised our glasses, and took a sip. I held my breath; all eyes turned to Madison.

She leaned into me, and our lips met. "Happy New Year," she whispered into my ear and gazed into my eyes. Before cuddling up to me for a second kiss, she reached out to put her glass aside. Did she see the ring? Is she ignoring it? All eyes remained on us. Think fast.

"Another toast to the New Year," I bellowed. Madison raised her glass with everyone.

"Here, here," Pat roared, and we all sipped again. Still, no response from Madison.

I took Madison's flute and held it at eye level. Thank God, the ring was still there. She glanced at the glass. Her eyes widened. She saw the ring!

"Will you marry me?" I said, my words rushed and desperate. Her eyes grew bigger, mouth open, she knit her brow, speechless. My eyes narrowed, sweat ran down my face. *How will she respond?* Self-doubt overcame me.

"Don't answer now," I blurted. My heart continued to race. "Everybody is watching."

"When do you want me to give you an answer?" she said, in a soft, coy voice. A long pause followed. "Yes, I'll marry you." She grabbed me and gave me a long kiss.

The room erupted in thunderous applause and cheers as I slipped the ring onto her finger. Sophie ran to congratulate us, followed by my friends.

I never did find out how much money was on the line, who won, and who lost. Madison and I danced and kissed and held each other tight, unwilling to let go.

At three a.m., we decided to call her parents, so I could formally ask her dad for his blessing. He still reminds me how I ruined golf for him the following day. When we arrived at my mother's apartment close to dawn, Mom met us at the door. She immediately inspected Madison's hand, then welcomed her daughter-in-law-to-be with a warm hug. Sophie and I joined in.

Madison peered over Mom's shoulder and mouthed, "I love you," and blew me a kiss.

About the Authors

Mary Adler escaped the university politics of "the ivory tower" for the much gentler world of World War II and the adventures of homicide detective Oliver Wright and his German shepherd, Harley. She lives with her family in Sebastopol, California, where she has created a garden habitat for birds and bees and butterflies—and other less desirable critters. Unintended consequences at work again. She does canine scent work with her brilliant dogs—the brains of the team—and loves all things Italian, especially Andrea Camilleri's Inspector Montalbano and cannoli, not necessarily in that order. Among the books she would be proud to have written are the Fred Vargas's Commissaire Adamsberg mysteries, set in Paris; Maurizio de Giovanni's Commissario Ricciardi mysteries, set in Naples; and Henning Mankell's Kurt Wallander mysteries, set in Ystad. She reminds herself daily of the question poet Mary Oliver asks: "Tell me, what is it you plan to do with your one wild and precious life?"

Jeff Baird is a natural redhead, a retired career educator at the secondary and post-graduate level, and a self-proclaimed technology junkie. He has published and presented at numerous state and national technology conferences. He now turns his attention to writing humorous memoirs such as about Mother Nature (waterfall chasing), pets, and life's vagaries. Check out his Amazon Author page for his collection of titles.

Dr. Peter J Barbour retired his reflex hammer to become a fulltime writer and illustrator. His works include *Loose Ends*, a memoir, three illustrated children's books: *Gus at Work, Oscar and Gus, Tanya and the Baby Elephant*, and over forty stories in e-journals and magazines. "The Fate of Dicky Paponovitch" earned him Raconteur of the Month from Susan Carol Publishing Company. He lives in Oregon with his photographer wife of over fifty years. They enjoy traveling and the outdoors. Please visit his website, Pete Barbour Stories and Illustrations, at PeteBarbour.com.

Paula Gail Benson is a legislative attorney and former law librarian whose short stories have appeared online and in anthologies including *Mystery Times Ten 2013; A Tall Ship, a Star, and Plunder; A Shaker of Margaritas: That Mysterious Woman; Fish or Cut Bait: a Guppy Anthology; Killer Nashville Noir: Cold Blooded; Love in the Lowcountry; Heartbreaks and Half-truths; Once Upon a Time; My Robot and Me; Malice Domestic's Mystery Most Diabolical; Dark of the Day;* and *Smoking Guns*. In addition to short stories, she writes and directs one-act musicals for her church's drama ministry. Her article on how to promote short stories is in *Promophobia*. She's a blogging partner at the Stiletto Gang and Writers Who Kill, and her website is paulagailbenson.com.

A. E. Decker writes fantasy and has been published in numerous venues, including *Fireside Magazine, Beneath Ceaseless Skies,* and over half a dozen anthologies. She likes octopuses and chocolate, but not chocolate octopuses, and recently can be found hanging out on the aerial silks.

Judge Debra H. Goldstein writes Kensington's Sarah Blair mystery series (*Five Belles Too Many, Four Cuts Too Many, Three Treats Too Many, Two Bites Too Many,* and *One Taste Too Many*). In addition to winning BWR prizes, her novels and short stories have been named Agatha, Anthony, Derringer, and Claymore finalists and received IPPY and Silver Falchion awards. Debra serves on the national board of Sisters in Crime and previously was a Mystery Writers of America board member and president of the Guppy and SEMWA chapters. Find out more about Debra at www.DebraHGoldstein.com.

Ralph Hieb is a short story author who enjoys reading and writing paranormal. His interests include travel and cryptozoology. He has taken a million pictures of things, but he can't remember where they were taken. He has been working on a novel for quite a number of years, hopefully to be finished this century, maybe. He is a member of the Horror Writers Association, the Pocono Liars, and the Bethlehem Writers Group.

ABOUT THE AUTHORS

D.T. "Dan" Krippene writes mystery, science fiction, paranormal, and alternate-world fantasy. His short story, "Hell of a Deal," appears in the 2019 Killer Nashville Finalist, *Untethered*; the 2021 Best Indie for Fiction, *Fur, Feathers, and Scales* with "Man's Best Friend"; and the 2023 Finalist Indie Award-winning, *An Element of Mystery* with "The Lost Gold of Rhyolite". He's been a featured author with the Bethlehem Writers Roundtable with "Snowbelt Sanctuary," "In Simple Terms," "Hot as Sin," and "Desert Buzz." You can find Dan on his website, dtkrippene.com, and his social media links on Facebook, Instagram, and Pinterest.

Jerome W. McFadden is an award-winning short story writer whose stories have appeared in fifty magazines, anthologies, and e-zines over the past ten years. He has received a Bullet Award for the best crime fiction to appear on the web. Three of his short stories have been read on stage by the Liar's League London and Liar's League Hong Kong. His collection of twenty-six short stories, titled *Off the Rails*, was published in October 2019 to great reviews.

Sally Milliken writes contemporary and historical mystery/crime and enjoys finding new ways to put amateur sleuths in difficult situations. Winning the Bethlehem Writers Roundtable Short Story Award was a first and great honor for her. Her stories have been published online in *Punk Noir* and *Stone's Throw*, as well as in the anthologies *Malice, Matrimony and Murder* and *Hook, Line, and Sinker: the Seventh Guppy Anthology*. Her flash fiction story "Adam-13" won the 2023 Golden Donut Award. She is working on her first novel, a historical mystery set in 1882 Massachusetts. Follow her @sallyhistorymystery. Find out more at www.sallymillikenauthor.com.

Emwryn Murphy is a writer, editor, and photographer based in Frederick, Maryland, where e lives with eir spouse and the world's most amazing children. Em is a fan of the Red Sox, ampersands, puns, and the Oxford comma. Visiting Em's author/editor website at www.EmwrynMurphy.com, or photography website at www.EmMurphyPhotography.com/.

Bettie Nebergall's short stories have appeared in many local anthologies and have captured top awards in local, state, and national competitions. On a lark, she collected seven of them and used Amazon's KDP service to create her book, *Everyday Deceptions*, now available on Amazon. Find her on Goodreads, Facebook, and LinkedIn, or visit www.bettienebergall.com. She and her husband live in a quaint tourist town in central Florida. They love to travel and recently completed visits to all fifty states. Space travel will have to wait until prices are reasonable, so the seven continents are next.

Christopher D. Ochs dove into speculative fiction with his epic fantasy *Pindlebryth of Lenland*. He then crafted a collection of mirthful macabre short fiction in *If I Can't Sleep, You Can't Sleep*. His latest novel is a gritty urban fantasy/horror, *My Friend Jackson*, a Finalist in Indies Today's Best Books of 2020. His short fictions have been published in GLVWG and BWG anthologies and websites, and by Firebringer Press. His current projects include: 'Eldritch, Inc.," the cosmic adventures of the world's most dangerous insurance agent; and a sci-fi/horror novel, "Sentinel of Eternity." Follow Chris's derring-do at www.christopherdochs.com and on Facebook @ChristopherDOchs.

Dianna Sinovic is an author, certified book coach, and editor based in Bucks County, PA. She writes short stories in several genres, including paranormal, horror, and speculative fiction. She is a member of Sisters in Crime, the Horror Writers Association, the American Medical Writers Association, and the Bethlehem Writers Group. Her website is www.dianna-sinovic.com.

Diane Sismour gave up her hard-hat to write dark, suspenseful stories that keep fans up at night. Her characters (and readers) never know what perils await them or the predicaments they must resolve. Unable to restrain her passion for storytelling to prose, she is now writing adaptations of her works for the screen. She lives with her husband in eastern Pennsylvania at the foothills of the Blue Mountains, where they own Leaser Lake B and B. Diane enjoys traveling to conferences to reunite with friends and meet fans. She's a member of national and local writing and screenplay groups.

Kidd Wadsworth has people in her head and likes to work in her pajamas. She found her career choices extremely limited: write or commit herself to an institution. www.kiddwadsworth.com

ABOUT THE AUTHORS

Carol L. Wright left a career in law and academia to write mysteries and more. Her debut traditional mystery, *Death in Glenville Falls: A Gracie McIntyre Mystery* was a finalist for two international book awards, and *Apple, Table, Penny . . . Murder*, her most recent novelette, was a finalist for a 2024 Next Generation Indie Book Award. Many of her short stories have appeared in award-winning anthologies and literary journals, and some of her favorites are collected in her book *A Christmas on Nantucket and other stories*. You can learn more at her website: CarolLWright.com.

Rhonda Zangwill has long flirted with the literary life, writing, editing, teaching and rabble-rousing for NY Writers Coalition, Writers Read, Girls Write Now, and The Moth. She now runs writing workshops for the Sirovich Center for Balanced Living, and 14Y. Some of her work is published in *Calyx, Natural Bridge, Common Unity, The Rainbow Project* and the *Arcade of the Scribes*. One of her plays was recently transformed into a shadow puppet show at Dixon Place. She enjoys reading around town, including at the National Arts Club, the Book Club Bar, and in some of her neighborhood's most charming community gardens.

Acknowledgements

The Bethlehem Writers Group acknowledges with gratitude the contributions of the Guest Judges for our 2023 and 2024 Bethlehem Writers Roundtable Short Story Award competitions. Barb Goffman, an Agatha, Macavity, Anthony, Silver Falchion, and Ellery Queen Readers Award winner and noted editor, served as judge for our 2023 competition, giving first place to "First Thanksgiving" by Sally Milliken. Marlo Berliner, multi-award-winning, bestselling author of *The Ghost Chronicles* series, served as judge for our 2024 competition, selecting "Oh! Christmas Tree" by Rhonda Zangwill as the first-place winner. Both stories appear in this volume.

In addition to these first-place winners, this anthology also includes the second- and third-place winners from our 2024 Short Story Award competition: "Just Ask Santa" by Bettie Nebergall and "Narragansett Nellie and the Transferware Platter" by Mary Adler, respectively.

Milton Keynes UK
Ingram Content Group UK Ltd.
UKHW040714141024
449705UK00001B/60